ROVERS

ALSO BY RICHARD LANGE

The Smack
Sweet Nothing
Angel Baby
This Wicked World
Dead Boys

ROVERS

A NOVEL

RICHARD LANGE

MULHOLLAND BOOKS

Little, Brown and Company

New York Boston London

Copyright © 2021 by Richard Lange

Hachette Book Group supports the right to free expression and the value of copyright. The purpose of copyright is to encourage writers and artists to produce the creative works that enrich our culture.

The scanning, uploading, and distribution of this book without permission is a theft of the author's intellectual property. If you would like permission to use material from the book (other than for review purposes), please contact permissions@hbgusa.com. Thank you for your support of the author's rights.

Mulholland Books / Little, Brown and Company
Hachette Book Group
1290 Avenue of the Americas, New York, NY 10104
mulhollandbooks.com

First edition: July 2021

Mulholland Books is an imprint of Little, Brown and Company, a division of Hachette Book Group, Inc. The Mulholland Books name and logo are trademarks of Hachette Book Group, Inc.

The publisher is not responsible for websites (or their content) that are not owned by the publisher.

The Hachette Speakers Bureau provides a wide range of authors for speaking events. To find out more, go to hachettespeakersbureau.com or call (866) 376-6591.

Excerpts from "Convoy," written by Bill Fries and Chip Davis © 1976 American Gramaphone Partnership. All rights reserved. Used by permission.

ISBN 978-0-316-54196-1
LCCN 2020951479

Printing 1, 2021

LSC-C

Printed in the United States of America

For Kim Turner

There are darknesses in life and there are lights, and you are one of the lights, the light of all lights.

—Bram Stoker, *Dracula*

Let faith oust fact; let fancy oust memory;
I look deep down and do believe.

—Herman Melville, *Moby-Dick*

Night is a world lit by itself.

—Antonio Porchia

ROVERS

1

JESSE DREAMS THE OLD DREAM FOR THE FIRST TIME IN MONTHS. He hasn't been sleeping much lately, and when he has, he hasn't dreamed. On bad days he lies there for hours, tossing and turning; on good ones he drops his lids and dies until the sun goes down. Today, though, one minute he's staring up at the water-stained ceiling of the motel room, listening to the maid argue with the manager out in the parking lot, listening to Edgar snore on the other bed, and the next, the dream! It reappears like a friend he hadn't known how much he missed until, hey, there he was again, the rascal. It's the only dream he dreams, so he's fond of it. It's the only time the world isn't just what it is.

He's walking down a road, always the same road, a road he's traveled in his waking life, but not one he can place exactly. Somewhere near Barstow maybe, somewhere outside Las Cruces. Scrubland, where the plants bristle with thorns and the hot wind never stops blowing, where train tracks slice across salt flats like ropy old scars, and the air is so clear what's ten miles away looks like it's two. He's walking alone on this road, and how he knows it's a dream is it's daytime.

He hasn't been outside during the day in more than seventy-five years. Seventy-five years since he's felt the sun on his face, seventy-five years since he's lain under a tree and run his fingers over leaf shadows flitting across a patch of warm grass, seventy-five years since he's squinted through his lashes to pin a cawing raven against the noon glare. For the past three-quarters of a century he's lived by night, in the ebon hours when monsters hunt and good folk keep to their houses. Since he turned, every dawn's been a death sentence, every sunbeam a white-hot razor.

That's why he's overjoyed whenever he dreams his only dream, when he finds himself walking that road under the blazing sun, under a few wisps of cloud unraveling across the sky. A bounding jackrabbit kicks up dust. A breeze brings a whiff of sage. He comes upon an empty pop can and gives it a kick. Light and warmth worm their way into the coldest, darkest thickets inside him, and if he never woke again, he'd be fine. This would be enough—the road, the sky, the sun— forever.

"Jesse."

Jesse opens his eyes. The ceiling is dark. Night has come down.

"Jesse."

"What?"

"I pissed myself."

Jesse sits up. His brother, Edgar, is lying in the other bed in his own mess. Even Abby, Edgar's cat, has more sense than that. At least she was smart enough to jump down to the floor. Jesse exhales his disgust. He doesn't mean for Edgar to hear it, but hear it he does.

"I'm sorry," Edgar says, and starts to cry.

"It's all right," Jesse says. "You've been doing better."

Ten years have passed since Edgar last had trouble holding his water, and Jesse can't figure out why the problem has returned. He asked Edgar if he was scared or worried about anything, and Edgar said no, so he supposes it's simply another of his bad behaviors that'll keep coming back now and then, like the shoplifting and the lying and the wandering off, something he'll be training out of him again and again for all eternity.

Can he really be that simple? You teach a dog a trick, a horse, and it remembers forever. So how come every few years he has to remind a grown man not to steal potato chips from the store? Could it be Edgar's messing with him and secretly reveling in his frustration?

Jesse makes him walk into the bathroom, take off his undershorts, and put them in the sink. Edgar's not crying anymore and seems to have forgotten he ever was. "Not too hot," he says when Jesse turns on the shower. He's a big fella, bigger than Jesse, over six feet tall, round as a barrel, and getting fatter every year. He'll always be fifty years old outside and ten inside his head, a child bearing a man's shell, and Jesse will always have to look after him, because he promised their mother he would. What else could he do, a dying woman's last wish?

He unwraps the cake of soap that came with the room and hands it to Edgar. Edgar smells it, licks it, and makes a face.

"It's soap, not candy," Jesse says.

"Smells like candy," Edgar says.

He sings while he showers, his current favorite song, about truck drivers who band together to outwit the Highway Patrol. He knows all the words, including the talking parts, and even cups a hand over his mouth to mimic the sound of a CB radio.

"Wash everywhere," Jesse yells over the singing. "Under your arms, your ass."

"Ten-four, good buddy."

Jesse strips the sheets off the bed. The mattress is already so filthy that one more stain won't be noticed. He tosses the sheets onto the bathroom floor, will wash them in the shower later.

Edgar stops singing. "I'm hungry," he says.

"There's Pop-Tarts," Jesse says.

"I mean *really* hungry."

The neon sign of the drive-in restaurant across the road from the motel is missing letters. H MBUR   SH K S FR S. The first time Jesse and Edgar traveled this stretch, it was part of the highway that ran from Chicago to Los Angeles. There was nothing but orange groves here then, and on that frigid January night when they passed through, they stopped to look at the smudge pots—crude oil-burning stoves kept blazing among the trees until dawn in an attempt to warm the air and prevent the fruit from freezing.

Thick clouds of greasy smoke billowed from the pots, smoke that scratched at Jesse's throat and blackened the faces of the men tending the fires. They looked like demons freshly sprung from hell as they slouched in the orange flicker of the flames, eyes and teeth shining out of the darkness. The sight scared Edgar, set him to whimpering.

"What's that? Haints?" he asked.

"No," Jesse said. "Just men."

They tore out the orange trees in the '30s and replaced them with motels and hamburger stands and filling stations.

Then they built a bigger freeway a few miles south that siphoned traffic off the old route, and the motels, burger joints, and filling stations started going under. Those still hanging on are struggling. There's no money to buy new mattresses or fix neon signs. Broken windows get boarded over, and owners opt to pay electric bills instead of replacing worn linoleum. Not that it matters to the customers they get these days.

The motel Jesse and Edgar are staying in is a horseshoe of ten cabins that hugs a gravel parking lot. Jesse looks back to make sure Edgar hasn't followed him out before crossing to the drive-in. The drive-in is where the local whores gather and where the truckers who detour over from the freeway come to find them. They favor this spot because there's room to park their rigs on a half acre of weedy asphalt next to the burger stand, an expanse that was once a used-car lot.

The whores and truckers conduct their negotiations at the drive-in's four wooden picnic tables. Two girls are on duty tonight. One sits at a table, nursing a cherry Coke and staring into the mirror of a compact; the other pretends to talk on the pay phone. Jesse goes to the window and orders an ice-cream cone from the old man who runs the place. The codger's paper-thin skin is drawn so tightly over his skull, he looks like he's about to scream.

"How you?" he says.

"Doing fine," Jesse says.

He takes his ice cream to an empty table and sits. The girls glance at him but quickly turn away. The one with the compact, a fat blonde, is wearing hot pants and a tube top. She's got a broken heart tattooed on one of her titties. The other girl is a little Mexican with a droopy eye.

"*Sí*," she says into the pay phone, "*sí*," all the while watching the road for potential customers.

A hot night wind blowing off the desert swirls trash. Bugs swarm the streetlights, and bats dart in to feed on them. The top of Jesse's table is rough with names and dates and dirty words gouged into the wood. BIG JOE + MARY. CARL WAS HERE. FTW 13/69 HELLS ANGELS. There's a pecker shooting jizz and a naked woman on all fours. Jesse runs his finger over the carvings and wonders about the people who made them.

An eighteen-wheeler pulls into the abandoned car lot next door. The engine gives a dusty cough and dies. The man who climbs down from the cab is a bandy-legged cowboy sporting a tiny paper American flag in the band of his Stetson. He does a couple of deep-knee bends before approaching the burger stand, where he tilts his hat to Jesse and the girls before ordering a cheeseburger.

Jesse walks to the liquor store next door. A patchwork Monte Carlo—maroon fender, white door, gray-primer hood—is parked out front. A buzzer goes off when Jesse enters the store. The clerk, a big black man, ignores him. He's looking toward the beer cooler in back. There, another black man—a pimp in platform shoes, green velvet trousers, and a silk shirt open to his navel—is arguing with a skinny white whore in tight jeans.

"You best not be holdin' out on me, bitch," the pimp says.

"He only gave me twenty, I swear," the whore says.

"That ain't what Trina said."

"Fuck Trina," the whore says. "I'm the one sucked the motherfucker's dick, and this is all he gave me." She waves a twenty. The pimp snatches it away from her.

"How you gon' say, *Fuck Trina*?" he says.

"Fuck Trina, fuck Trina, fuck Trina," the whore says. "Fuck her in her motherfuckin' ass."

The pimp backhands her. She crashes into the glass door of the cooler and slides to the floor.

"Take that shit outside," the clerk shouts.

The pimp comes up the aisle toward the counter without another glance at the whore. Instead he focuses on Jesse, bugging his bloodshot eyes. Jesse stares right back.

"The fuck you lookin' at?" the pimp says, moving in so he and Jesse are chest to chest.

"Nothing," Jesse says.

"She your sister?"

"No."

"Your mama?"

"No."

"Then keep to yourself."

The pimp leaves the store, gets into the Monte Carlo, and roars out of the parking lot.

"You want something?" the clerk says to Jesse.

"Give me a half pint of Old Crow," Jesse says.

The whore is still sitting on the floor. "Can I use the restroom?" she says.

"The facilities is for customers only," the clerk says, handing Jesse his bottle and change.

"Come on, man," the whore says. "I need to clean up."

"Buy something, then."

The whore reaches into her purse, fishes out some coins.

"You sell loosies? Kools?"

"No loosies."

"I ain't got enough for a pack."

"I don't give a fuck."

Jesse lays a dollar on the counter.

"Give her her cigarettes," he says. "And let her use the bathroom."

"Thank you, man," the whore calls after him as he walks out the door.

He's leaning against a telephone pole and looking up at a sliver of orange moon when the whore comes out of the store. He's been nipping at the whiskey and is feeling like he's ready to do what he has to.

"Are you waiting for me?" the whore says. She's pulled herself together after the beat-down, got her sass back.

"Maybe," Jesse says.

The whore takes a drag off her cigarette, exhales smoke, and does a little thing with her hips, a little sway.

"You want a date?" she says.

"Who was that guy, the one that hit you?" Jesse says.

"Sugar?" the whore says. "He's nobody."

"Is he gonna cause me trouble?"

"He's nobody, I said."

Another truck, as big as a couple of elephants, pulls into the lot. The whore's eyes dart to it. "What kind of party you looking for?" she says to Jesse.

"It's not for me," Jesse says. "It's for my brother."

"He can't do his own thing?"

"He's slow."

The whore makes a face. "I don't mess with retards," she says.

"I'll pay extra."

The whore glances at the truck again, thinking maybe that'd be easier money. She swats at a moth that bounces off her face.

"Where's he at?" she says.

"Across the road, in the motel," Jesse says.

"You have to give me ten to walk over, and I'm not promising anything until I see him," the whore says.

Jesse takes the money out of his shirt pocket and hands it to her. He considers offering her some whiskey but doesn't want her mouth on the bottle.

2

THE LITTLE DEVIL'S GOT A GROUCH ON KICKING AND CLAWING and screaming, *Feed Me You Sonofabitch.* I curl up on the bed lay on my front lay on my back but nothing helps. He keeps raging in the pit of my stomach a fat spiked toad with possum teeth and a snapping snake for a tongue. There's nothing but black holes where his eyes should be but he can smell blood a mile off. His skin oozes poison that burns worse than fire.

Jesse brings a girl in. She's got blond hair and skinny legs. She's got torn blue jeans and a yellow shirt that shows her belly button. Her eyes are blue too but different blue from the jeans. Abby hisses and crawls under the bed. The girl says, Somebody doesn't like me much. I say, She don't take to strangers. The girl nods at the TV and says, What're you watching? A story about a giant tarantula, I say. Truth is I ain't been paying attention to the show. Been too busy rassling the Little Devil. He comes on fast and he comes on mean gnawing at my bones and itching me deeper than I can scratch.

This is Candy, Jesse says, get up and make your manners. I stand and stick out my hand and say, Pleased to make your acquaintance Miss Candy you sure are pretty. Candy says to Jesse, This is your brother? Looks more like your dad. Our daddy's dead, I say, our mama too. My mom's dead too, Candy says. Did you cry when she died? I say, I cried when my mama died. Candy smiles. One of her teeth is broke. Give me twenty more and I'll take care of him, she says to Jesse.

Want to hear me sing? I say. Candy looks to Jesse. He nods okay. What songs do you know? Candy says. Do you like old ones? I say. Sure, Candy says so I sing Mama's favorite. *I would not die in springtime when all is bright around and fair young flowers are peeping from out the silent ground.*

Jesse steps behind Candy with his stiletto. He claps a hand over her mouth yanks her head back and sticks her in the throat. He hits a gusher on his first try. A jet of blood shoots across the room. Candy's blue eyes get real big. She tries to pull Jesse's hand off tries to wriggle free but ain't going nowhere. Another spurt and her legs buckle. Another and her hands flutter and fall.

Jesse sits on the bed with her in his lap. Get over here, he says, don't let it go to waste. I fasten my lips to the hole in Candy's throat. Hot blood fills my mouth. I suck and swallow suck and swallow. You got to work fast to drink as much as you can before the heart gives out. Abby feeds too. She comes out from under the bed and licks up the blood on the floor. Candy was a bad girl. Her blood tastes like dirty water. The Little Devil don't care. He gets his fill and settles and I'm not hungry anymore neither not hurting.

Sometimes Jesse lets me play the radio when we're driving sometimes he don't. Tonight he wants quiet. Won't even let me tap my fingers. There's no other cars on the road. It's dark and dark and darker. Nothing to look at but the dotted line. I pretend it's ears of corn and the Ford's a hog gobbling them up. I pretend it's rabbits and the car's a hound.

How far are we from Hollywood? I ask Jesse so bored I don't care if he gets mad at me for talking. We ain't going to Hollywood, he says. I want to see Daniel Boone and Mingo, I say. Daniel Boone died a hundred years ago, Jesse says. That's an actor on TV pretending to be him. I know that, I say. No you don't, Jesse says. You think he's real.

Jesse says there can only be one boss and it's him. Says he makes the rules and I'm to follow them. Like a dog. If he's so smart how come he don't know you can only kick a dog so long before he turns and bites?

We swerve onto a rough dirt road. I hang on so I don't bang my head. Jesse drives deeper into the dark and pulls over and shuts off the engine. An itty-bitty moon silvers the rocky hills the sand and the trees that look like badmen surrendering. Jesse opens his door and gets out. A coyote yips close by. Abby's ears is back and her tail's aswishing. She'd whup a coyote's ass.

What're you waiting on? Jesse says. Drag your lazy butt out here.

I'll do anything to get out of shoveling. I've played sick. I've lied about a bum leg. It don't sound like Jesse's in the mood for foolishness tonight though. I climb out and meet him at the trunk. Miss Candy's in there with a bedsheet for a shroud. Jesse hands me a shovel.

We walk out a ways and commence to digging. Six foot is Christian but we never go that deep. Ain't no preacher looking. You got to bury your bodies or burn them. Make them disappear. That's a rule for all rovers: cover your tracks. Otherwise folks'll put two and two together and that'd be the death of us all. That's what happened in Europe in the old days, Jesse told me. Rovers there got sloppy and people caught on and hunted most of them down or run them off.

That's when the first ones come here to the United States of America.

I say I wish we was rich so we could hire a man to dig for us. Jesse says to wish in one hand and shit in the other and see which fills faster. Or we could turn someone and make *him* dig, I say. We ain't turning nobody, Jesse says. There's too many of us as it is. I ask when he's gonna take me to Disneyland like he promised. Why? he says. You want to visit Mickey Mouse? You think he's real too? Mickey Mouse is a cartoon, I say, and a cartoon ain't real. If you can't talk and dig at the same time don't talk, Jesse says.

After we lay Miss Candy to rest I say a prayer over her. Jesse tells me to hurry it up we got to steal a new car before we hit the road. 10-4 good buddy, I say, I'm about to put the hammer down. I know he won't let me drive tonight so I don't ask.

3

June 24, 1976, Portland, Oregon

COFFEE AND DOUGHNUTS FOR BREAKFAST. I PICKED UP NEW enlargements of the photos of Benny to replace the ones ruined by the rain and took them to a place to be laminated. The man there recommended a print shop that could run off more copies of the flyer.

The guy at the print shop looked at the flyer, then at me.

"Who was this boy to you, the one who was murdered?" he asked.

"He was my son," I replied.

The man's eyes flickered like candles about to go out.

"I lost a son too," he said. He gestured at a photo hanging on the wall, a kid in a Boy Scout uniform, giving the peace sign.

"Vietnam," the guy said. "Eighteen years old."

So much grief. So many people in mourning. Souls everywhere bent double under the weight.

"I'm sorry for your loss," I said.

"And I hope you find who killed your boy," the guy said. He wouldn't let me pay for the flyers.

I drove the Econoline to a park on the Willamette River and ate a can of deviled ham and a sleeve of Ritz crackers for lunch. The sun sparkled where it hit the water, and Mt. Hood floated on a layer of haze. A bunch of hippies sprawled on a patch of grass nearby, white boys with long hair and beards, white girls in Indian-print skirts and headbands. Someone had a guitar, someone else a Frisbee. A couple of the girls got up to dance. A big, yellow dog joined them, barking excitedly. One of the girls took hold of the animal's front paws and waltzed it in a circle.

I went over with some flyers and handed them around, asked if anyone had seen Benny.

"This says he was killed in L.A.," one of the boys said. "Shouldn't you be looking there?"

"He hung out here too," I said. I have the postcard he sent, the one with the river and the mountain on the front and *Doing fine, don't worry* on the back. Like all the rest of the cards, it's addressed only to you, his mother.

"I bet the fuzz are useless," the boy said. "I bet they could give two shits about a dead black kid."

What the hell do you know about anything? I wanted to reply, but I've learned to keep my mouth shut. "There's a telephone number there for an answering service," I said. "I'm offering a reward for information."

"Money makes the world go round," the boy said. He tapped another kid with the Frisbee and told him to go long. Even with the hair, the beads, and the beard, he dreamed of being a quarterback, an all-American hero. The other kid sprinted across the grass. The quarterback sailed the Frisbee to him and whooped and clapped when he made a diving catch. The girls went back to dancing with the dog.

I spent the rest of the afternoon in the park. I wiped down the side of the van and used shoe polish to reapply the messages: SON MURDERED, REWARD FOR INFO, PLEASE HELP.

I put up the photos of Benny and the poster I made that lays out everything I know about his death. A path ran right past the Econoline, and everyone who used it, the bicyclists, the joggers, the dog-walkers, could see the display.

Then I lay down on my cot in the back of the van and went through the local newspapers. An alcoholic living in a boardinghouse had gone missing. I scissored out the story and pasted it in my scrapbook. The corpse of a young woman had been fished from the river, the body too decomposed to determine the cause of death. I saved that one too.

And then I came upon one about a little girl murdered a month ago. Suzy Byrd, age ten, left home to walk to school. Her body was found a week later in a junkyard. Her throat had been cut. James and Molly, her grieving parents, were begging for the public's help in finding the killer. Anyone who knew anything about the crime was asked to call a police tip line.

Another atrocity for the book. After only a year, it's almost full. Every city I pass through has had a mysterious death or disappearance, and I still believe that if I gather enough of these stories and peruse them closely enough they'll lead me like a trail of blood to whoever killed Benny.

I ate a peanut-butter sandwich for dinner and drove to the Memorial Coliseum, where a rock band was playing a concert. I parked out front but a cop made me move, said I was blocking a fire lane. I found another spot and walked back to pass out flyers to the kids when the show ended.

They were an unruly bunch, mostly white, mostly high. The majority of them dropped the flyer without looking at it, and those who did take the time to read it were no help. One girl cried and hugged me and wouldn't let go. "It's so sad," she kept wailing. Her boyfriend finally dragged her off, saying, "Sorry, man. She's tripping." Another kid raved about satanic cults. He was stoned on something too. His eyeballs wheeled, and he fidgeted like a horse tormented by flies.

"Did you know Satan was an angel?" he said. "A fallen angel. Can you dig it?"

When the crowd thinned, I drove to a quiet neighborhood, parked the van, and crawled into my cot. I write this by flashlight after 373 days in the wilderness, feeling farther than ever from the truth. I don't know if you'll ever read this, but it does me good to keep a record, helps me organize my thoughts, helps me remember where I've been, and gives me someone to talk to. Good night, Wanda. I miss you. Good night, Benny. I miss you too.

TODAY'S PASSAGE: I am the man that hath seen affliction by the rod of His wrath. He hath led me and brought me into darkness, but not into light.

—Lamentations 3:1–2

June 25, 1976, Weed, California

Coffee was all I could handle this morning. My stomach was as tight as a clenched fist. After calling the service from a pay phone in the library to see if anyone had responded to yesterday's flyers, I dialed the tip line from the story about the little girl who'd been murdered. The cop who answered was suspicious when I said I wanted to talk to the girl's parents.

"Do you have information about the crime?" he said.

"Not specifically," I said.

"What's that mean?"

"I'm conducting an investigation."

"Into what?"

"That's classified."

"Classified?" the cop said. "Are you with law enforcement?"

"It's an independent investigation."

"What's your name?"

"I'll tell that to the parents."

"You're not gonna talk to the parents if you don't give me your name and tell me where you're calling from," the cop said.

I hung up and quickly left the library in case they were running a trace. After what happened last time, I should know better than to go through official channels. You remember that, in Seattle, when I first tried to contact the family of someone murdered in a way similar to Benny. It was a teenage boy there, and I stupidly agreed to meet his mother at the police station after phoning the tip line. When I showed up the cops took me into custody and interrogated me for forty-eight hours before escorting me to the city limits. I never got to talk to the mother, but I read later that the father ended up confessing to the killing.

This time I drove to another phone booth, at a gas station on the other side of town, and looked in the directory hanging there. I quickly found the address for Mr. and Mrs. James Byrd. Rather than calling, I'd visit in person.

I cruised past the house, checking for police. The small wooden bungalow looked as if it was about to be set upon by the hulking, ivy-covered trees surrounding it. It hadn't been painted in who knows how long, and the yard was strewn with junk—a rusted washing machine, a crumpled fender, milk crates full of empty beer bottles. The place fit right into the neighborhood, a poor-white ghetto made up of houses that had seen better days and known better residents. Even on a serene sunny morning, the street oozed melancholy and regret. Satisfied the coast was clear, I parked down the block.

The pink kiddie bicycle lying on the porch brought tears to my eyes. I picked it up and propped it on its kickstand before knocking at the door. When I heard the lock click, I stepped back, giving whoever was about to answer plenty of space. It was a woman, or rather what was left of a woman whose heart had been torn out and whose brain had been scrambled by loss. I could have put my finger right through her.

"Yes?" she said in the softest of voices.

"I'm sorry to bother you, ma'am, but are you Suzy Byrd's mother?" I asked.

"I am," the woman replied. "Who are you?"

"My name is Charles Sanders, and I wondered if I might talk to you about what happened to your daughter."

"She was murdered," the woman said.

"I know that, ma'am," I said. "My son was murdered, too, in the same way, two years ago, in Los Angeles. The police gave up trying to find the killer, but I've been working on my own, retracing my son's path in the last year of his life, gathering information and searching for anyone who might know something about what happened to him."

Confusion clouded the woman's face. "Why would you think *I'd* know anything?" she said.

"No, no," I said. "Excuse me for not making myself clear. The reason I'm here is, as part of my investigation, I'm talking to people whose loved ones died under similar circumstances on the chance there might be a connection the police aren't seeing."

"What connection?" the woman said.

"One theory I have is that the same person might be committing a lot of these murders," I said. "They're identical in many ways. I've got some clippings I could show you."

"I don't...I don't—" the woman said. She raised a trembling hand to her mouth.

"Your daughter's throat was cut, right?" I said.

"What?"

"Was her body drained of blood?"

"Oh, my God," the woman said. "How could you?"

A man appeared behind her, a big man with three days' stubble and red eyes.

"What's going on?" he said.

"He asked if Suzy's blood was drained," the woman said.

"How do you know that?" the man said.

"As I was telling your wife, the same thing happened to my son," I said. "A small incision over the jugular vein. Very neat. Very precise."

"Stop," the woman wailed.

"Call Sergeant Emory," the man said to her and stepped onto the porch. He reached for me, but I slapped his hand away and backed down the stairs.

"I want to help you," I said.

He kept coming. I grabbed his arm, turned, and flipped him over my shoulder with a throw I learned in the Army. He landed hard, air whooshing out of him in a beery gust. I ran to the Econoline, climbed in, and sped away.

Figuring the police would be looking for me, I got on Interstate 5 headed south. This was my second visit to Portland in the past year, and I think it's time to admit it's a dead end. I'm not even sure how much time Benny spent there. It could have been a month, it could have been a quick layover on a bus on his way to somewhere else. The next postcard he sent you after Portland came from Reno. I've been there *three* times already, but I'll go back and poke around again before working my way down to L.A.

I pulled into this truck stop shortly after crossing into California, parked between two big rigs, took a shower, and had chicken fried steak for dinner. Afterward I sat in the restaurant and read the local paper but found nothing new to add to the scrapbook.

I know what you're thinking, baby: I need to work on my approach if I'm going to continue talking to folks who've been through what we have—and I *am* going to continue talking to them, because that might be the key to finding Benny's killer. My desperation got the better of me today, and I came on too strong. I'll ease into the subject next time, use more tact. I bought a book in the store here, one of those self-improvement guides. Maybe that'll help.

TODAY'S PASSAGE: Always lead with a smile. A smile will open more doors (and hearts!) than the slickest patter.

—*Listen, Respond, Win: A New Path to Success*
by Dr. Christine Pellegrino

THE FIENDS ORDER BEER AND WHISKEY: SEVEN LONE STARS, seven shots. The old man behind the bar pours the Jack with a shaky hand.

"He scared or just decrepit?" Real Deal jokes with Yuma.

Yuma twists a lock of her long red hair around a finger and smiles at the bartender. "Kinda dead in here tonight, ain't it?" she says.

There's only one other customer besides the Fiends, another old man, this one in an Astros ball cap. He's trying hard not to stare at the seven leather-jacketed savages who burst through the door of this nowheresville roadhouse and charged the air with evil electricity.

"Yup," the bartender says. "I was about to close before you all rolled in."

"We won't keep you too late," Yuma says. "Promise."

Bob 1 and Bob 2 are getting ready to shoot pool, lagging for the break. Johnny Kickapoo studies the jukebox. Antonia and Elijah, the leaders of the gang, sit head-to-head at a small round table, apart from and somehow above everybody else. Antonia is tall and thin, with icy blue eyes that tell you nothing unless you know her and blond hair she keeps cut short.

Elijah is the biggest, burliest dude in the gang, but also the most graceful. Behind his unruly black beard is the face of a king or a prince from a 500-year-old painting.

Pedro, keeping watch out front, opens the door and pokes his head in. "He's here," he says, and steps aside to let George Moore's man pass. George Moore's man is a Mexican cowboy in a big straw hat. Everybody watches him walk to Antonia and Elijah's table.

"You're to come with me," he says.

Antonia looks at Elijah, and Elijah looks at Antonia. They've been together so long, they don't need words to make a decision. They stand at the same time.

"Hold down the fort," Antonia says as she and Elijah follow the man out the door. Johnny drops a dime into the juke and punches a couple of buttons. Bob Wills's "Take Me Back to Tulsa" comes blaring out so loud, everybody jumps.

Out in the parking lot Antonia and Elijah put on their helmets, climb onto their Harleys, and kick them to life. The rumble of the engines shakes the ground and agitates the very atmosphere, waking every slumbering critter for miles around. Neon ricochets off chrome as the Fiends follow the Mexican's pickup out of the lot and on down the road. It's so dark out here in the wilds between San Antonio and Laredo, so desolate, they might as well be racing through a black tunnel.

Ten minutes later the truck's brake lights flare. There's no sign for Moore's ranch. Antonia and Elijah would have zoomed right past the turnoff if the Mexican wasn't with them. He unlocks a gate and waves the bikes through, then drives through himself and gets out to lock the gate before taking the lead again.

The road is dirt now, and the truck throws up a cloud of

dust the bikes' headlights can't penetrate. Antonia and Elijah hang back so they can breathe. Eventually they turn off the road, following the pickup down a driveway lined with spectral cottonwoods. The driveway ends at a Spanish-style hacienda with thick walls, covered verandas, and a tile roof. The Fiends park their bikes and kill the engines. The silence that replaces the roar is profound, broken only by a dog grousing in the distance.

The Mexican walks up the stairs to the porch and waits for Antonia and Elijah. They slap the dust off their jeans, stomp it off their boots, and join him. He opens a heavy wooden door onto an entry hall coated in honey-colored light. Old portraits look down on old furniture, a scene from another time, except for the canned laughter of a sitcom coming from somewhere upstairs.

The Mexican slides a panel aside and nods the Fiends into the room revealed, a library with leather armchairs, floor-to-ceiling bookshelves, and a cold, dark fireplace. An oil lamp flickers on a wide desk at the far end of the chamber, behind which a shadowy figure waits.

"Welcome," the shade says.

Antonia and Elijah approach the desk, their footfalls muffled by the thick carpets covering the tile floor. The man at the desk stands. "George Moore," he says. "And you must be the Fiends I've heard tell about." He shakes Elijah's hand, kisses Antonia's.

He's tall and fat. Fat fingers, fat thighs, fat face. In age, he could be anywhere between forty and sixty. It's hard to read with all the extra flesh. He's wearing a rich man's getup from a hundred years ago: waistcoat, watch chain, string tie. His hair is oiled, and his big bushy sideburns look like they're straining to hold up his chins.

"I apologize for the gloom," he says. "But I can't abide electric light. I was born in 1806, and as far as I'm concerned, the world's been going to hell since 1860."

"We try to keep up with the times," Antonia says.

"I heard," Moore says. "You sounded like Judgment Day coming up the drive."

"It does put the fear of God in you, doesn't it?" Elijah says.

"Is that what this is all about?" Moore says with a contemptuous wave. "The motor scooters, the jackets, the attitude?"

"Doesn't hurt to have people wary of you," Antonia says.

Moore takes a skinny cigar from a carved wooden box on the desk and tilts the box toward Elijah. "Care to join me?"

"Never took it up," Elijah says.

Moore starts to close the box. Before he can, Antonia darts out a hand and grabs a cigar. Moore raises his eyebrows but recovers quickly, striking a match and holding it out to her.

"Is smoking part of keeping up with the times?" he says.

"Oh, hell," Antonia replies. "Ladies have been smoking as long as men have."

"Not in my circle," Moore says. "Not ladies." Antonia makes a face but holds her tongue. Moore sees this and smiles. "Then again, I don't know much about how things are these days," he continues. "I haven't left this ranch in a hundred years—haven't had to." He motions to two chairs in front of the desk. "Let's relax, shall we?"

The three of them sit. Antonia is still perturbed.

"No lights, but you've got television," Elijah says.

"A concession to my wife," Moore says. "She claimed she was bored out here. *Oh, George, I'm so bored.*" He mimics her voice. "Now she stares at the damn thing so long and so hard, it's a wonder she's not blind."

"Is she your cow too?" Antonia says.

"What a question," Moore says.

"Just wondering how you get by. You said you never leave."

"I feed off her, yes. I have an arrangement with her family. They're aware of my needs and sympathetic to them. Lupita is my fifth Sanchez wife. The man who fetched you here, he's a Sanchez too. They've been in Texas two hundred years and have worked for my family most of that time."

"Must be nice having people who are so understanding," Elijah says.

"I pay them well," Moore says. "I wouldn't be suited to the life most of our ilk live, always on the move, always on the hunt. I'd be worn out in no time. Luckily, I have the means for a more settled existence."

A clock chimes softly on the mantel. Antonia blows a smoke ring at the ceiling. She's tired of the chitchat. "Monsieur Beaumont told us you had a job that needed doing," she says.

Moore shoots a glare at her, peeved at being hurried. "Perhaps the rules of interacting with hired help have changed too," he says. "I was taught it was polite to engage in a bit of small talk before issuing my marching orders, in order to avoid appearing imperious."

"You're not talking to your ranch hands," Antonia says. "Spit it out."

Moore purses his lips, then turns slightly, enough so Antonia will notice, to address Elijah only. "I want you to kill a man for me," he says.

"All right," Elijah says.

"Not just any man. He's one of us. Do you have a problem with that?"

"Not if the money's right."

"You'll be amply compensated."

"Where would we find him?"

"Right now he's in Phoenix. The man I have tailing him says he'll be there for another three days. Can you make it by then?"

"We can."

"And have time to do the job?"

"That part doesn't take long."

"Why not have your man dust him?" Antonia says.

"He's afraid of our kind," Moore says. "Believes all those campfire tales." He reaches into a drawer and pulls out a stack of money. "I'll give you twenty-five thousand now," he says, "and twenty-five when McMullin is dead."

"That's not enough," Antonia says. "A rover's harder to sneak up on than your average sonofabitch. And there's the travel."

"I wasn't finished," Moore says. He gestures to the man, Sanchez, who came for Antonia and Elijah at the roadhouse. He's been standing at the door to the library but now leaves the room.

"What did this guy do to you?" Antonia asks Moore.

"That's not your concern," Moore says.

"Not usually," Antonia says, "but this time, with you, I want to know. Tell me why you want him dusted or get someone else to do your dirty work."

Moore looks to Elijah, who shrugs. He turns back to Antonia. "While a guest in this house, he seduced my previous wife, fucked and fed off her," he says. "I'm a proud man. Too proud to let that kind of betrayal go unpunished. My wife, I staked out in the desert and let the sun and ants and coyotes have their way with her. McMullin escaped, though, and I've been hunting him for five years. Last week my man finally caught up to him."

Sanchez comes back into the library. He approaches the desk, carrying a drawstring sack.

"Ahh, here we are," Moore says. "I believe this and the money will be more than sufficient."

Sanchez opens the sack. Antonia and Elijah peer inside. A naked baby wriggles at the bottom, a tiny brown baby girl. The Fiends exchange glances.

"When you bring my man in Phoenix proof you've killed McMullin, he'll hand over the rest of the money and this little treat," Moore says.

"Looks like we're in business," Elijah says.

The trouble starts when Real Deal notices a Confederate battle flag hanging on a wall of the roadhouse, up there with the beer signs and girlie pinups. He nudges Yuma.

"Don't," she says.

Ignoring her, Real Deal calls to the bartender, who's been sitting sullenly with the other old man, the one in the ball cap, giving him and Yuma dirty looks. He probably doesn't like seeing a curvy, freckled redhead cuddling a big black man. The bartender gets up, shuffles over, and opens the beer cooler, thinking they want another round.

"You ever hear of Baxter Springs?" Real Deal says.

"I don't believe so," the bartender says. "Is it in Texas?"

"Kansas," Real Deal says. "Baxter Springs, Kansas."

"Don't know it."

"How about Quantrill's Raiders? Heard of them?"

"Them, yes, I've heard of."

"I bet you have," Real Deal says. "Stories about how they gave the Federals hell. How they ambushed Jayhawkers and Red Legs and other nigger-lovers and shot 'em to pieces. I bet you think they were pretty goddamn great, real heroes."

"Look, friend," the bartender says. "I don't know what you're getting worked up about. That's ancient history."

Real Deal grabs the bartender's forearm and presses it to the bar. "Ancient history?" he says.

The Bobs and Johnny Kickapoo look over, sensing trouble. Real Deal stares into the bartender's eyes.

"October 6, 1863," he says. "Me and my little brother, Henry, were teamstering, hauling the possessions of General James G. Blunt, who was transferring his command from Fort Scott to Fort Smith. We were being escorted by a unit of the 14th Kansas Cavalry and some men from the 3rd Wisconsin. Between the soldiers, us teamsters, and a few civilians, we were one hundred souls.

"Henry was eighteen. I was twenty. He looked so much like me, people thought we were twins. He was the best horseman I ever saw, even young as he was. All he had to do was think something, and a horse'd do it. He was Mama's favorite. Mine too."

Real Deal's voice seizes. He takes a sip of beer.

"This ain't worth it, baby," Yuma says.

"We were on the Texas Road, the old Shawnee Trail, a quarter mile north of Fort Blair, where we were supposed to overnight," Real Deal continues. "General Blunt called a halt. He had his regimental band with him, and he ordered them into their dress uniforms. He wanted to make an emperor's entrance at the fort, put on a show.

"It was late in the afternoon. Me and Henry were laid up against a wagon, smoking and speculating how cold it was gonna get once the sun went down. All of a sudden a hundred Federal troops rode up on us. We first thought it was an escort from the fort, but something didn't feel right, something about their hats, their beards, even the way they sat in their saddles.

"'Those ain't soldiers,' Henry said. 'They're bushwhackers.'

"The general knew something was wrong too. He yelled for the troops to mount up, but it was too late. Quantrill and his cocksuckers charged, wearing stolen uniforms, howling like hellcats, and slinging shot. Behind that first wave came even more raiders. Some of the soldiers put up a fight, but most broke and ran, and Quantrill's wolves set about chasing them down. Me and Henry, unarmed and scared shitless, ducked under the wagon.

"'What's our play?' Henry said. 'Stay or go?'

"Some of the teamsters were trying to get away, hauling ass across the prairie. The wagon we were hiding under joined the stampede, leaving me and Henry with no cover. There was nothing for it but to scatter with the rest of the chickens.

"I've been roaming this earth for 133 years. I've forgotten cities I once knew, the faces of women I've loved, the names of men I've despised. But I remember that day like a slap still stinging my cheek. Running through the tall grass and it trying to trip me. The puffs of smoke and the smell of powder. The gunshots and the screams. And I remember seeing a yellow butterfly and a sea of blue flowers and thinking, *This is too pretty a place to die.*"

Real Deal pauses again, again swamped by the past.

"Let's go outside and smoke a fatty," Yuma says.

"We're talking ancient history," Real Deal says. "Don't make me lose my place." The bartender tries to ease out of his grip. Real Deal clamps down and continues. "We ran up one gully and down another, and it looked like we might be getting away until we came upon the general's band. They'd tried to escape, but their wagon lost a wheel. The bush-whackers had caught up to them, had them kneeling in the dirt, ten men and a little Negro drummer boy. You ever heard a man beg for his life? It's pitiful, something to give even the meanest motherfucker pause. Not those Rebs, though. They shot every one of the poor bastards, whooping and hollering like it was squirrels or cats.

"Henry couldn't bear it. He jumped up and ran, and they chased him down. They shot him twice in the back and a bunch after he fell, and it was like they'd killed me too. I lay there like one more dead man and watched the Rebs pile the corpses onto the band's wagon and put a torch to it.

"Someone started screaming, someone alive in the pyre, the drummer boy. He untangled himself from the other bodies and crawled out of the fire. Flaming from head to toe, he dragged himself on his belly like a glowworm, leaving a trail of burning grass. The bushwhackers wagered on how far he'd get and pissed on him to put him out when he finally dropped.

"I laid there all night, hollow as an old cow carcass, while the Rebs drank themselves to sleep. They packed up at day-break and rode off, and sometime later a scout from the fort out looking for survivors found me."

Real Deal releases the bartender, sits back, and strokes his goatee.

"Eighty-two good men were massacred that afternoon, slaughtered without mercy by four hundred piece-of-shit Reb bushwhackers," he says.

He points at the Confederate flag.

"Take that fucking thing down."

"This is my place," the bartender says.

In a dark flash Real Deal pulls his pearl-handled switchblade and sticks the point of it under the bartender's chin.

"Take it down, or I'll drain you dry," he says.

Pedro comes in from outside. He's big for a Mexican. His mom used to tell him he was part mountain and part tree. He's got a thick, black horseshoe mustache that hangs six inches off his chin. "Antonia and Elijah are back," he says. "Time to go."

Nobody moves. All eyes are on Real Deal and the bartender, the tension in the room like a finger tightening on a trigger.

"I said let's roll!" Pedro roars, trying to break the spell. "Samuel!"

Samuel is Real Deal's true name. Hearing it makes him blink. He takes his knife from the bartender's throat, goes over to the flag, and yanks it off the wall. Neither of the old men say anything as the Fiends walk out the door, Real Deal carrying the flag. Yuma's the last to leave. She tosses a hundred-dollar bill on the bar and says, "Ain't you lucky."

Out in the parking lot, Real Deal uses a siphon hose to pull enough gas from his bike's tank to soak the flag. He tosses a match. Flames claw at the stars, and the flag burns to nothing as the Fiends clatter off into the night.

5

Jesse can't sleep. Every time he dozes off, a jolt shoots through him, zapping him back to wakefulness. He gives up after an hour, crawls out of bed and sits at the little table in front of the motel room's curtained window. He thinks about putting on the television but doesn't want to disturb Edgar, who's snoring away on the other bed.

Abby is curled beside Edgar, protective as a good dog, yellow eyes blazing in her coal-black head. Edgar turned the cat twenty years ago behind Jesse's back. Jesse hates the damn thing and she knows it, hissing whenever he gets near and swiping at him, claws out, if he makes to touch her. He'd have gotten rid of her a long time ago if she didn't calm Edgar. Petting her brings Edgar out of his worst tantrums and brightens him when he's at his bluest. So Jesse puts up with the hissing and the scratching, the foul-smelling food and even fouler shit box.

He picks up Edgar's deck of cards, intending to play Klondike. A slash of sunlight that's pushed between the curtains cuts the table in half. He stares at the beam while he shuffles, tracks the dust motes schooling in it like fish in a lustrous sea. Then, as if in a trance, he puts down the cards and slides his index finger into the light.

The pain is sudden and intense. He grits his teeth against it. A wisp of smoke rises from a knuckle, the flesh blackens and chars, a blister swells. He pulls the finger back, and as soon as it's out of the sun, the burn begins to heal. A few seconds later he can't even tell where the damage was. *Enough,* he thinks, but can't stop, is never able to. He thrusts his finger into the beam again, again it starts to cook, and again he pulls it back as he's about to scream. He repeats the ritual until he's finally worn out enough to sleep.

He asks the desk clerk what's going on in town. He and Edgar have passed through Phoenix countless times, and he's sick of the same old pool halls and miniature golf courses but doesn't feel like spending another night in front of the television.

"You can still catch the game at Municipal Stadium," the clerk says.

Jesse's wary of taking Edgar anywhere there's a crowd. He never knows how he'll react to the noise and confusion. But sitting outside, drinking cold beer sure sounds like a nice way to pass the evening. He asks Edgar what he thinks, and his response—bouncing with excitement—convinces him to take the chance.

"If you start making monkeys, I'll drag you out so fast your head'll spin," he warns his brother.

"You're the boss," Edgar replies.

They drive to the stadium and settle into a couple of cheap seats. It's the bottom of the fourth inning. The stadium lights shine down as bright as the sun on the green grass and red dirt of the field, transforming it into an oasis that defies both the darkness and the desert.

The players' uniforms gleam, music throbs in the warm air, and wherever Jesse turns he sees happy faces. He allows himself the briefest fantasy that he's safe among these people, but the reality is, if they knew he and Edgar were rovers, they'd tear them to pieces.

Edgar's thoughts are nowhere near as bleak. He's enjoying the game even though he barely understands what's going on. Jesse's explained the rules to him a hundred times, but they never stick. Instead, he looks to other spectators for cues, cheering when they cheer, stomping and chanting, "Let's go, Giants, let's go," when they stomp and chant.

He spots a boy eating a hot dog and decides he wants a hot dog too.

"I'll get you one later," Jesse says.

"I'm hungry now," he says. "Come on, good buddy."

Jesse looks for a vendor, but none are nearby. What he does see is a man in the row below theirs taking beer orders from his friends.

"How many?" the man asks. "You want one? You?" His pals hand him money, and when he pulls out his wallet to cram the bills inside, Jesse notices a lot of cash already stashed there. The guy's been drinking. He knocks his ball cap off scratching his head and nearly falls picking it up. His friends send him on his way with catcalls and good-natured shoves.

"Wait right here," Jesse says to Edgar.

"Attaboy," Edgar says. "Mustard and ketchup. You know how I like 'em."

Jesse follows the drunk down the stairs. The man takes the steps slowly, one at a time. When they reach the echoey concourse, he hurries to a bathroom, and Jesse enters right behind him. Men and boys piss into a long metal trough, lined up like cows at their feed. The drunk slips into an open spot and unzips his trousers. He stares at the wall above the trough, humming whatever song is playing outside. Jesse wedges in beside him and mimes taking out his prick. Then, quick as a robin plucking a worm, he reaches over and lifts the drunk's wallet from his back pocket and sticks it into his own.

The drunk is still pissing, still humming, when Jesse leaves the bathroom. Jesse walks some distance along the concourse before ducking into an alcove, where he pulls the money from the wallet and drops the wallet to the ground. He counts the bills while waiting in line at a concession stand. Fifty dollars, a decent score.

The announcer reminds everyone about the upcoming Bicentennial Fireworks Spectacular, "a night of patriotic fun for the whole family." Jesse was born in the centennial year—1876—and he'd swear more than a hundred years have passed since then. It feels to him he's been on the roam forever. He steps up to the counter and orders a dog for Edgar and a beer for himself.

Back in the stands the drunk is on his knees, searching for his wallet. He tosses aside empty popcorn boxes and drink cups and brushes peanut shells off his palms. "I know I had it," he says. "You guys saw." Jesse, coming up the steps, freezes. Not because he's worried about the drunk fingering him, but because Edgar isn't in his seat.

He scans the crowd, trying to recall what his brother is wearing. Jeans and his favorite Mickey Mouse T-shirt. He's been going on about catching a foul ball, so maybe he moved closer to the field, but there's no sign of him on the rail either.

He's slipped away before, and Jesse usually finds him within a few minutes, quaking with fear, his wanderlust having faded as soon as he got out of sight of his brother. Three years ago, though, things played out differently, in a way that's troubled Jesse ever since.

They got separated at a county fair in Butte, Montana, and when Jesse eventually tracked Edgar down, he was walking hand in hand with a little boy toward the exit.

"What are you doing?" Jesse asked Edgar.

"I'm hungry," Edgar replied.

It had been only two weeks since he'd last fed—too soon for bloodlust.

"Let the boy go," Jesse said.

"I won't," Edgar said and pulled the kid closer. The boy started to cry.

"Let him go, or I'll dust you where you stand," Jesse said.

Edgar hesitated, reluctant to give in, but he could see Jesse meant business. He released the boy, who dashed off, and Jesse grabbed Edgar by the neck and hustled him out to the parking lot before there was any trouble.

Back at their motel, Jesse alternated between punching and threatening him.

"I say when it's time for you to feed, and I do the hunting," he said.

"I know," Edgar said.

"You don't have the brains to do for yourself. You'll get us both killed."

"I know."

Edgar's never again shown an inclination to satisfy his bloodlust on his own, and Jesse's been hoping that what happened was a one-time thing. But what if it wasn't?

He sprints down the concourse, calling for his brother into every restroom and pausing at every concession stand to make sure he's not there trying to wheedle a hot dog. When he gets to the end, he turns around to make another pass, his heart kicking at his ribs, and his mouth so dry, it's work to swallow. He wonders if Edgar's in the parking lot, looking for the car, wonders if he remembers they swapped the Ford for a Grand Prix last night.

He comes to a door he missed before and pushes it open to reveal a stairwell.

"Edgar!" he shouts.

An echo, then silence.

"Don't be scared, buddy. I'm not mad at you."

He hears a shuffle and a faint "I ain't scared." Edgar peers over the rail of a landing two stories up.

"What's going on?" Jesse says.

"I seen a rover."

"You sure?"

"He glowed black."

He's talking about the dark aura surrounding rovers that only other rovers can see.

"What did you do?"

"What you always say to: took cover."

Because there are berserkers out there, rovers who wouldn't hesitate, who would in fact relish the opportunity, to dust another rover with an eye toward cutting down on the competition for prey. It's for this reason Jesse avoids others who've turned and why he's tried to instill a fear of strangers in Edgar.

"You did good," he says. "Let's get our asses out of here."

As Edgar starts down the stairs a commotion rattles the walls. Cheering, stomping. A home run.

"What about my hot dog?" Edgar says.

"I'll get you one on the way out," Jesse says.

"Can I pay for it myself?"

Jesse fishes a dollar out of his pocket and hands it to his brother.

"A dollar'll buy two," Edgar says.

"So get two," Jesse says. He pulls open the door and leads Edgar through the crowd. If he really did see a rover, the rover likely saw him, so the quicker they leave the stadium, the better.

Jesse isn't quite ready to go back to the motel. He's all wound up and could use a drink. He and Edgar drive down Central Avenue. The street is clogged with cruisers, a slow-moving procession of greasers gunning cherry hot rods and high-school kids packed into sedans and lumbering station wagons borrowed from their parents. Every window is down, every radio is on, and a sticky-sweet Top 40 cacophony floats above the revving engines and car-to-car sass. "Take the Money and Run," "Love Machine," "Jive Talkin'"—Edgar knows all the songs and sings along.

They come to a bowling alley. That'll do. Edgar likes to bowl, or try to anyway. Most of his throws end up in the gutter, but toppling even a few pins is enough to make him happy. Jesse rents shoes for him and helps him pick out a ball, then parks himself at the bar where he can keep an eye on his lane.

The girl tending bar asks what he'll have. He starts to order a beer but is struck dumb. The bartender is the spitting image of Claudine, beautiful, doomed Claudine, dead, oh Christ, some seventy years now. The only woman he ever loved, the only woman he'll ever love.

"Need a minute?" this bartender says.

Same skin the color of red-elm heartwood, same green eyes that shine as if lit from behind, same long, black hair, only not worn loose, but plaited into two braids that hang past her shoulders.

"I'll have a Coors," he manages to say.

"Jesse! Hey, Jesse!"

He turns to see Edgar pointing at five pins he's downed and gives him the thumbs-up.

The girl sets a bottle in front of him. "Is that your friend?" she says.

"My brother," he says. He keeps staring at Edgar so he doesn't stare at her.

"Why aren't you playing too?"

"He has more fun on his own."

"Nah. You're afraid he'll beat you."

Jesse smiles. Claudine liked to joke around too. He gathers himself and turns to face the girl.

"Ain't you smart," he says.

"And don't you forget it."

"What's your name, smarty-pants?"

"Johona. It's Navajo."

"You're an Indian?"

"My mom is. My dad's Dutch."

Claudine kept changing her story. Sometimes she was Spanish, sometimes French, sometimes a gypsy princess.

"How'd that happen?" Jesse asks Johona, talking about her parents.

"My dad came over here to study Indians," Johona says. "He's an archeologist. You know what that is?"

"Someone who studies old things," Jesse says. "Ancient civilizations."

"You're pretty smart yourself," Johona says. "What's your name?"

"Jesse."

"Pleased to meet you, Jesse."

Johona goes off to see to other customers. Jesse watches

42

her out of the corner of his eye, can't stop. Claudine in tight jeans and a black tank top. She's got an easy way with people, knows what to say to make them feel good. A nice girl. Claudine wanted to be nice, but because she was a huntress at heart, used kindness mainly as a lure.

Jesse checks on Edgar. He's getting ready to roll. He apes the form of the bowler next to him, but his ball still ends up in the gutter. The clatter of falling pins from the other lanes is as sharp and startling as firecrackers. It bounces off the high arched ceiling and returns twice as loud.

Johona replaces Jesse's empty bottle with a full one.

"On me," she says.

"Thanks."

"Where you from?"

"Guess."

"Not here. Somewhere down South?"

"West Virginia. But it's been a while since I've been back."

"So you live in Phoenix now?"

"Passing through. Got work in Denver."

"Doing what?"

"Construction."

"Construction?" Johona says. "You're as pale as a ghost. Give me your hand."

She runs her thumbs over Jesse's palm, his fingers. He remembers Claudine's touch and breaks a little inside.

"You aren't a construction worker," she says.

"What am I then?" Jesse says.

"You're a bank robber."

"You get a lot of bank robbers in here?"

"No, but we get a hell of a lot of construction workers. I'm on the lookout for something more exciting."

"Exciting can go different ways."

"At this point, I'm up for anything."

Two drunks at the end of the bar call for another round. Jesse forces himself to get up when Johona goes off to serve them. He could stay here all night, watching her and seeing Claudine, but what's the point? She's not Claudine. Claudine's dead. He joins Edgar, who's sitting at the scorekeeper's desk and drawing stick figures on the acetone sheet, grinning to see them projected overhead.

"Ready to get your ass whupped?" Jesse says. He picks up a ball, hefts it.

"You ain't no good," Edgar says. "You ain't no better'n me."

They start a game. Every once in a while Jesse looks toward the bar and catches a glimpse of Johona, and every time it makes him smile. Even better, once or twice he catches her looking at him, and she's smiling too.

6

THE ONLY THING ON THE TELEVISION IS A WAR STORY WITH John Wayne. Sometimes Jesse'll talk like him joshing me but not tonight. He's been quiet since we got back from bowling. I ask him does he want to play Crazy Eights or Nickle Nock. Watch your show, he says, I'm thinking.

I lay there petting Abby and thinking too. I think about Mama. I'm having trouble remembering her again. I can see her shape but where her face should be is like rippling water. Same with Daddy and J.P. and Peggy and Aunt Beulah. They're fading away.

Mama used to say all we got is family. Which means I got nothing now. Nothing but Jesse and him barely. He tells me I'll grow into being alone. But that's him not me. We ain't all alike. There's good men and bad men. Brave men and cowards. Some are on the run from the past and some want to keep it with them.

I can't help it I'm crying. Abby climbs on my chest and licks my face. What's the matter? Jesse says. I don't want to tell but it busts out of me. I'm missing Mama. You want to look at the pictures? Jesse says. He goes to his grip and takes out the album and I sit with him on the bed.

He points to the first picture. This is Mama and this is Daddy, he says. On their wedding day, I say. They went to Mr. Borden's studio directly from church to get a photograph made and Mama said to Mr. Borden, I better look pretty in it or we ain't paying. I got the same eyes as her the same nose. Jesse always says whenever I forget her I can look in a mirror. Jesse favors Daddy. Not so tall but seeming bigger. Crow-black hair and eyes. A girl's pouty lips. He's got a smile like Daddy's too. One you don't see much but when you do makes you smile too. I think he looks like Elvis Presley. He says I need glasses.

The next picture's the whole family. Mama Daddy Jesse when he was seven sister Peg when she was five brother J.P. when he was three and me just born. Jesse says, You remember what we called you? You all called me Butterbean, I say. 'Cause you looked just like one, Jesse says. I say, You know what they should've called you? What? Jesse says. Turd, I say, 'cause that's what *you* look like.

Jesse turns the pages. Daddy kissing a shovel at the mine. Peg in her coffin after a fever took her. All us on a trip to the ocean. I say to Jesse, You're fourteen here and I'm seven. See, Jesse says, you remember. I say, I like this picture of Mama where she's smiling. I run my finger over her face. You're my special child, she told me, the one'll be with me forever. The one'll take care of me when I'm old. I will, Mama, I said, don't you worry. And I did. I was the one took care of her after J.P. moved to Norfolk to work at the shipyard and after Jesse went away. He run off one night and we didn't see him again for thirty years.

'Cause you turned, I say to him. It wasn't safe no more for him in Monongah. He had to hit the road. He had to light out for the territory. I asked him was he an outlaw in those days. He said, Buddy I was whatever I had to be. Claudine the girl who turned him the one he run off with got dusted somewhere along the way and he's been sad ever since.

In Monongah the world kept turning as Mama would say. Daddy got blown up in the explosion at the mine. J.P. broke his neck falling off a destroyer he was building. Aunt Beulah ate a bad mushroom and her liver quit. In the end only me and Mama was left. When she got sick she sent for Jesse. Turned out she knew all along where to write him. I asked why she was calling him home. I said, I can keep looking after you. I don't doubt that hon, she said, but who's gonna look after you?

It snowed the day she died and for a week after. The grave-digger said he got blisters on blisters planting her in the frozen ground. Jesse bought her a new dress to be buried in and a casket with white silk lining. I didn't tell nobody he was back. Only me and Cousin Ray knew. Jesse said he'd give Ray the house for holding the funeral and keeping his mouth shut. If you give him the house where'm I gonna live? I asked Jesse. He told me not to worry.

The next night he sat me at the kitchen table and said he was leaving again but this time taking me with him. I asked where we was going. Out West, he said. Where the buffalo roam. I asked him could I get a horse because I didn't know nothing then. I hadn't been anywhere or seen anything. That's why he was able to trick me like he did.

He made a cut on his arm and told me to drink the blood that come up. Said it was a ceremony we had to do before we left. Like when you was baptized, he said. Mama made pan-cakes when I got baptized. That's what I was thinking while I did what he asked: *Maybe I'll get pancakes.* I put my mouth to the cut and drank the blood never guessing my own brother was fucking me.

Because that's how the Little Devil snuck inside. He hid in a bubble and I swallowed him down with the blood. A week later he started whispering in a voice so soft I first thought it was my own mind. Every day he got louder until finally he was howling so I couldn't hear myself think and thrashing about like a salted slug. *Feed Me You Sonofabitch You Cocksucker You Fool.* And I been grappling with him ever since.

I feel better after looking at the pictures. I can see Mama again hear her laughing at my foolishness. I tell Jesse we should get a camera. What for? he asks. I tell him to make pictures to remember things. There's nothing worth remembering, he says. All right, I say, how about a CB radio? He puts the album back in his grip. We don't have any use for a CB radio either, he says. Firecrackers then, I say, for Fourth of July. How about that? That's all I need, he says, for you to blow your fingers off.

I try not to hold against him what he did to me. I understand it's the only way we could stay together and I understand that's what Mama wanted. But if I knew in the kitchen in Monongah what I know now that I'd be at the beck and call of a blood-sucking monster till the ocean dries up and the sun falls out of the sky I'da taken that knife and cut Jesse's heart out right there. That's a sin even to think but a small one considering.

7

June 27, 1976, Near Truckee, California

OVER THE LAST TWENTY-FOUR HOURS THE SCAB OF CIVILIZATION has been torn away and the rot that festers beneath revealed to me. I learned there are monsters that pass as men and that the night nurtures unspeakable crimes, and my own hands have been stained with blood. You'll think I've gone crazy as you read what I'm about to set down—I'm having trouble believing it myself—but Wanda, baby, every word is true.

I spent yesterday morning parked on Virginia, Reno's main drag, a street lined with casinos and souvenir shops. Hungover tourists glanced at the poster and the photos of Benny, but none took me seriously. Neither did the street preacher who thrust his sweaty Bible into the air, laid a hand on my shoulder, and bellowed a prayer before asking for a donation.

I called Howard and let him know I was in town. It seemed only right. As he did last time I passed through, he invited me to stay with him and Mary, and as I did last time, I said I was fine sleeping in the Econoline.

"That's hurtful," he said. "You're my brother-in-law.

Wanda'll never forgive me for not talking you into bedding down at our house."

"She'll forgive you," I said. "She knows better than anyone I'm not fit company these days."

"At least meet me for lunch," he said.

I felt I could handle that. He's family, after all.

He chose the place, the Gold 'N Silver Inn, a greasy spoon near the freeway. He was already sitting with a glass of ice tea in front of him when I got there. He had a badge pinned to his chest with his name and the title *Supervisor, Physical Plant* on it, so he must have come directly from work.

You know I've always liked Howard. He'll talk your ear off, but he also listens, and you can see he's thinking about what you're telling him rather than just waiting to go on about himself. You once told me he never got to be a kid because he had to step up when your father died and take care of the younger children while your mother worked. Cook for them, bathe them, see they got off to school. That stuck with me, because I was a hellion as a boy, a heedless fool who didn't give a damn about anybody but myself. While Howard was changing diapers and washing dishes, I was swiping cigarettes and chasing tail, and I'll bet he's probably still a better person than me.

He waved me to his table when he saw me come in, ignored the hand I stuck out and gave me a hug instead.

"Look at that scruff," he said.

I tugged at my beard. "It's easier just to let the damn thing grow when you're always on the move," I said.

"It's cool," he said. "You got kind of a Moses thing going on or, hey, Marvin Gaye."

"I'd rather be Marvin than Moses," I said. "Moses had God's ear, but Marvin, he's got all the money."

Howard gave the joke a heartier laugh than it deserved. I could tell he was uncomfortable behind his smile. We sat and fumbled with our napkins and silverware.

"How you been?" he said.

There was no sense in lying. "It's been rough," I told him. "Lonely days and lonelier nights."

He nodded like he understood and said, "How long do you think you can keep it up?"

"As long as it takes to find out who killed Benny," I said. "Nobody's gonna do this if I don't."

"The police—" he began.

"The police have given up," I said. "They gave up a long time ago. 'Do you know how many murders go unsolved every year?' one of the detectives had the gall to ask me. 'That's the way it is sometimes,' he said."

The waitress brought me a cup of coffee. Howard waited in silence while I stirred in cream and sugar. Someone was playing a slot machine in the bar. I heard the lever being pulled and the reels spinning and clicking.

"Listen," Howard said. "I'm not gonna pretend I know what it's like to lose a child, and I admire your dedication, but maybe there comes a point where you have to accept the tragedies life throws at you."

I took out my wallet and opened it to a photo of Benny. "You remember this kid, don't you?" I said. "That laugh he had that made everybody else laugh? At what point am I supposed to forget that?"

"I'm not saying you have to forget him," Howard replied.

"He hid a stray dog in his room for a month," I said. "Wanda hates dogs, but he convinced her to let him keep it. He was tenderhearted, couldn't stand to see anything suffer. I took that for weakness and was hard on him when I shouldn't have been. I said things to him that haunt me, things that made him leave home."

Howard reached across the table and laid a hand on my arm. "Charles," he said. "Charles, listen to me. Benny was a drug addict. He was a prostitute. He got into a car with the wrong person. That's the truth of it. The ugly truth. You feel guilty about what you said to him, and maybe you should. But you also gotta know that whenever someone dies, someone else always wishes they'd set things right with them before."

I felt my anger building. It doesn't take much to set me off these days. All of a sudden it was all I could do to keep from pounding my fist on the table.

"So you're another one like that detective," I said. "Gonna tell me how it is."

"I'm here for the sake of my sister," Howard said. "You feel bad about Benny, but what about Wanda? You cleaned out the bank accounts when you left, and while you've been running around conducting your investigation, she's been working sixty hours a week to keep up the mortgage on your house. She's been busting her ass to pay bills and buy groceries. She's been going to bed every night not knowing where you are and wondering if you're ever coming back. When's the last time you even called her?"

"To say what?" I asked him. "I'm failing out here? I'm chasing my own tail?"

"What you need to do," he said, "and I'm telling you this with nothing but love, is get your ass home and take care of the living instead of obsessing over the dead."

What he said made sense, but sense has no place in the new world I woke into the day I got the call about Benny's murder. For a year afterward I pretended things were the same as they'd been before, that *I* was the same. I went to work every day, I came home and sat down to dinner with you, and I went to bed at nine every evening. Most nights, though, I lay wide awake, begging God to let me sleep.

I tried hard, baby, but I realized I was fooling myself. I realized the old world I'd been living in died along with Benny, and I'd been stranded in a new one where madness and cruelty were the norm. How to explain this to a good woman like you, though? All you'd have heard would've been the raving of a lunatic. So I didn't try. I snuck off instead, set out on this mission of mine.

And it would have been just as impossible to explain myself to Howard. I finished my coffee, stood slowly so as not to explode, and spoke softly lest I shatter every window in the place.

"Good to see you," I said.

"Hold on, now, goddammit, hold on," Howard said.

"Give my love to Mary and the boys."

I tottered out of the diner, feeling like I was carrying a thousand extra pounds. I started breathing easier when I reached the Econoline, but fresh air wasn't enough. I needed something more to keep me going. I needed a sign I was on the right path.

Be careful what you wish for, they say.

As I fumbled for my key, desperate to escape before Howard got it into his head to follow me out and press his case, I noticed an old white man standing nearby. His arms were crossed over his chest, and he regarded me through one squinted eye, the other hidden behind a black patch.

"You all right?" he said. His voice sounded like gravel in a garbage disposal.

"I'm fine," I replied.

He jerked his chin at the shoe polish pleas scrawled on the van. "Your son was murdered?"

"He was."

"How?"

"What's it to you?"

"Throat cut? Bled out? Killed one place, dumped another?"

I examined the man more closely. He wore blue coveralls and had the steel-gray flattop haircut and broomstick-up-the-ass posture of an ex-soldier.

"They found him in a trash bin in Los Angeles," I said. "Two years ago."

"My wife was buried in the desert outside Tonopah," he said. "Coyotes dug up her remains, and a crew of linemen happened upon them."

"I'm sorry to hear that," I said.

Hot wind blasted across the parking lot, scattering trash and rocking the Econoline. The sky was the color of dirt, the sun missing in action.

"Let's go to my house and talk," the man said.

"I don't think so," I replied. "You can say what you have to say here."

"I could," the man said. "But I won't. And besides, it's not so much what I've got to say as what I've got to show you."

In my search for Benny's murderer, I've wasted time on mad scientists, fallen under the spell of false prophets, and been led to lots of dead ends by conspiracy theorists of every stripe. This one-eyed man was different, I could tell. Those of us in pain are sensitive to pain in others. We're tuned to the distinctive frequencies of grief.

"How far?" I said.

"Twenty miles," the man said. "My name's Czarnecki. Follow me in your van."

He walked to an old green Ford pickup crowned with a camper, got in, and pulled out of the lot. We headed up into the hills south of town. He drove fifty miles an hour whether he was on the freeway or on a twisty two-lane mountain road. We turned off onto a dirt track somewhere near Truckee. The road ended a few miles and a couple of creek crossings later at a cabin and some outbuildings spread over an acre of sagebrush and Ponderosa pines.

Czarnecki parked in front of the cabin. A blue jay harangued me from the top of a tree as I joined him. The cabin was old but solid. A rocking chair waited on the porch next to a coffee can full of sand and cigarette butts. An American flag hung next to the front door.

Czarnecki led me into the one-room structure. A sofa, a TV, a bed in one corner with a sleeping bag on it instead of sheets. A sink, a refrigerator, a stove, a table with two chairs. There was some clutter—antique bottles lined up on the mantel above the stone fireplace, rusty branding irons, taxidermied animals—but everything looked to have been arranged, not strewn haphazardly.

"Want a beer?" Czarnecki said, going to the refrigerator.

"No, thanks," I said.

He tore the tab off a can of Budweiser and took a seat at the table. "I don't suppose you'll sit, either," he said.

"I'm fine where I am," I said. I wanted to be ready to make a quick getaway if necessary.

Czarnecki lit a cigarette and contemplated the match after he'd blown it out. "How long have you been looking for your boy's killer?" he said.

"It's been a year now," I said.

"Got any suspects?"

"No, but I have some theories."

"The circumstances do make a man ponder," Czarnecki said. "Abducted somewhere. Killed and drained of blood somewhere else. Body left somewhere else. That's not a robbery, that's a ritual. I like to drove myself nuts ruminating over it."

He paused to take a hit off his cigarette, a long, deep drag he released with a hiss.

"Then I found Mr. Otto," he said. "Or, rather, Mr. Otto found me. He turned up one day at my old place in Carson City, the house I shared with Marjorie, my wife. This was a couple years after her murder, a couple years where I hadn't been doing much but drinking. Drinking and pondering. 'I'd like to talk to you about your wife,' Mr. Otto said. 'What about her?' I said, skeptical, like you."

He paused again, and I realized he was fighting tears. "Everything changed for me that day," he said. "And every-thing's gonna change for you today." He finished his beer in a gulp. "Come with me."

I followed him outside. The jay was still squawking. A warning, I now realize. Nature raising an alarm. I should have heeded it. I should have gotten into the Econoline and driven away as fast as I could. But Czarnecki had hooked me, piqued my curiosity. We went to a concrete-block shed with a thick wooden door. Czarnecki opened a padlock and folded back a steel hasp. The door creaked when he pushed it. Blood was racing through my veins. I could feel it in my wrists, in my throat.

The big, orange afternoon sun shot fire into the window-less shed. In the middle of the tomblike space was a cot; on the cot, a blanket; under the blanket, what?

Czarnecki stepped into the shed and yanked off the cover. The sun shone on a figure lying on the cot. A white man—a kid, really—naked except for underwear. He was in handcuffs, and his feet were shackled, too, at the ankles. The restraints were attached by a chain to an eyebolt embedded in the concrete floor.

When the sunlight hit him, he screamed like a wounded animal and writhed in agony. "What the fuck?" he wailed. "What the fuck?" He threw his arms up to protect his face from the glare, and his flesh started to smoke.

Czarnecki pulled me into the shed and slammed the door shut, plunging the room into darkness. He yanked a string to turn on a bare bulb dangling from the ceiling. The kid quieted. He was twenty or so, with blond hair and blue eyes. The skin on his forehead, his arms, his legs—wherever the sun's rays had touched him—was black and blistered. The stench of it made me retch, and I retreated in horror until my back was against the door.

Before my eyes, the wounds began to heal. The charred areas flattened and softened, and new flesh spread like melting wax to cover the lesions.

"Isn't that something?" Czarnecki said.

I had no response.

"You can shoot them, stab them, run over them with your car, and they'll come right back from it."

Pretty soon it was as if the boy had never been burned at all. As his pain eased, he regarded me with a disdainful sneer that revealed a gold tooth up front. He was so thin, his elbows and knees were swollen knobs, and you could count his ribs. There was a tattoo of a butterfly on his chest.

Enough for now.

My fingers are too weak to hold this pen, my mind too tired to remember clearly. I'll get some sleep and set the rest down later. Unless I wake and find this has all been a bad dream. Please let that be so.

TODAY'S PASSAGE: Everyone that doeth evil hateth the light, neither cometh to the light, lest his deeds should be reproved.

—John 3:20

8

THE FIENDS MAKE THE RIDE TO PHOENIX OVER TWO NIGHTS, with a stop in Alpine to wait out the sun. They keep to deserted back roads, hogging both lanes and rocketing through sleeping one-horse towns.

At one point they come upon a pickup truck rattling home from some late-night mischief and speed up to overtake and surround it. Eight black Harleys ridden by eight leather-clad devils materialize out of the darkness, and the truck's driver is buffeted by the bone-jarring rumble and soul-deep throb of the bike's engines. The Fiends laugh at the yokel's jaw dropping beneath his cowboy hat and roar off—disappearing, the driver swears later, in a cloud of smoke and swirling sparks.

They get to Phoenix just before dawn and check into the Apache Motel. That evening Antonia calls George Moore's man. The guy is some kind of hawkshaw, some kind of bounty hunter. He doesn't offer his name.

"McMullin is flopping at the Sandman on Van Buren," he says. "But he's at a ball game tonight, at the stadium."

Antonia hangs up and joins the rest of the Fiends by the motel's swimming pool, drops onto a chaise next to Elijah. Real Deal, Bob 1, and Johnny Kickapoo are roughhousing in the water like unruly children. The rest of the gang slam dominoes on a round metal table with a metal umbrella hovering above it. A transistor radio blares a rock 'n' roll station. The motel's owner has asked them twice to turn the music down, but they crank it back up as soon as he returns to the office. Nobody's worried about him calling the cops. The motel is lousy with hookers, thieves, and dopers.

Johnny Kickapoo climbs out of the pool. He got his nickname because he hung around the Kickapoo reservation while growing up in Oklahoma. He doesn't have a drop of Native blood in him—his black hair and eyes come from his Italian mother, his prominent nose from his German father—but he pretends he's part Indian, even wears a feather in his hair. He bares his ass at the other swimmers and jumps back in with his knees pulled to his chest. The resulting explosion sends the pool's pale blue light skittering over the dying palms drooping overhead. Above them the stars, unmoved, as Antonia and Elijah discuss the hit.

Normally, the next team up in the rotation, in this case Real Deal and Yuma, would do the job and split half the payment—minus ten percent to Monsieur Beaumont—and the rest of the gang would divide the remaining half equally. The baby Moore has promised throws a wrench into the works. An infant is special for a rover. Feed on one and instead of having to feed again the next month, you can go a whole year. Something about the blood.

You'd think, then, it would be open season on babies, but in the same way that con men are known to be as gullible as their marks, rovers are a superstitious lot, and a venerable bit of lore keeps most of them away from infants: Steal a child, the warning goes, and you'll wind up dusted soon after.

Antonia scoffs at this fear. She understands that it's simply the childish spookifying of the real danger connected to snatching babies: The disappearance of an infant upsets the public much more than if a vagrant or a whore suddenly drops off the face of the earth. It makes people much more likely to form posses, mount searches, and scrutinize strangers, all of which could mean disaster for a rover.

But since the Fiends didn't grab the baby in question—and in fact have no idea *how* Moore got it—they'd all be comfortable feeding on the child. Even if it's shared with a partner, that's still six months of not having to hunt, not having to wonder where your next get-right is coming from, and not having to worry about being caught draining some rummy. Six months when you could get off the road and relax if you wanted to.

That's why Antonia tells Elijah it's only fair they make an exception to the rotation this time and allow everyone a chance at the jackpot.

"That won't go over well," Elijah says.

And he's right.

"You can't be changing how we do things whenever you want," Real Deal says when Antonia has gathered everyone around the umbrella table. "It's me and Yuma's turn. We do the job, and the baby's ours."

"Right," Yuma says. "Luck of the draw. It could've been any of us."

"If you two weren't up, you'd be begging for a chance at the brat," Pedro says.

"But we don't have to beg," Yuma says. "Because the rules are the rules."

Bob 2 tosses a beer can. Pedro shakes a finger in Yuma's face. War's about to break out. Antonia raps her knuckles on the table to quiet the shouting.

"We'll take a vote," she says. "Do we stick with the regular rotation, or do we give everybody a shot at the kid?"

Everyone but Yuma and Real Deal votes to make an exception. The pair sit there steaming, but what can they do? They're outnumbered.

"How do we decide who makes the hit?" Bob 1 asks.

"We'll roll for it," Antonia replies. "One person per team. Winners do the job and get the kid, the rest split the money."

Elijah grabs a pair of dice out of the domino box. They agree to let Yuma go first. She shakes the bones and tosses them on the table, gets a seven for her and Real Deal. Johnny rolls a nine, and Antonia throws a three for her and Elijah. Then it's Bob 1's turn. He whispers to the dice, blows on them, shakes them over his head. When he finally flings them, he gets two sixes.

"Boxcars!" Bob 2 shouts.

The party breaks up. Too much disappointment and resentment in the air. Everyone shuffles off to their rooms except the Bobs, who celebrate their good fortune until the first rays of sunshine, leaping over the horizon, chase them inside.

"See it?" Bob 2 says.

He points out a giant rat, a foot long from its nose to the tip of its tail. The beast creeps up on a Kentucky Fried Chicken bucket lying in the gutter. Poking its head inside, it pulls out a half-eaten drumstick and rears back on its haunches to gnaw it.

"What the fuck did you show me that for?" Bob 1 says. "You know I can't abide vermin."

They're sitting in an ice-cream parlor across the street from the Sandman Motel. They've been here almost an hour, since right after sunset, came over as soon as it was safe. Their table has a view of McMullin's room, and of the rat, which is rooting in the bucket again.

"A rat's got to be smart to get that big," Bob 2 says. "Got to be able to sniff out poison, fight off dogs, think on its feet."

"Fuck 'em," Bob 1 says. "They should all die. You never heard of the Black Death?"

"I tried to feed on a rat once."

"Stop right there."

"I got so desperate, I went to a dump and chased one down. It tasted like shit and didn't help at all."

"It's a good thing you hooked up with me, isn't it?" Bob 1 says.

"I was doing okay on my own," Bob 2 says.

"Feeding on rats is not 'doing okay.'"

The men have been partners for twenty-five years. Bob 1 was born in 1904 in Key West. He grew up working on fishing boats, got married, had a kid. At 22 he fell for a Cuban girl he met on Mallory Square, a Cuban girl who'd come out only at night. They decided to run away to Havana, and Bob had her turn him, thinking they'd be lovers until the end of time. The night before they were supposed to sail, the girl disappeared, and Bob never saw her again.

Bob 2 is from Brooklyn, born in 1923. He fought in France during the Second World War, killed a lot of men and saw a lot of men die. This triggered his first and only existential crisis: What was the point of grubbing through life when the only possible ending was death? When a hooker he was jungled up with after returning to the States confided that she was a rover and would likely live forever, he saw a way to ease his mind. He forced the girl to turn him, then dusted her so nobody in the world knew his new secret. His plan worked perfectly: He hasn't worried about dying since.

The Bobs met in Kansas City and started traveling together. When your survival depends on hunting down and killing another human being every thirty days, it's smart to have someone watching your back. They make quite a pair. Bob 1 is tall and thin and fair, and Bob 2 is short and round and dark. Bob 1 is kind of quiet, but Bob 2 talks enough for both of them. They get on each other's nerves but also make each other laugh more than anyone else can.

One night a few years into their relationship one thing led to another, and they ended up rolling around in bed. It was more like fighting than fucking, and both of them felt okay afterward, so they've kept it up. It's nothing they plan, just something that happens now and then. Four years ago they fell in with the Fiends, again thinking about safety in numbers, but also looking to make some money, and it's been a wild ride ever since.

Bob 2 finishes his coffee and scrutinizes the menu board on the wall.

"The Bicentennial Special," he says.

"What?" Bob 1 says.

"Cherry, vanilla, and blueberry on a sugar cone."

"Knock yourself out."

Bob 2 goes to the counter. The high-school girl scooping sundaes and working the register is scared of him and Bob 1, he can tell. Their long hair, their beards, their tattoos. Good. The more scared people are, the better.

"Gimme that Bicentennial thing," he says.

Movement at the motel catches Bob 1's eye. He straightens from his bored slouch and puts his face to the window. A man steps out of the room they've been watching. He matches Moore's description of McMullin, and a black rover aura shimmers around him. He makes sure his door is locked, shoves his hands in his pockets, and walks toward the ice-cream parlor.

Bob 1 stands and calls to the girl, "Where's the back door?"

He and Bob 2 dash through a storage room and out into an alley behind the shop. Hurrying to the end of the alley, Bob 1 peeks around the corner and watches McMullin enter the ice-cream parlor. A bell rings when the door opens. Bob 1 pulls his head back and takes a bag of sunflower seeds out of his pocket. He tosses some into his mouth and cracks them between his teeth.

"You aren't gonna keep an eye on him?" Bob 2 says.

"You didn't hear that bell?"

A few minutes later the bell rings again. McMullin leaves the shop, carrying a cup of coffee. He crosses Van Buren and gets into a Dodge Dart parked in front of his room, starts it up, and pulls out of the lot.

The Bobs dash to the Hornet they stole in order to be less conspicuous than they would on their Harleys. They keep a car between them and the Dart as they follow McMullin. He makes his way to a drive-in theater and turns into the entrance. Bob 2 pulls to the side of the road. The jittery red and yellow neon on the back of the giant movie screen dances across the hood of the Hornet.

"What now?" Bob 2 says.

"I guess we're going to the show," Bob 1 replies.

They join the line of cars waiting to enter the drive-in, pay the admission fee at the booth, and cruise the lot, looking for McMullin. When they find where he's parked, they pull into an empty slot two rows behind, between a couple of teenagers in a Volkswagen Beetle and a family sitting in lawn chairs in the bed of a pickup. Bob 2 takes the speaker off the post and hangs it from the window but turns the sound down. The film has already started. Clint Eastwood, fifty feet tall, squints and draws his gun.

Bob 1 watches McMullin's car while Bob 2, imitating a play-by-play announcer, keeps up a running commentary on the action in the Volkswagen.

"Here we go, folks," he says. "Johnny Fuckerfaster is making a move on Susie Rottencrotch. He's got his hand up her blouse and is trying to sneak under her bra. Meanwhile, Susie's petting his trouser snake. Young love, ladies and gentlemen, young love. You can't beat that."

McMullin gets out of the Dart and heads for the cinderblock snack bar. He's a little guy with an unruly mop of curly red hair.

"There he goes," Bob 1 says.

"I've got a plan," Bob 2 says.

"Clue me in."

"Come running when I signal."

Bob 2 slides out of the Hornet and walks to the Dart. A gunfight erupts on the screen, and shots ping out of every speaker on the lot. The driver's door of the Dodge is unlocked. Bob opens it and pops the lock on the rear door. Opening that, he climbs in and lies down behind the front seat. He made the garrote he takes from his pocket himself—a length of thin wire with wooden handles at both ends.

Crunching gravel telegraphs McMullin's return. Bob grips the garrote tighter. The front door opens, and the overhead light goes on. The Dart rocks as McMullin slides in with his popcorn and soda. He closes the door, and the light goes out.

Bob sits up, slips the loop of wire over McMullin's head,

and yanks the handles. The wire digs into McMullin's throat. He drops the popcorn and struggles silently, the garrote cutting off his voice as well as his air. He claws at the wire, trying to pry it from his windpipe. His legs spasm, and his feet kick the underside of the dash.

Bob uses all his weight to draw the wire even tighter, nearly pulling McMullin into the back seat. McMullin's eyes bulge. His tongue protrudes from his mouth like a snail stretched to its limit. Bob takes both handles of the garrote in one hand and with the other draws a hunting knife from a sheath on his belt. He leans forward and drives the knife into McMullin's chest, angling it so the blade slides between two ribs and plunges into the man's heart. McMullin's arms drop, his eyes close, and he slumps in his seat.

Bob climbs out of the back of the Dart and opens the front door. He pushes McMullin over and slips behind the wheel. The keys are in the ignition. Two flashes of the car's brake lights bring Bob 1 running. He's carrying a duffel bag.

"Get him?" he says.

"What's it look like?"

Bob 1 dives into the back seat. Bob 2 hangs the speaker on the post and makes for the exit, leaving the Hornet behind. He takes it slow, but McMullin's head still bounces off the passenger window a few times. When they're in the clear, Bob 1 leans over the seat to look at the body.

"It go easy?" he says.

"I hit him like an A-bomb," Bob 2 says.

"Boom."

"Boom."

They pull over on an empty stretch of road outside town. Saguaros stand out against the starry sky, and jagged black hills disrupt the horizon. Bob 2 drags McMullin's body out of the

Dart and drops it on its back. Bob 1 unzips the duffel bag and takes out a Polaroid camera. He snaps a couple of photos as proof for Moore (*click, whirr, click, whirr*)—McMullin's face, a tattoo on his forearm—then goes back into the bag for a hatchet.

"You want me to dust him?" he says.

"My hit," Bob 2 says. "I'll do it."

He grabs McMullin's hair and lifts his head. Bob 1 passes him the hatchet, and he raises it high and brings it down on McMullin's neck. Flesh splits and bone crunches. The guy's head comes off so suddenly after only three whacks that Bob nearly loses his balance. He drops the head, and he and Bob 1 watch it and McMullin's body disintegrate into gray powder, leaving only his clothes.

Bob 1 goes through the pockets of the pants, removing a wallet and motel key. The shirt yields a pack of chewing gum. The wind gusts and carries away most of the ash. Bob tosses the shirt high in the air, and it sails flapping across the desert, all the ghost McMullin will have.

"You want his shoes?" Bob 1 says.

"You ever see me wear sneakers?" Bob 2 replies.

They drive into town, abandon the Dart in a shopping mall parking lot, and ride their Harleys back to the Apache.

9

EDGAR SWAYS AND GRUNTS AND JABS AT THE FLIPPER BUTTONS on a pinball machine. Jesse's at the bar. They've returned to the bowling alley after Jesse lay awake all day, buffeted by a flood of memories triggered by meeting Johona, memories he thought were lost to him for good.

There Claudine was, humming French songs in the moonlight; there she was sipping champagne in a San Francisco hotel, New Year's Eve 1902; there she was, the shine of her hair, the swish of her skirts, the seaside rhythm of her breath in sleep.

Time devours memories, gnaws the meat off them and crunches the bones. Jesse's always considered this a blessing. Better to be focused on the here and now when you're forever on the hunt, forever being hunted. Better not to be daydreaming about Mama's peach pie or a departed lover's touch. But maybe he's been wrong. Because tonight, for the first time in a long while, he doesn't wish he was dead. In fact, after spending hours caught up in the torrent of reminiscence, he felt as if a crust of mud that'd been weighing him down had cracked and fallen away. That's why, as soon as the sun set, he roused Edgar and said, "Let's go back to that place we were last night."

Johona was behind the bar, as he'd hoped. "Howdy, stranger," she said, and he'd be damned if she didn't even have the beauty mark on her lip Claudine had. He set Edgar up in front of the game and went back to the bar and ordered a beer. Johona's been busy ever since, however. The place is packed, and there are drinks to be poured, jokes to be laughed at. Jesse doesn't mind. It's a thrill watching her scoop ice, watching her make change.

She stops by whenever she gets a chance, sighs and says, "You good?" and, "I'm about to lose my voice, screaming over all this noise." She lights a cigarette, takes two quick puffs, and stubs it out in an ashtray with a conspiratorial wink. She shakes her hips to the beat of a song and glances over to make sure he saw. When her hand brushes his, time collapses in on itself, old feelings and new crashing head-on.

At ten she slaps the bar and says, "So where are we going?"

"What do you mean?" Jesse says.

"I'm off," she says. "Where you taking me? And don't you dare say another bar."

Jesse hesitates. He should end this flirtation now. As much as he's drawn to the girl, going any further will only be courting trouble. Nothing good ever comes of the turned consorting with the unturned. But then she smiles Claudine's smile again, and a worry she's misread him ripples across her face, and in the second between the needle of the jukebox dropping onto a record and the song starting to play, he throws caution to the wind.

"Are you hungry?" he asks.

"Always," she replies.

"I've got my brother with me."

"He can chaperone. Meet me in the parking lot in ten minutes."

Edgar's run out of quarters and so is pretending to play the pinball machine, making sounds with his mouth. He whines about having to leave but brightens at the mention of food.

"Now, listen. There's a girl coming with us," Jesse tells him.

"You gonna feed?" Edgar says.

"No. She's a friend of mine."

"You ain't got any friends."

"You best behave yourself."

"I know how to act," Edgar says. He stands up straight, clicks his heels, and bows like someone he's seen on television. "May I kiss your hand?" he says.

"No fucking around, I mean it," Jesse says.

They wait for Johona in the parking lot, Jesse so nervous that he's bouncing on his toes. Johona comes through the door, laughing and waving goodbye to someone inside.

"You're here," she says to Jesse, kidding like she thought he wouldn't be.

"This is Edgar," Jesse says. "Edgar, this is Johona."

"Pleased to make your acquaintance, Miss Johona," Edgar says. "You sure are pretty."

They walk to the Grand Prix.

"You ride in back, let Johona up front," Jesse says to Edgar.

"I got shotgun," Edgar says. "I always got shotgun."

"It's cool," Johona says. "I like riding in back."

"He has the mind of a child," Jesse says as he opens the door for her.

"Me too," Johona says. "We'll get along great."

She directs Jesse to a Mexican restaurant that's the last business hanging on in a dying strip mall, says it makes the best chimichangas in the world. The hostess seats them in an orange vinyl booth. A menagerie of piñatas hangs from the ceiling, and the Coors sign on the wall has a moving waterfall. Jesse and Johona order beers. Edgar wants one too, but Jesse says, "He'll have a Coke."

Johona talks nonstop, flitting from subject to subject so quickly that Jesse gets lost sometimes. When he does, he just smiles and nods, content to let her enthusiasm wash over him without worrying about keeping up. "You've never heard of Neil Young?" she says. He hasn't, nor Led Zeppelin, *Slaughterhouse Five, Charlie's Angels,* or any of the other things she chatters about. When she asks, "What TV shows do you watch?" he's embarrassed not to have an answer.

"I like wrestling," he says. "I see *Dragnet* sometimes. *The Lone Ranger.*"

"*The Lone Ranger?*" Johona says. "Okay, Pops."

Edgar is pretending his straw wrapper is a snake, slithering it between the salt shaker and the basket of tortilla chips. He doesn't like spicy food, so Jesse orders him a hamburger.

Johona moves on to stories about her friends—Tracy and Pam and Eddie and Carlos. One of them was busted for a joint, but his dad knew the judge and got him off. Another works at a drugstore where the pharmacist keeps cornering her in the back room and telling her he and his wife have an open marriage.

"He's so gross," Johona says. "He looks like Jackie Gleason. You know who that is, don't you?"

Edgar pipes up with, "To the moon, Alice."

Johona laughs and says to him, "Well, *you* know, anyway."

When the food comes, she sits back and claps a hand over her mouth.

"I haven't shut up since we got here," she says.

"I don't mind," Jesse says. "My life's boring compared to yours."

"I don't believe you," Johona says. "Tell me about it."

"There's not much to tell."

"You do construction?"

"Sometimes."

"What about the other times?"

Jesse makes up something new. "I sell cars."

"Man," Johona says. "I really wanted you to be a bank robber."

"How come?"

"So when I'm an old lady I can say I went out with one. I'll say, 'We only had one night together, but it was glorious.'"

She's trying to be funny, but Jesse hears something sad in her voice. For the first time since they sat down, there's a silence. She sips her beer and avoids looking him in the eye.

"Why'd you ask me out if you're taking off for Denver?" she says.

"I believe it was you who asked me out," Jesse says.

"Which was a totally slutty thing to do."

"You aren't a slut."

"How do you know?"

"I know."

Johona scoffs at this. "Anyhow, why'd you say yes then?" she says.

"You remind me of someone," Jesse says.

"A girlfriend?"

"More than that. You could be her twin."

"So she was super foxy."

"She was beautiful."

Johona wasn't expecting a serious reply. She pauses, then says, "What was her name?"

Claudine. Claudine Dejardin. Though the night Jesse met her, she called herself Pythia.

★　　★　　★

SEES ALL, KNOWS ALL promised the signboard on her booth, one of many lining the midway of a traveling fair set up in a pasture on the edge of Monongah. A month earlier the same field had been the site of a weeklong outdoor revival meeting, which hadn't interested Jesse in the least. The fair, though, with its faintly sinister, faintly salacious air and maze of colorful wagons and patched canvas tents, strummed a restless chord in him. So one Saturday, after ten hours of drudgery at the sawmill where he'd been working since he'd been old enough to work, he hurried over to see what he could see.

The encampment was lit by flaming torches and strings of electric bulbs that shone like little suns. A steam calliope whistled out "A Picture No Artist Could Paint" and "My Wild Irish Rose," the music so loud, you stopped trying to be heard over it after a while and pointed instead. Pointed at the sword swallower and the fat lady, pointed at the shooting gallery and Jacob's ladder, pointed at the horse that could count. The lights, music, and frenzied whirl of strangeness worked magic on the crowd. Normally stoic farmers grinned around penny cigars, their stone-faced wives tittered like young girls, and their kids gaped goggle-eyed at the spectacle of an honest-to-God African Pygmy sitting on the shoulder of the World's Tallest Cowpoke.

Jesse bought popcorn and watched folks ride the pleasure wheel and the roundabout. He blew two bits throwing baseballs, trying to win a vase for Mama but walking away with only a Chinese finger trap. A barker spieled him into laying down a nickel to see a flicker projected onto the wall of a tent, ghostly footage of a parade in New York City. In another tent—GENTLEMEN ONLY—two sleepy girls danced the hoochie-coochie in peekaboo harem getups for most of the male parishioners of the First Baptist Church.

Too shy himself to stare openly at the dancers, Jesse pretended to look at the ground, sneakily raising his eyes to watch without lifting his head. He was starting to enjoy the show when a coworker of his, Wade Finney, sidled up with his tongue hanging out.

"The redhead'll suck your pecker for three bucks," he whispered like someone who knew something.

"That so?" Jesse said.

The notion of sticking his pecker anywhere Wade's had been held no appeal. He waited until the fool was absorbed in the show again and slipped back out onto the midway. Claudine was standing outside her booth.

"You want me to tell your fortune, Monsieur?" she called to him, playing up her French accent.

Her eyes were rimmed with kohl, her lips painted red. Wild black hair spilled down her back, and silver stars decorated the blue robe she wore, stars that glittered under the torches like the real thing. Right then and there Jesse's map was redrawn. All roads would lead to her forever after.

He sat across from her in her candlelit stall. Sweet smoke curled out of a brass incense burner shaped like a dragon. Claudine gestured at the deck of tarot cards and the crystal ball on the table between them.

"What is your question?" she said.

"Are you really a gypsy?" Jesse said.

"Among other things."

"We got an old woman around here who about drowned when she was a girl. She can tell your future by looking in a teacup."

"There are many ways to lift the veil."

Jesse pointed at the crystal ball. "You can see the future in that?"

"Those with the gift of prophecy can," Claudine said.

Jesse leaned forward to peer into the ball. "It's true," he said. "I see it clear as day: You and me are gonna fall madly in love."

Claudine told him later that she tried to call a roustabout to bounce him for his sass but couldn't get her mouth to work right.

"You'd already laid me low," she said.

A mariachi band approaches the booth where Jesse, Johona, and Edgar are sitting. A man wearing a sombrero and strumming a guitar asks if they'd like to hear anything special. Johona makes a request.

"What's this?" Jesse says when the band starts to play.

"'Paloma Negra,'" Johona says. "My dad always asks for it."

"What's it about?"

"Fuck if I know."

Johona gives the musicians a dollar when they finish, and they move on to the next table. Edgar is done eating and getting restless.

"I want to play more pinball," he says.

"We'll get a move on soon," Jesse says. "Hold your horses."

"I know something else fun we could do," Johona says.

"What?" Edgar says.

"It's a surprise," Johona says. "You up for a surprise?"

"I guess I am," Edgar says, like he's accepting a challenge.

"What about you?" Johona says to Jesse.

He feels uneasy, as if he's wandered too far out onto thin ice. At the same time he's not yet ready to end the night. So he's going to ignore his misgivings and take Johona where she wants to go, spend a while longer courting Claudine's ghost.

As they get up to leave, Edgar sings softly.

"'I've been to Hollywood, I've been to Redwood.'"

"Hey!" Johona says.

"I know Neil Young," Edgar says. "Jesse don't, but I do."

They drive out of town and wind along a narrow road up the side of a mountain. Johona has Jesse take a turnoff that ends at a wide, flat overlook with a view of the city.

"Park in the bushes in case the cops cruise by," she says.

Jesse pulls into a hollow in a mesquite thicket where the Grand Prix will be hidden from view. He, Johona, and Edgar get out and walk back to the viewpoint. The ground is littered with cigarette butts, crushed beer cans, and McDonald's wrappers. Broken glass glints in the uncannily bright light of a bit of moon blazing overhead. Edgar bends and comes up with an empty shotgun shell.

"People party here," Johona says.

She leads the brothers up a short trail to a natural bench on top of a boulder. The three of them sit against the rock, which even now is still warm from the sun. Phoenix sparkles below like diamonds strewn across the desert. The night is perfectly calm, not even a tickle of a breeze. A helicopter hovers silently above downtown, tethered to the earth by the beam of its spotlight.

"I can see all the way to Monongah," Edgar says. He tosses a rock, another, another.

"Quit it," Jesse says.

Johona lights a cigarette. Jesse can smell the bowling alley on her behind the perfume she's wearing.

"Tell me more about Claudine," she says.

"What do you want to know?" Jesse says.

"How long's it been since you two were together?"

They met at the fair in June 1900. Jesse was twenty-four, Claudine looked to be twenty or so but said she'd been born in 1727 or '28 somewhere in France. She'd once carried a baptism certificate as a reminder but lost it on one of the many occasions she'd had to run for her life. "What does it matter now anyway?" she said. A birthdate was important to someone plotting a course across time, but since turning, she drifted in eternity, a sea without shores.

Johona blows a smoke ring, waiting for an answer.

"It's been a long time since I last saw her," Jesse says.

"Were you in love?"

"I'd say so."

Every turning is a love story. Love for a woman, a man, a child, for life itself, for darkness and the things found only there. Jesse fell for Claudine the moment he saw her. She fell for him just as quickly. They made love that first night in a bed of tall grass on the bank of Booth's Creek.

Jesse had been with other girls, but it was nothing like being with Claudine. She breathed fire into him that raced through his body, burning every dead tree and tumbledown shack, every briar patch and bog inside him. After he came white hot, he lay beside her gloriously empty, gloriously free, for the first time in his life.

Claudine hurried away before dawn that morning and the next and the next. He asked to see her during the day, but she refused. He knew she was hiding something, thought it might be a husband or a child. "Tell me," he urged her again and again. "Tell me what's wrong," and on what was supposed to be their last night together—the fair moving on the next day—she finally revealed her secret.

They were down by the creek again, but she wouldn't let him touch her this time. Many years earlier, she said, she'd made a choice. In exchange for eternal life and health, she'd infected herself with a sickness—an unholy, incurable sickness, the pain of which was dulled only by drinking the blood of other humans. She and others like her were called rovers. They lived like nomads, keeping constantly on the move in order to avoid detection and surreptitiously stalking victims in the night.

Jesse wonders still how she knew he wouldn't raise an alarm or kill her himself after hearing her story, how she sensed the despair and loneliness plaguing him and his intense, near-violent desire to escape the drudgery and hopelessness of Monongah. He wasn't frightened or repulsed when she finished her confession; he was buzzing with strange excitement.

"You've witched me somehow," he said.

"Why?" Claudine replied.

"Because none of what you told me changes how I feel about you."

"If I was a witch, I'd make you disappear," Claudine said. "I'd fix it so I'd never met you."

Jesse grabbed her hand and pulled it to his chest. "I want to come with you," he said.

"You'll have to leave everything behind, your whole life," Claudine said. "You'll be an outcast. You'll live by new laws."

"Your law," Jesse said. "I'll live by your law."

Claudine turned him that night. He remembers her blood trickling down his throat, the heat of it, the stink of it. He remembers the thunder in his brain and the lightning in his veins as he was destroyed and reborn.

"How long did you go out?" Johona says.

"Not long," he says.

"Did you break up with her, or did she break up with you?"

More memories come, memories Jesse doesn't want to revisit. "Tell me something about you now," he says.

Johona puffs on her cigarette. "I've been thinking I'd like being a chef," she says. "Not a cook, a real chef."

"You any good in the kitchen?"

"I burn water, but I could learn. My plan is to go to cooking school somewhere cool like L.A. or New York, somewhere something's happening. Have you ever been to L.A.?"

"Lots of times," Jesse says.

"Isn't it bitchin'? My old boyfriend and me went once. Venice Beach, Universal Studios. We got stoned with this old hippie and walked all the way down Hollywood Boulevard."

"L.A.'s too big for me," Jesse says. "I'm a country boy."

"I love that it's big. I love that you can get lost there."

Edgar stands and points.

"Skunk," he says.

Johona stands too.

"Where?"

"Down in them bushes."

Johona squints.

"It's too dark," she says.

"A mama and a baby."

"Can you see them?" Johona says to Jesse.

Jesse gets up to look. The disgruntled mutter of powerful engines held in check catches his attention instead. Someone's coming up the road. Headlight beams bounce across the overlook.

"Duck," Johona says. "If it's cops, they'll bust us."

Jesse crouches and pulls Edgar down with him.

10

I KNOW MICKEY MOUSE IS A CARTOON. HIM AND MINNIE AND Tom and Jerry. Yogi Bear and Boo-Boo. Woody Woodpecker and Fred Flintstone. Popeye Bluto Olive Oyl Wimpy and all them.

But the folks that show the cartoons are real. You got Quick-Fire McIntyre in Birmingham Uncle Bob in Tucson Mr. Patches in St. Louis Happy Herb in Indianapolis Fred and Fae in Denver Captain Delta in Stockton Cactus Vick in Little Rock and Lorenzo in Tulsa.

I know radio and TV come through the air but the telephone needs a wire. I know everything costs money plus tax. Ten pennies makes a dime. Ten dimes makes a dollar. So do four quarters. I can pump gas and wash bugs off the windshield. I can drive if there's not too many curves. I bet I can change a tire.

If you want to win a fight kick a man in the balls. It ain't real fighting in the movies. They got bottles that break easy. A king beats a queen a queen beats an ace an ace beats everything. If you shake a pinball machine too hard you'll tilt it.

Stars are cold so's the moon. The sun's hot. Hotter than hell. It can cook you just like that. Don't drink out of cricks 'cause cows shit in them. If your kid has asthma stick a lock of his hair in a hole in a sourwood tree a little higher up than the kid is tall. When the boy grows taller than the hole his asthma'll be gone.

Some people are sad and some ain't. Jesse's sad. He got sad when Claudine got dusted and stayed that way. Daddy was happy most the time. Mama was happy. I'm happy except when the Little Devil starts in. He ain't happy nor sad nor mean nor nice. All he is is hungry or not hungry. He's nothing but need and teeth and claws.

I saved a dog once and I saved a man.

The dog belonged to Mr. Sayre. I was hunting crawdads down by the crick and I heard some pitiful howling and whining. I first thought to run home but said to myself, *You ain't yella*, and snuck to the noise keeping well hid.

Mr. Sayre's pup Queenie had one of her paws stuck in a beaver trap. She was crying and thrashing and snapped at me when I come close. I had the idea to use the tow sack I was carrying for the crawdads to cover her muzzle so she couldn't get at me. She took off when I sprung her and run crying all the way back to Mr. Sayre's house. He give me a dollar coin and a bag of peppermint sucks for setting her free and said she'd've died if I didn't come along. Her leg was broke too bad to fix but she got around fine on three.

The man I saved was a miner that turned up missing at the end of a shift. A wop named Scalo. The bossman called everybody in to search. Daddy wasn't none too happy about it. Said, The bastard's probably drunk in some tavern.

He was pulling on his boots getting ready to go and I was playing with ants on the porch drawing a finger across their trail to watch them scatter when a blackness come crashing down on me. Daylight turned dark and I thought I'd been struck blind but little by little like they do when you go from inside to out at night my eyes started working again. Only I wasn't on the porch no more I was down in the mine.

Daddy took me into the pit when I was a boy. We rode a car down then got off and walked along a tunnel. We had lanterns but the light from them didn't do nothing but make the dark darker. Coal dust swirled and water dripped. Daddy told me about blackdamp and whitedamp—poison gases that'll kill you after one whiff—and the deeper we went the harder it got for me to breathe.

Daddy dropped a rock into a shaft and told me to listen for it to hit bottom. It never did. I got the notion Daddy was gonna toss me down the hole next. This give me a fright and I run off down the tunnel. I didn't get far before I tripped and my lantern went out and I fainted dead away. Daddy had to carry me back up top.

On the porch I wasn't scared at all. I could see in the dark as good as in day. And what I seen was the wop. A beam had fallen and trapped his legs. There was his lantern and there was his lunch pail. The lantern had gone out. He banged his pail against the wall and called for help then lay down and prayed in Italian.

When the dark lifted a figure popped into my head: Number 8 Left Heading. I run in the house to tell Daddy. I told him I seen the wop and told him the figure. He grumped and said he ought to whup me for lying.

What is that? Mama asked. Number 8 Left Heading? It's a drift in the mine, Daddy said. Mama's eyes got big. You got to take him to tell someone about this, she said. What am I supposed to say? Daddy asked her. My idiot son had a vision? Twenty-two years old and can't shave himself? Can't go to the store without getting lost? That was a lie. I knew the way to the store. And if you don't say something and that man dies? Mama said.

They fought on it a while longer till Mama put her foot down. If you don't take him I will, she said. Goddammit, Daddy said and me and him set off for the mine.

Daddy talked to the bossman. He was busy telling crews to search here and search there and busy telling guards to keep the townfolk who came to see the commotion back from the adit. Daddy pulled him aside and said, I'm sorry, and, I know it sounds crazy, and, The wife you understand.

The bossman looked at me looked at Daddy and looked at me again. He had a map of the mine in front of him. Number 8 Left Heading, he said tracing it with a finger. That section's been closed for a year. Still he sent a crew to check. They found the door to the tunnel ajar and the wop pinned by a fallen timber where he snuck in to take a nap.

I saved him but I couldn't save Daddy. A year later the mine exploded when he was down there with three hundred others. They went looking for survivors and Mama begged me to try again to see into the darkness. Nothing came to me hard as I thought. They brought Daddy's body up four days later. What was left of it. Barely enough to bury, Mama said.

I know proper is a coffin. I know proper is a stone and flowers. The folks we kill don't get none of that 'cept for sometimes a prayer. I know one or two good ones.

11

June 27, 1976, 3 p.m.

AFTER A FEW HOURS' REST I FEEL STRONG ENOUGH TO FINISH setting down the events of the past day. It's more important than ever there's some kind of record now that things have turned strange.

After Czarnecki showed me the boy chained in the shed, we returned to the cabin. The old man poured himself a tumbler of bourbon, and we sat at the little table.

"What's wrong with him?" I asked.

"They call themselves rovers," he said. "I think they're some kind of vampires."

"Come on," I said.

"It's not what you're picturing, all that pointy teeth and turning into a bat Dracula bullshit. They're predators, pure and simple. They stalk humans, cut their throats, and drink their blood. One of them killed my wife, and one killed your son."

I'd have thought the old man was insane if not for what I'd just witnessed: Sunlight opened wounds on the kid's flesh, and those wounds healed instantly in the dark. In any other context, you'd call that a miracle.

"I use the kid as a pointer," Czarnecki said.

"A what?" I said.

"These things look like just another person to you or me, but they recognize each other—give off some kind of glow only they can see—so I use the kid to sniff them out. It's something Mr. Otto taught me. The kid finds rovers, and I kill them."

Mr. Otto again. I asked who he was.

"Mr. Otto ran a feed lot in Omaha," Czarnecki said. "His daughter, Iris, disappeared one day in I believe it was 1922 and turned up later drained of blood. The police couldn't come up with any suspects, and after a while they stopped looking. Mr. Otto started searching on his own, determined to find whoever'd killed Iris. What he eventually uncovered was something almost beyond his ken."

"Vampires," I said, mockingly.

"Call them that, call them rovers, call them whatever you want," Czarnecki said. "But they do exist: bloodthirsty creatures that prey on humans. Once Mr. Otto discovered them, he set out to destroy as many as he could. It was a crusade, good against evil, and he'd been at it thirty years when he visited me in Carson City and showed me this."

Czarnecki reached under his shirt for a gold ring hanging on a chain around his neck.

"This belonged to Marjorie," he said. "One of the monsters Mr. Otto killed was wearing it. Her name and mine are engraved inside, and that's how he tracked me down. I was skeptical, as I said before. I even thought he might have killed Marjorie himself. But then he took me on a hunt, and I pretty damn quick became a believer."

Czarnecki paused to catch his breath. I noticed how his hands shook when he lifted his glass, how dull his eye was. He's sick, I thought. He's coming to the end of his time.

"Mr. Otto was sixty then," he continued. "He was looking for someone to take over for him. We hunted together until he passed away, and I kept going on my own. I knew I'd never get the fucker that murdered Marjorie, but there were plenty more to send to hell. My aim was to wipe out every bloodsucker on the planet. I didn't get there, but maybe you will."

"Me?" I said. "Not me."

"What was your son's name?" Czarnecki said.

"Leave him out of this," I said.

"Benny," Czarnecki said. "You hear Benny calling to you, don't you? You hear him begging for revenge."

"I don't hear anything except the nonsense of a crazy old drunk," I said.

The stuffed head of a bear snarled at me from above the fireplace, and the wooden floor quaked beneath my chair. My hands were balled into sweaty fists as I stood and hurried for the door. I felt like I was walking with somcone else's feet.

"I'm going hunting tonight," Czarnecki said. "If you want more proof what I've told you is true, come along."

I left the cabin without another word and locked myself in the Econoline. Then I sat there, sat there for hours, mind racing. I sat there until the sun went down and the air grew chill. I sat there until night blacked the trees and a light came on in the cabin. I sat there until Czarnecki called out, "There's an extra can of stew, if you want it."

When I returned to the cabin, the old man put a bowl in front of me and didn't say anything until I'd eaten my fill. Then all he asked was, "You ready?"

I answered with a nod.

★   ★   ★

I followed him out to the shed, him carrying a bowl of Dinty Moore for the kid. The boy was sitting on the cot in the dark, the blanket draped over his bare shoulders. The only other thing in the shed was a reeking five-gallon bucket that served as a toilet. Czarnecki slid the bowl and a spoon across the floor. The kid snatched them up and shoveled stew into his mouth. When he finished, Czarnecki threw him a ring of keys.

"Get dressed," he said.

"I need more than that slop," the kid said. "It's been over a month since I fed proper."

Czarnecki drew a pistol, a .45, from the pocket of his coveralls and pointed it at the boy. "Get dressed," he said again.

The kid unlocked the shackles on his ankles and pulled on a pair of jeans that lay neatly folded on the floor, then sat on the cot to tie his sneakers. He reshackled his ankles, took off his handcuffs, and donned a T-shirt and a denim jacket. When the cuffs were back in place, Czarnecki ordered him to undo the chain from the eyebolt in the floor and return the keys.

"Stand clear," the old man said, waving the .45 at me. "Never let him get too close. They're no stronger than us, but because they can heal, they'll take chances you wouldn't and fight a lot harder. If this one tried to jump me, I'd shoot him in the head. The round wouldn't kill him, but it'd put him down long enough for me to finish him off, and there are a few ways to do that. I could stop his heart with a knife and leave him to rot, I could drag him into the sun, I could burn him, or I could starve him of blood. The quickest and easiest way is to hurt them enough they can't fight back, then cut off their heads. They'll turn to dust in an instant."

The kid emptied the slop bucket in the bushes, then carried it to the truck and put it inside the camper bolted to its bed. He was so skinny, he had to hold his pants up when he walked. Czarnecki kept the gun on him until he had climbed in on the passenger side of the cab and secured himself to an eyebolt on the floor. We slid in on either side of him, Czarnecki behind the wheel. I leaned against the door, nervous at being so close to the kid. He stunk, and the whites of his eyes were pus yellow and shot through with veins.

"So who are you?" he asked me.

"Nobody," I replied.

"Nice to meet you, Nobody. I'm Nobody too."

"Leave the man alone," Czarnecki said.

"Yessir," the kid said, meaning *Fuck you.*

Czarnecki turned on the radio. A sportscaster was cracking jokes about Ali's fight with that Japanese wrestler. A "Bicentennial Minute" came on, the story of a Revolutionary War battle fought on this very day exactly 200 years ago.

"Don't let me die listening to this," the kid groaned. "Put on some music."

Czarnecki dialed in a country-and-western station and played that the rest of the way to Reno. It was all noise to me. Between my fear of the kid and bracing myself as the old man raced down the mountain, I couldn't hold a thought in my head. I finally took to reading road signs to have something to focus on.

When we got into town, the kid started looking for rovers. We cruised the streets for hours, from one end of Reno to the other, past the casinos, past the tourist motels, past the flophouses and dives. Every time we spotted a bum blowing his nose or a hooker preening on a corner Czarnecki would bark, "How about that one?" and the kid's reply was always the same: "Nope."

Czarnecki grew frustrated.

"If you don't earn your keep, you're not worth keeping," he said.

"I'm all messed up," the kid said. "I need to feed."

"You know the deal. Find me a monster first."

"I can't see straight."

"Find me a monster."

The kid's chains rattled as he slumped, dejected. We made our third pass down Virginia. I asked Czarnecki if they found rovers every time they went looking.

"I used to get a couple a month," he said. "Places like Reno draw them, lots of trash for them to feed on. Things have slowed down the last few years, though. I don't know why. We've been out fifteen times in the past sixty days and had no luck. Sometimes I think this asshole is goldbricking." He slapped the kid on the back of the head. "Are you slow-playing me, boy?"

The kid didn't reply, just kept staring out the cracked windshield. Czarnecki slapped him again and said, "Better not be."

Around 2 a.m., as we were crawling through a stucco-and-cinderblock barrio, the kid leaned forward so suddenly, I threw my arms up to protect myself.

"There!" he said.

He pointed at a Mexican wearing a black cowboy hat and ostrich-skin boots. The man's unsteady gait showed he was drunk. He nearly toppled over stepping off the curb to cross the street.

"Get out and tail him," Czarnecki said to me.

"What?" I replied.

"I'll circle the block so he doesn't get wise."

Caught up in the moment, I hopped out of the truck and fell in behind the man, keeping a careful distance.

Czarnecki drove past and disappeared around the next corner.

The street was deserted, all the stores shut up behind steel gates. The only place still open was a beer bar with a cracked plastic sign, CLUB TANGO. Mexican music oompah-pahed from behind a heavy curtain drawn across the doorway. The man I was following paused out front, stood there swaying like a palm tree in the wind, then suddenly continued on his way, stumbling as if an unseen hand had shoved him. The lights of a passing bus pinned his shadow to a brick wall, his hat enormous.

A couple blocks later he came to a two-story fleabag motel fronting a parking lot full of dusty, dented cars and trucks. After a few fumbling stabs with a key, he let himself into a ground-floor room.

I turned to look for Czarnecki's pickup. Parked down the street, the old man flashed his headlights.

"What room?" he said when I rejoined him and the kid.

"Eight," I said.

"Ha!" he said, as if addressing the Mexican. "Got you, you sonofabitch."

"What happens now?" I said.

"We wait," Czarnecki said.

"How long?"

"Till daybreak. They're weaker then."

I could have ended the hunt at that instant, forced the old man to take me back to his place, gotten into the Econoline, and put this madness behind me. I could have, but I didn't. You see, baby, Czarnecki was right: I *do* hear Benny demanding vengeance. I've heard it every day since learning of his death, and to have shied away from a possible lead to his killer because of my own fear would've been another betrayal of him and made me even more of a failure as a father than I've already been.

So.

Czarnecki got out of the truck. I stood behind him as he drew his .45 and threw the kid the keys. The kid freed himself from the bolt on the floor, slid out of the cab, and walked back to the camper.

Czarnecki opened the door. Inside was a plywood crate resembling a crude coffin. The kid climbed into the camper, opened the hinged lid of the crate, and lay down inside. Czarnecki closed the lid and secured it with three padlocks. He covered the crate with a canvas tarp. Winded by even this bit of exertion, he sat at the camper's small table to catch his breath.

"You stick him in here if you're gonna be out during the day," he said, patting the crate. "Keeps him out of the sun."

We returned to the cab, and Czarnecki moved the truck so we had a clear view of the Mexican's room. The motel had quieted for the night. There were no lights anywhere except for the flicker of a TV in the office. Czarnecki lit a cigarette, blew the smoke out his window. He asked if I'd been in the military.

"The Army," I said. "From '51 to '55."

"So you're used to blood and guts."

"I was a clerk, a typist."

"What do you do for a living now?"

I laughed. For the first time in a long time, I laughed.

"I teach typing," I said. "I've come far."

"You must be fast," Czarnecki said.

"A hundred and twenty-two words a minute."

The old man whistled, pretending to be impressed.

"I was in the Army too," he said. "Enlisted at eighteen and stayed in until I was thirty."

"Long haul," I said.

He shrugged. "The pay was decent, and I learned a trade. I was a mechanic after I got out, before Mr. Otto came along."

"Did you like that kind of work?" I asked.

"It made sense," he said. "This part does this, that part does that. You figure out what's not working, replace it, and you're back in business."

He slipped two fingers under his eye patch and scratched while staring with his good eye at what we could see of the night sky through the windshield.

"Do you know the constellations?" he said.

"I knew some when I was a kid," I replied.

He pointed. "There's Hercules. His arms, his legs, his club. Scorpius, the scorpion. Cygnus, the swan. Those four in a square there with the bright one on top? That's Lyra, the lyre."

"Well, well," I said, impressed.

Czarnecki tossed his cigarette out the window and opened his door.

"I'm gonna grab a couple hours of shut-eye," he said. "There's another bed in back if you want to sleep too."

There was no way I was going to be able to sleep, especially not lying five feet from the kid, no matter how many locks were on the crate. I told Czarnecki I'd stay up front, keep watch. He gave me a mocking salute and said, "Blow reveille at sunrise if I'm not up already."

The truck trembled and squeaked as he climbed inside the camper and settled down. I made myself as comfortable as I could and tried not to think too much about what morning would bring. The door to the Mexican's room was painted brown, the number white. Below the number was a silhouette of a covered wagon.

Sometime around 4 a girl emerged from one of the other rooms, a big girl wearing pajamas and pink slippers. She walked to the pay phone in front of the motel and dialed the operator. Slouched in the soul-bleaching fluorescent bubble of the booth, she looked like a criminal or a victim. She told the operator she wanted to make a collect call and pressed her forehead to the glass wall, listening to the rings, waiting for someone to answer.

"Mom," she said when someone finally did, "I'm married," and started to weep.

Czarnecki woke me by banging on my window. I'd nodded off somewhere near dawn, slid into a half dream of running, falling, and running again. I was relieved to be startled out of it, but as soon as I remembered where I was, I wished I'd come to a million miles away.

The sun was rising over the scarred foothills to the east. A few wispy clouds blushed pink. All the decisions I'd made the day before seemed like bad ones, and I was full of dread. I climbed out of the truck and stomped away the stiffness in my legs. I needed coffee. I needed aspirin. I needed a way out.

Czarnecki hocked and spit and lit his third cigarette of the morning. One foot dragged a bit as he walked up and set a duffel bag on the hood.

"Let's get to it before everyone's up and about," he said.

I didn't ask any questions. It was too late for that. The match had been struck, the lake of gasoline shimmered beneath it. I followed Czarnecki across the parking lot to the Mexican's room. He unzipped the duffel and took out a crowbar. I felt like I had a sponge stuck in my throat.

Thirty years fell off the old man as he turned and gave me a wink. He wedged the hooked end of the bar into the crack between the door and the jamb. The flimsy lock broke with one tug, and the door swung open to reveal the Mexican lying on a bed in his underwear. He started to sit up, but Czarnecki was on him in a flash. He pushed him back onto the mattress and plunged an ice pick into his chest, and he died without a sound.

Czarnecki struggled to his feet, a sick old man once again.

"I like to use a pick," he said. "Less blood." He took a few deep, wheezy breaths, then said, "Come here."

I obeyed like someone hypnotized, stepped into the room and closed the door. Czarnecki grabbed the man's legs and ordered me to help move the body into the bathroom. I took hold of the Mexican under his arms, and we lifted him off the bed. After we'd laid him in the tub, Czarnecki got a hacksaw from his bag of tricks and held it out to me.

"Cut off his head," he said.

I finally found my voice. "No."

"You're here for proof what I've told you is true," he said. "Cut off his head, and you'll have it."

I'd already crossed a line. If I left at that moment, the only thing I'd know for certain was that I was an accessory to murder. My sole hope of redemption was that the old man was telling the truth about the rovers, and one way to verify that was to do what he'd ordered.

Beating back fear and revulsion, I grabbed the saw and bent over the tub. I pressed the blade against the neck of the corpse, closed my eyes, and went to work. The sound of the saw's teeth chewing through flesh and bone brought bile gushing into my mouth. I peeked through slitted lids to check my progress, caught a flash of bloody muscle and tendon, and nearly fainted.

The moment I was sure I couldn't continue, the head came loose. I dropped it, backed away, and forced my eyes open in time to see both the head and body collapse into dust. One instant they were there, and the next nothing was left of the Mexican but his underwear and a mound of feathery gray ash.

Czarnecki's monsters were real. While I grappled with the enormity of this, the old man turned on the water and washed the ashes down the drain, using the dead man's skivvies to wipe the tub clean. I didn't react when he said let's go, so he grabbed me by the arm, and we hurried to the truck and made our getaway along empty early-morning streets.

We left the kid in the camper when we got back here to the cabin. The old man will return him to the shed after dark. I've spent the day in the van, trying to sort things out. Right now I'm lying in the warm glow of a golden afternoon, but I'm chilled to the bone by what I've seen and what I've done. I've been searching for the truth about what happened to Benny, and I believe I've found it. I have no proof it was a rover that killed him, no hard evidence like Czarnecki's ring, but I'm almost sure that's how he met his end. There's no happiness in this certainty, but there is the satisfaction of having solved the mystery, which is at least something after so much disappointment and frustration.

But a storm still roils within me. Because now I have to make a choice. Do I join Czarnecki in his war against the rovers, even though the chances of encountering the one that murdered Benny are slim? Or do I return to you and step back into my old life, knowing that the monsters that murdered our boy and God knows how many others are out there continuing to kill?

Truthfully, I feel whichever road I choose is going to lead to my destruction, and all I can do this evening is pray that you, at least, are at peace.

TODAY'S PASSAGE: Stand in awe and sin not. Commune with your own heart upon your bed and be still.

—Psalm 4:4

12

Antonia and Elijah meet George Moore's man at a diner. "I'll be the ugliest sonofabitch in the joint," he said when Antonia asked how they'd know him, and he wasn't lying. He looks like a possum with acne scars and a greasy pompadour, has the beadiest black eyes Antonia's ever seen.

The waitress is refilling his coffee when the two Fiends walk up to his table. He motions for them to sit and proceeds to stir half the sugar in the dispenser into his cup.

"Nice bikes," he says, nodding at the Harleys parked out front.

"Do you ride?" Elijah asks.

"Not me," the possum says. "If I fell off and cracked my skull, they'd be washing my brains off the road with a fire hose. You, you're good as new in five minutes." His grin reveals a mouthful of crooked brown teeth. "Do you have the pictures?"

Antonia reaches into the pocket of her denim vest and brings out the Polaroids Bob 1 took of McMullin, tosses them on the table. The possum squints at the one of the tattoo.

"*Mors tua, vita mea,*" he says.

"Your death, my life," Antonia says.

The possum's lips purse like he's tasting something sour.

"That about sums you rovers up, doesn't it?" he says.

"And you're somehow better?" Antonia says.

"At least I'm still as God made me."

"God?" Antonia says. "You fucking child."

"I dig blondes, but why's your hair so short?" the possum says. "You trying to look like a man?"

Antonia slaps her hand on the table, smirking when the possum jumps.

"We'll have what you owe us," Elijah says.

The possum sets a paper bag on the table. Elijah picks it up and glances at the stack of bills inside.

"And the other?" he says.

"Meet me out back," the possum says.

He downs his coffee and gets up to pay at the register. Antonia and Elijah walk outside. The diner's neon sign puts on its show, flashing pink—TRUCK—flashing green—TOWN—flashing red—CAFÉ. A semi pulls into the gas station next door and stops, brakes hissing, at a diesel pump. A uniformed attendant runs out and shouts, "Good evening, sir. How can I help you?"

"If you could go anywhere, where would you go?" Antonia asks Elijah.

"Wherever you were," Elijah says.

"What if I was in Japan?"

"I'd go to Japan."

"Italy?"

"Italy."

"Atlanta?"

"Don't make me go to Atlanta."

The possum comes out and says, "Follow me."

Antonia and Elijah start their Sportsters and ride around behind the restaurant. A bright orange light burns at the top of a pole, but the possum's Lincoln is parked away from it, deep in the shadows. He reaches the car as the Fiends pull up beside it.

The car's dome light goes on when he opens the door. He grabs a cloth drawstring sack from behind the front seat and passes it to Elijah like it's got something that stinks in it. Elijah looks inside. The baby is lying at the bottom. Elijah can't tell if she's dead or alive until he pokes her with a finger and she opens one eye.

The possum pulls out another bag, this one from Safeway.

"There's formula in here, Pampers," he says.

Antonia takes this bag, though she's thinking the kid won't be around long enough to need what's in it. The possum slides into the Lincoln and drives across the parking lot to the frontage road. Beyond that, cars and trucks zoom past on the freeway, bound for better places.

Elijah opens one of his Harley's saddlebags and lowers the sack containing the baby into it.

"Think it'll be okay in here?" he says to Antonia.

"Why are you asking me?" she says. "I don't know anything about babies."

That's not true. Elijah knows she had two children before she turned, both of which died of the pox. In all the years they've been together she's never told him more than that, not even their names, but he can tell she's thinking of them now as she pulls on her gloves. He wishes he could say, *It wasn't your fault. Those babies were taken from you by nature, not because you were a bad mother,* but they aren't that way with each other.

Instead he says, "I hope they haven't burned down the motel while we've been gone."

Antonia listens to the traffic on the freeway, which sounds tonight like wind blowing through trees. "Are we really stuck riding herd on these shitheads forever?" she says.

"We can do whatever you want," Elijah says.

"Let's feed on the baby ourselves and take off," she says. "Let's go to Japan. Let's go to Italy."

Elijah knows she's just talking. They've never been as safe as they've been since they joined with the others, never been as powerful. In addition, the only human thing the rest of the Fiends have left is their pride, and they'd never forgive an insult to it. If he and Antonia swiped the baby and ran out on them, they'd have six wild animals on their tails, animals that wouldn't rest until they tracked them down and exacted revenge. Elijah's not ready to die yet, and he's pretty sure Antonia isn't either, but he's still trying to come up with a response when she says, "Got ya."

"What do you mean?" he says.

"That was a test."

"Did I pass?"

"I'm not telling."

However she wants to wriggle out of it is fine with Elijah. She stomps her Harley to life, pops it into gear, and roars off. Elijah follows right behind her.

Bob 1 and Bob 2 are by the pool when they get back to the motel. The rest of the Fiends are playing cards in Pedro and Johnny Kickapoo's room. There's been tension between the Bobs and the others since the Bobs won the right to make the hit and claim the infant. In the hours since they returned from the killing, Yuma has refused to give them enough weed for a joint, and Bob 2 and Johnny almost came to blows because Johnny didn't laugh at one of Bob's jokes.

Elijah suggests they pay the Bobs off separately from the others, but Antonia says no, they're adults, and they're going to act like it. She calls a meeting in her and Elijah's room. Everybody files in looking glum except the Bobs.

The baby is lying on the bed. She's been crying since Elijah took her out of the sack.

"Did you check its diaper?" Yuma asks. She was a nanny in another life, looked after the children of the richest man in Cincinnati.

"I just changed it," Elijah says.

"Then it's probably hungry."

Elijah hands her the bag containing formula and diapers. "This came with it," he says.

"Any of you fuckers know how to mix formula?" Yuma says.

"Just give it a tit," Bob 2 says, trying to be funny.

Grumbling, Yuma sets about preparing a bottle.

Antonia brings out Moore's original $25,000 and sets it on the table next to the twenty-five she and Elijah got from the possum. Minus Beaumont's ten percent, everyone but the Bobs will receive $7,500. Johnny and Real Deal do the divvying, licking their fingers and dealing the bills into six stacks.

Yuma finishes shaking the formula. She picks up the baby and sticks the nipple of the bottle in her mouth. The kid stops crying and starts sucking.

"Enjoy your last meal," Bob 2 says.

"You ever had a child?" Yuma asks him.

"Depends how you mean."

"You're a sick fuck."

"The sickest," Bob 2 says. He pulls a big hunting knife from his belt. "How about I nick the brat right now and make you sore losers watch us drink?"

Real Deal draws his knife.

"How about I cut you in half?" he says.

Bob 2 glances at Bob 1—who, with a tiny shake of his head, tells him to back down. Bob 2 twirls his knife like a gunslinger playing with his pistol before returning it to its sheath. He leans against the wall and crosses his arms over his chest. Real Deal puts his blade away too.

"We need to take a vote," Antonia says, looking to ease the tension. "We're pulling out of here tomorrow night. All in favor of New Orleans as our next stop, say *aye*."

A chorus of *ayes* rings out. It's unanimous, as Antonia knew it would be.

"New Orleans it is, then," she says. "Now, who's next to feed?"

They've worked things out so their feedings are staggered, thereby leaving a narrower wake of dead and disappeared behind them.

Pedro raises his hand. "I'm up."

"Seems like it's been a while."

"Forty-five days, but I can't go much longer. I'm getting itchy."

"We'll find something along the way, set you right."

Johnny gestures at the piles of bills on the table in front of him. "Come and get it," he says.

Pedro, Antonia, and Elijah grab their stacks. Real Deal pockets his.

"Snag mine, doll," Yuma says to him. She's still feeding the baby.

"Go on," Bob 1 says to Yuma. "I'll take the nipper."

Yuma hesitates, primal reflex tightening her grip on the

child, but she quickly overrides it. Bob 1 rests the kid in the crook of his arm and tosses the bottle away. He picks up the drawstring sack and slips the infant back inside.

"Feed somewhere else," Antonia says.

"We've got a good place," Bob 2 says.

"And bury it deep when you're done."

The Bobs put the sack in one of Bob 2's saddlebags and blast off. They take Central south. Bright and bustling downtown gives way to dark warehouses and auto-body shops, which give way to brand-new tracts of homes bounded by freshly planted palm trees. Out past these they ride across the desert until the road narrows and climbs a mountain. Near the top they turn onto a dirt road that leads to a spot overlooking the city.

They've been here before, to drink beer and get stoned. Teenagers use it as a lovers' lane, but tonight they have it to themselves. They park at the edge of the flat and dismount. Bob 2 takes the sack out of his saddlebag.

The ruins of an old adobe cabin sit on a ledge fifty feet downslope from the overlook. The Fiends sidestep along the steep, slippery trail leading to it. Rocks and dirt loosed by their passage cascade down the mountain. Bob 2 trips, and the jolt startles the baby. She lets out a yell Bob swears will be heard all the way back in town.

"Shut it up," Bob 1 says.

"You know of a magic word?" Bob 2 says.

"Try singing."

"I'll try stomping its brains out if it doesn't stop soon," Bob 2 says. He cradles and rocks the sack, quieting the kid to a fuss.

The Fiends enter the cabin by ducking under a low

doorway. The roof has collapsed, and the floor is littered with rubble. The walls still standing are spattered with graffiti. A pentagram, a skull and crossbones, a broken heart. Bob 2 sets the sack down, and he and Bob 1 step through a breach in the north wall to where there's an old rock garden. Bob 1 pulls out a pint of Seagram's, has a sip, and passes it to Bob 2. The men catch their breaths while contemplating the lights of Phoenix.

"I remember this town when there were still horses on the streets," Bob 1 says.

"You *are* as old as dinosaur shit," Bob 2 says.

"Don't I know it. I see twenty-two in the mirror but feel a hundred and twenty-two."

"It's all in your mind."

"I'm not so sure. Years have weight."

"Look at Elijah, born in seventeen-something and still going strong."

"Maybe it's the pace I'm living at, always on the run."

Bob 2 nods toward the cabin, toward the baby.

"Wait'll you suck on that," he says. "You'll be raring to go again."

"I've been thinking," Bob 1 says.

"Uh oh."

"I want the kid to myself. I want a whole year where I don't have to hunt, not just six months."

"To do what?"

"I'm gonna go to Cuba and find the girl who turned me."

Bob 2 is shocked by this, hurt even. "Are you serious?" he says.

"I need a purpose."

"You need not to complicate things."

"Maybe so, but I want to go to Cuba."

"And what about me?" Bob 2 says. "That bitch left you high and dry, but I've been loyal for twenty-five years, never once let you down, always had your back."

"You're a good dude for sure. The best."

"But fuck me anyway, right?"

Bob 1 looks away, uncomfortable.

"Well, I'm not just giving the kid up to you," Bob 2 continues. "I made the hit and earned the right to feed too."

"I know that," Bob 1 says, "and that's why I'm willing to gamble for it, double or nothing."

"Gamble how?"

"Liar's poker, roshambo. We can flip a coin, if you want."

The baby cries again, a reminder to the Bobs that every minute they draw this out is one more when trouble might find them. An idea comes to Bob 2, one that'll put Bob 1's resolve to the test. He draws the snub-nosed .38 he carries.

"The game's Russian roulette," he says.

"Jesus," Bob 1 says.

"It's that, or let's get to feeding."

"You don't think I'm serious, do you?"

"Prove it."

Bob 1 stands there chewing his beard. He's played Russian roulette a few times before, wagering with other rovers. He won twice and lost once, took a bullet to the brain. The pain was excruciating, and he's always wondered if he's not a little dumber now than before. But he's determined to see Maria again and get answers to the questions that have tormented him for half a century.

"Roulette it is then," he says.

Bob 2 is nervous. He only suggested the game thinking the other Bob would back down. With trembling hands, he opens the cylinder of the revolver and drops the cartridges into his palm. Retrieving one, he slides it back into an empty chamber, closes the cylinder, and spins it.

"Who's first?" he says.

Bob 1 takes the gun from him. Might as well get it over with. He presses the muzzle to his temple and pulls the trigger.

Click.

Relief weakens his knees, but he keeps a blank face as he spins the cylinder and passes the gun to Bob 2.

"Goddammit," Bob 2 says. He swipes at the fear sweat dripping off his nose. "Goddammit." He puts the gun to his head. "Goddammit!"

Click.

"Ha!"

He spins the cylinder and thrusts the gun at Bob 1, who moves a little slower this time, who takes a deep breath and twists the tension out of his neck before raising the pistol.

Blam!

The echo of the shot caroms and fades. Bob 1 crumples to the ground, blood spurting from a hole in his head. Bob 2 picks up the Seagram's and guzzles what's left. He won, but he's still angry at the other Bob for ruining their partnership. Even if they keep riding together, things will never be the same. The baby stopped crying when the gun went off but bawls again now. Fuck it—it'll be quiet forever soon enough.

Bob 1's foot twitches. His mind restarts in stages, like lights going on floor by floor in a skyscraper. He sits up with a groan and touches the crater where the bullet exited his skull, flesh and bone regenerating even as he does so.

"You lose, motherfucker," are the first words he hears when his ears stop ringing.

"Yeah, yeah," he replies, relieved to find his tongue works.

The baby is still crying, but softly now. Bob 2 draws his

knife. "To the victor go the spoils," he says, and enters the cabin. A second later he shouts, "Where's the kid?"

"What do you mean?" Bob 1 says.

"The kid. It's—" Bob 2 checks the floor of the cabin again. "Where the fuck is it?"

13

Two motorcycles circle the overlook and stop at the brink. Jesse worms on his belly for a clear view. The bikes' engines cough and die, and two bearded men—one tall, one short—step off the Harleys. Jesse's heart freezes. Rovers. There's a patch on the back of their jackets, a grinning skull with goat horns. A banner above it proclaims FIENDS, another below HELL. Jesse's heard stories about the Fiends, rovers who travel in a pack, killing anyone, turned or unturned, who crosses them. Bad news all around.

Johona creeps over to lie beside him.

"Biker trash," she says.

The shorter Fiend takes a sack out of a saddlebag on his bike, and he and the other start down a path that ends at the bones of a cabin on a ledge below the outlook. Jesse can just make out the crumbling structure from where he and Johona are hiding.

Edgar, back at the boulder they were sitting on, stands to look at the bikers too.

"Rovers!" he says.

"Get down," Jesse whispers.

It'd be too risky to try to sneak back to where the car

is hidden. Better to lie low and wait until the Fiends leave. "We'll sit tight—" Jesse begins but is interrupted by the piercing cry of an infant in distress.

The Fiends halt on the trail. There's a baby in the sack they're carrying. They discuss how to quiet it, and when one threatens to stomp it, Johona gasps. The infant settles, and the bikers continue their descent.

Johona asks what they're doing with a baby. Jesse says he doesn't know, but he's pretty sure he does.

The Fiends reach the cabin and slip from view inside it.

"Maybe they're devil worshippers," Johona says.

The bikers reappear behind the cabin and pass a bottle. Jesse hears a rustle and turns to find Edgar on his feet again. "Those sonsofbitches are gonna do us in," he says and sets off for the car at a run. Jesse throws an arm around his neck and drags him to his knees. Edgar twists and turns, trying to free himself, extra strong because he's scared.

"Easy," Jesse croons. "Easy."

His brother bucks a few more times, then collapses, breathing hard. Jesse strokes him like he would a spooked horse.

"We're safe up here," he says. "All you have to do is keep quiet."

"Give them the girl," Edgar says.

"We're not giving them the girl," Jesse says. He spies a small cave at the base of the boulder, a niche barely visible behind a creosote bush.

"Look," he says. "An Indian hideout."

Edgar lifts his head, intrigued.

"They'll never find you in there."

Edgar crawls to the cave and backs into it.

"Can you see me?" he says.

"Not a hair," Jesse says.

"There's room for you."

"I'll keep watch. Soon as it's clear, I'll come for you."

When Jesse gets back to where he left Johona, she's gone. He spots movement below, on the overlook. The girl is sneaking toward the trail that leads to the cabin. The Fiends are still on the ledge behind the ruin. One of them has a gun.

The baby starts crying again as Jesse races down to retrieve Johona. She's crouched at the edge of the overlook, straining to make out what's happening below, but the cabin blocks the Fiends from view. She flinches, startled, when Jesse appears out of the darkness and kneels beside her. "Come with me," he whispers, but then the *click* of a revolver's hammer on an empty chamber rings out. He and Johona watch the cabin, holding their breaths. One of the Fiends yells "Goddammit," and another *click* rebounds off the surrounding hills.

Jesse's worried. He and Johona are on the path the Fiends will use to return to their Harleys, and they'll see them as soon as they leave the cabin. He needs to move the girl now, while the bikers are occupied. He tugs her arm, but she frowns and pulls away.

"The baby," she says.

A gun goes off, making them both jump. The child stops bawling mid-wail.

"Oh, my God," Johona says.

What Jesse sees is Claudine. Claudine confused, Claudine terrified. He flashes back to her final moments, and when Johona jumps up and starts down the trail to the cabin, he follows without hesitation, thinking only that she'll not die in front of him like Claudine did.

They're completely exposed on the mountainside, no cover at all, and flying blind, their view of the Fiends still obstructed by the cabin. Jesse catches up to Johona. *Me first,* he mouths, and squeezes past her to take the lead. She rests a hand on his shoulder to steady herself, and he goes as slowly as he dares.

They take cover behind a stunted palo verde tree when they reach the ledge. The baby cries again, the wails coming from inside the cabin. Jesse sees the shorter, stockier Fiend through a gap in the wall, facing away from them. There's no sign of the tall one. Jesse twists to look over his shoulder, worried he might be creeping up on them, but the only thing moving is a sheet of plastic caught on a rock.

He turns back to find Johona crawling across the open ground between the palo verde and the cabin. He starts after her, then thinks better of it, staying hidden and keeping an eye on the Fiend out back instead. Johona pauses when she reaches the doorway. Jesse waves for her to return, but she shakes her head and continues into the cabin. The next thing Jesse knows, he's in the doorway, watching her grope for the baby in the darkness. He sees where the child is lying, still closed up in the sack, but doesn't dare risk directing Johona to it, not with the shorter Fiend ten feet beyond, grinning down at the body of his companion on the ground beside him.

"You lose, motherfucker," the shorter Fiend says as the taller one sits up and shakes his head.

Jesse wonders whether he should grab Johona and flee or rush the bikers. The choice is made for him when Johona finds the sack, snatches it up, and crawls back toward the door.

The short Fiend pulls a knife. "To the victor go the spoils."

Jesse yanks Johona to her feet and hurries her to the palo verde. They drop behind it as the Fiend enters the cabin. Finding the sack missing, he yells, "Where's the kid?" Any second now, he'll spot them. The best Jesse can do is give Johona a fighting chance.

"Go," he says.

She hugs the sack and runs up the trail toward the overlook. The shorter Fiend sees this and starts after her. Jesse pops the blade of the stiletto he carries. He covers the yard of the cabin in two leaps, ducks when the Fiend slashes with his knife, and plants the stiletto in the biker's barrel chest, leaving it there when the man sinks to his knees and flops onto his back.

The tall Fiend staggers through the cabin, brandishing his own knife. Jesse blocks an overhead stab and punches him in the face. The biker's legs wobble. Jesse hits him again. He drops his knife, and Jesse dives for it. The man is too quick. He falls on the blade, covering it with his body.

Jesse tries to roll him over, but he grabs Jesse's hand, twists it, and snaps a bone in his wrist. The pain makes Jesse woozy. He runs out the door, stepping over the shorter biker's body. Johona is halfway to the overlook when he catches her. He takes her arm and forces her to speed up.

The tall Fiend is on his feet. He recovers his knife and steps outside the cabin, where he sees Jesse and Johona scrambling up the mountain. He bends over his partner and pulls Jesse's stiletto out of him before giving chase.

Jesse and Johona near the overlook, the tall Fiend closing on them. Jesse hands Johona the keys to the Grand Prix, meaning to stand and fight. Even if he goes down, he might hold the bikers off long enough for the girl to escape.

"Get to the car and go," he says. "Don't stop, don't look back."

Johona continues up the trail as Jesse picks up a rock and turns to face the tall Fiend's attack. He's smaller than the man, lighter, and he hopes faster. The biker's knife flashes like a shooting star as he raises it, running full tilt.

Jesse fakes like he's going to meet the man upright but ducks in the instant before the Fiend crashes into him and jams his shoulder into his belly. All the wind goes out of the biker, and he doubles over. Jesse brings the rock down on the back of his head, hitting him again and again until he feels the man's skull give way.

Somehow managing to keep standing, the biker staggers backward. Jesse rushes him, only to run into a whistling haymaker that smashes into his temple and sends him to the ground cockeyed, ears ringing. The Fiend lifts his knife, but as he's about to bring it down, his eyes roll back, and he topples, the blows from the rock finally taking their toll.

Jesse looks toward the cabin. The shorter Fiend has healed enough to sit. He spies Jesse, struggles to his feet, and stumbles to the trail. Defying dizziness and pain, Jesse grabs the taller Fiend's blade. He tilts the man's head back to expose his throat and begins to saw. Blood spurts, slicking the handle of the knife. Jesse tightens his grip and keeps cutting. Soon all that's keeping the head attached is the spine. Jesse wedges the knife between two vertebrae, bears down, and twists the head free. He's startled when the man turns to ash. He knew it would happen, but he's never dusted a rover before.

The shorter Fiend is coming quickly up the trail. Jesse dashes the last fifty feet to level ground and turns with the dusted biker's knife in his hand. The shorter Fiend plows into him like a bull before he can get set. He goes flying and lands hard but pops up ready to fight. The Fiend spits as he approaches. He's smaller than the dusted one, but beefier and has a bigger knife. He tosses it in the air and catches it by the handle, showing off. There's a grin on his face, but his eyes are rage-fueled furnaces.

"Greetings, *brother*," he says, sarcastic. "How long have you been tailing us?"

"I've never seen you before," Jesse says.

"Bullshit."

"It's the truth."

"Were you stealing the kid to feed on, or were you trying to save it?"

"Does it matter?"

"No. No it doesn't."

Everything inside Jesse wants to run, but he goes into a crouch and cocks his knife arm. The Fiend charges, aiming to bowl him over again. Jesse drops and rolls out of his path. As he passes, Jesse slashes one of his calves to the bone. The man stumbles but regains his balance. He shuffles sideways, circling Jesse, stalling while the wound mends. Jesse turns to keep him in front of him.

He spots an opening, darts in, feints right, goes left, and stabs the Fiend in the side. The Fiend strikes at the same time, jabbing his knife into Jesse's upper back, the blade puncturing one of Jesse's lungs. Jesse lurches out of reach, coughing blood. The Fiend limps toward him, but Jesse can't work up the momentum to run. Every time he moves, it's like he's being stabbed again.

He waves his knife. The Fiend slaps it away and raises his own blade. Jesse bows his head to await the strike, but it doesn't come. The Fiend grunts, and Jesse looks up to see that Edgar—twice as big as the biker and twice as strong—has him in a chokehold.

"Don't let go," Jesse says.

He picks up his knife and dashes toward Edgar and the Fiend. His haste makes him careless. The Fiend lifts both feet off the ground and, supported by Edgar, kicks with all his might. Jesse takes the blow in the stomach and falls backward.

The Fiend turns his attention to Edgar, stabbing blindly over his shoulder. Edgar bellows in pain but keeps choking him. The biker weakens, can't keep his knife up. The blade slips from his fingers, and he sags in Edgar's arms.

Jesse runs at him again. His thrust is deflected by a rib, though, and with a final, desperate spasm, the Fiend snaps his head back and slams his skull into Edgar's face. Edgar releases the biker and presses his hands to his broken, gushing nose.

The Fiend pauses—panting, thinking—then says, "You know you're a dead man, don't you? Wherever you go, we'll find you." He turns and bolts for the edge of the overlook. Running full speed, he hurls himself off the precipice.

Jesse, right behind, pulls up short. The Fiend soars briefly out into the night, a black angel bound for the stars, before falling. He slams into the mountain two hundred feet below and tumbles another hundred before finally skidding to a stop, a bloody sack of broken bones and ruptured guts.

There's no easy way down to where he is to finish him off, so Jesse decides to flee. Edgar moans when he crouches beside him.

"You all right?"

"I got blood all on my shirt."

"I'll get you a new one."

"Mickey Mouse?"

"Whatever you want. You did good, buddy."

Johona watches wide-eyed from the thicket where the Grand Prix is hidden. The baby, freed from the sack, sucks one of her fingers.

"Get in the car," Jesse calls to her, but she doesn't move.

He tells Edgar to come with him. They walk to the Fiends' motorcycles. He takes hold of one and has Edgar grab the other. They roll them to the edge of the overlook and push them off, sending them crashing down the side of the mountain. Edgar whoops and pounds his chest like a gorilla. Jesse hurries him to the car.

Johona backs away as they approach. She's just watched Jesse cut off a man's head and seen that man disappear. "Please don't hurt me," she says.

"I'm trying to save your life," Jesse replies.

"I want to get out of here."

"So do I. And I want to get the baby out of here, too. So let's go."

Johona moves cautiously to the Grand Prix, keeping plenty of distance between her and the brothers. She slides into the back seat, and Jesse gets behind the wheel. Edgar climbs in on the passenger side. Checking constantly for more Fiends, Jesse backs out of the thicket, squeals onto the road, and races down the mountain.

14

JESSE WON'T LET ME HOLD THE BABY. I ASK HIM TWICE TILL HE tells me to shut up. It's in Johona's lap in the back seat. I reach my hand out and it grabs my finger. I ask if it's a boy or a girl and Johona says it's a girl. What's her name? I ask. I don't know, Johona says.

She wants to take the baby to the police. No police, Jesse says, we'll drop her at a hospital. Johona's shaking. Drop me there too, she says, please. I promise I won't say anything about what I saw. Jesse looks at her in the mirror and says, It's not us you've got to worry about it's that biker. He runs with a gang called the Fiends. He'll be coming back to life and him and the rest of them will be after me for dusting that man and you for grabbing the baby.

The child makes a noise and Johona lays it over her shoulder. They won't find me, she says, Phoenix is a big city. Not big enough, Jesse says. There's a story about someone stealing one of their motorcycles. They chased the man for two years and when they finally caught up to him killed him and the woman he was traveling with and five other people two of them children who happened to be in the house. That's how they are.

Johona looks like she's gonna cry. What are they? she says. What are you? Jesse tells her most of it. How we can't go out in the day. How we heal when we get hurt. How we ain't never gonna die. It's too much talking and I know it already. I want to play pinball. They got Space Time at the bowling alley and Quick Draw and Fireball. I'm good at all of 'em.

Johona asks Jesse if he kills people and drinks their blood like the Fiends do. He tells her no. He tells her me and him are a different kind of rover. He's lying but I don't squeal. Me and him have secrets. You got to be careful. You got to keep your mouth shut.

Johona sits back and strokes one of her braids. My dad'll know what to do, she says, he'll help me. What are you gonna tell him? Jesse says. Monsters are after you? He'll think you're crazy. And if the Fiends find out where your family lives they'll kill them too. So what should I do? Johona says. Get out of town for a couple months at least, Jesse says, for good if possible. You were talking about going to California. Go now. I don't have any money, Johona says, and my car's a hunk of junk.

We're back in the city. Out the window there's a giant holding a giant tire. There's a building that looks like a castle and another with a blinking antenna on top. There's a Ford pickup painted like it's on fire. What are *you* gonna do? Johona asks Jesse. We're getting out of here tonight, he says, driving as far as we can before daylight.

The baby starts bawling again. She's burning up, Johona says. We've got to get her to a doctor. Jesse says we need to clean up first. We stop at a Gulf station and he takes me to the bathroom. He scrubs the blood off his face and makes me do the same. Johona and the baby ain't in the car when we get back. She's run off, I say. Quiet, Jesse says. He waits jingling coins and whispers okay when Johona comes out of the ladies' room.

She gives him directions to the hospital. He parks away from the lights. She goes to get out but Jesse stops her. Better if I do it, he says. He asks for her shirt 'cause his is bloody. Johona thinks on it and takes off her top. Her brassiere is pink and shiny. A girl I fed on in Kansas City had one just like it. Jesse wearing Johona's shirt makes me laugh. You sure are pretty Miss Jesse, I say.

He gets out of the car takes the baby from Johona and runs off across the parking lot. An ambulance drives past quiet but with its red and blue lights going. I ask Johona does she want me to sing Neil Young. She says no thanks watching where Jesse went. Don't worry, I say, he's real smart.

Jesse comes running back and strips off Johona's shirt. We drive out of the hospital so fast I take hold of the dash. Jesse gave the baby to a nurse. She didn't have any questions? Johona says. I imagine she did, Jesse says, but I got the hell out of there before she could ask them.

Everyone's quiet for a spell.

Johona lights a cigarette. Can I go with you? she says. We aren't going to Los Angeles, Jesse says. Anywhere'll do, Johona says, I'll get a bus from wherever we wind up.

We can't have a woman with us. They're bad luck, Jesse always says. He don't even like Abby. But I can see he's mulling it. I poke him and shake my head. He tells me to quit. Bad luck, I whisper. He don't pay me no mind.

We'll drop you in Denver, he says to Johona, but you have to do exactly what I tell you to while you're with us. We can't even stop at your place. Anything you need we'll pick up along the way. Fine, Johona says.

We get to the motel and go inside. Johona sits on Jesse's

bed while he showers the rest the blood off him. You want to play Nickle Nock? I ask her. You need three cards that add up to 31. We can play for money or candy. She shakes her head no. You couldn't shut her up before and now she's got nothing to say. Abby's in a corner watching her with hate in her eyes.

Jesse comes out of the bathroom and says it's my turn. Hot water, he says. I scrub and scrub. Blood don't come off easy. The water's pink going down the drain. After I dry off I do a peek into the room. Jesse's sitting with Johona on the bed. His arm's around her and he's talking sweet. She smiles but won't laugh. The Little Devil pipes up. *Him and her are going off together gonna leave you all alone,* he says. Goose bumps rise on my arms. I yell for Jesse to help me get dressed.

Stop playing around, he says when he comes in. You know how to put your clothes on. Don't leave me, I say. What're you talking about? he says. You got Johona now, I say. We're driving her to Denver that's all, he says. You know I can smell a lie, I say. I'm not going anywhere without you, he says.

He carries our grips out and puts them in the trunk of the Grand Prix. I give Abby a bowl of Meow Mix and stand by while she crunches it. How old's your kitty? Johona asks me. Twenty-five or thereabouts, I say. That's ancient for a cat, she says. I turned her, I say. What? Johona says. I turned her into a rover, I say. She starts to cry. Jesse comes in and asks what's wrong. You changed the cat? Johona says. Jesse gives me a look like he wants to kill me and sits down to sweet-talk her again. I'm glad she's crying. The more you cry the less you have to piss.

We set off when she quiets. Pretty soon there's no more buildings no more cars no more town. Everything's dark except for the speed meter inside and headlights outside. Jesse checks the mirror over and over. Johona falls asleep laying across the back seat. I sing to myself real quiet. Mama's song. *I would not die in summer, when music's on the breeze, and soft, delicious murmurs float ever through the trees.*

15

June 27, 1976, 10 p.m.

FOR THE THIRD TIME TODAY I'M PUTTING PEN TO PAPER, THIS time to set down what happened in just the last hour while it's fresh in my mind.

I stayed here in the Econoline after my last entry earlier today, reading my Bible and trying to figure out my next move, had cold chili for dinner. Shortly after dark, as I was about to settle down to sleep, Czarnecki came out of the cabin mushmouth drunk.

"There's something else I need to show you," he said.

I got out of the van reluctantly and followed him to his pickup. He climbed into the camper, undid the locks on the crate, and opened it. The kid had been chained inside since last night and looked like hell. Dark circles ringed his eyes, and his bones would've torn his thin skin if he'd moved too quickly. Czarnecki backed out of the camper and stood beside me.

"Come on," he snapped at the kid.

"I need—" the kid began.

"I know what you fucking need."

The kid lifted himself slowly out of the crate. He took a second to reset his balance, then stepped onto the bumper and down to the ground.

Czarnecki had his .45 in his hand. "The shed," he said.

The kid staggered to his prison, walked inside, and yanked the string to turn on the bulb. The light it threw was the color of a flophouse bedsheet. The kid sat on the cot and fastened his ankle chain to the bolt in the floor. Czarnecki passed the .45 to me.

"If he tries anything, put a bullet between his eyes," he said.

I qualified for a marksmanship badge in the Army, but that was twenty years ago. I was as likely to hit him as the kid if I had to shoot.

He drew a hunting knife from a sheath on his belt. Grabbing a bottle of rubbing alcohol off a shelf, he doused the blade and pulled up the sleeve of his coveralls. The inside of his forearm bore a series of short crosswise scars, twenty or so, some old, some freshly healed. They followed the arm's main vein from elbow to wrist. He laid the blade on a patch of unmarred skin and sliced into it. Blood dribbled from the cut. Stepping to the kid, he held out the arm. The kid grabbed it and pressed his mouth to the wound.

"You have to give him a little every now and then to keep him going," Czarnecki said. "He'll tell you he needs it once a month, but I make him go two. Doesn't matter to me how lousy he gets to feeling. I want him weak."

"How long has this been going on?" I said.

"I trapped him in '67, so nine years or so. Me and Mr. Otto had a couple others, but he's lasted longest."

The image of the old man offering his blood to the kid, the sucking sound, the smell of shit and sweat that clung to the concrete walls—this and the other horrors of the past few days hit me all at once. The urge to flee was powerful, but I was so woozy I barely made it to the doorway before sinking to the ground in a stupor.

"You look like you've seen a monster," Czarnecki said with a laugh.

He was a foolish man, or, I don't know, maybe a brave one, joking like that while I was holding the gun. Maybe he's taken my measure and decided I'm not the kind that'll lash out no matter how far I'm pushed. Maybe he's had my number since he approached me in the parking lot and I agreed to follow him here.

In any case, I didn't shoot him. I sat against the doorjamb and stared out at the light spilling from the cabin, at the trees against the sky, at the stars sharp as needles. I inhaled deeply, trying to flush the filth from my lungs and refill them with clean air.

The sound of a scuffle made me turn back into the shed. Czarnecki was struggling to pull his arm away from the kid.

"Let go, motherfucker," he growled.

I stood and pointed the .45. "Should I shoot?" I said.

"Should he?" Czarnecki yelled. "Should he?"

The kid released him and backed away. He ran a finger over the blood on his lips, sucked it clean, and showed his gold tooth in a defiant smile, then stretched out on the cot and rolled to face the wall.

Czarnecki turned off the bulb, and we stepped outside. He closed the door and locked it.

"Might be time to get a new hound," he said, loud enough so the kid could hear. "You can't keep a biting dog."

He pressed a handkerchief to the cut. I held the .45 out to him. "Bring it inside," he said.

"I'm all wrung out," I said.

"Five minutes," he said. "Sit with me while I patch this nick."

I could barely keep my eyes open, but I followed him to the cabin.

*   *   *

He poured himself some whiskey and brought out a cigar-box first-aid kit. After painting the cut with iodine, he asked me to lay a bandage over it. My fingers brushed the scars on his arm—waxy pink worms spaced regularly as fence posts—and I pulled my hand away, repulsed.

He smiled and lifted his other sleeve to show more scars.

"My rosary," he said. "Each a mystery to be contemplated."

"You're religious?" I said.

"I was, then I wasn't, but I might be trending back. You?"

"I believe in God," I said. "I believe Jesus Christ died for our sins."

"How do rovers fit into your system?"

"There are demons in the Bible."

"Demons," he said. "So you won't have any problem killing them?"

It's a question I haven't answered for myself yet, so I wiggled out of answering it for him by replying, "That's not what I said."

Czarnecki leaned back in his chair. "Here's one way to look at it," he said. "Before Jesus, you got rid of sin through sacrifice. For every sin you committed, you slaughtered an animal and offered it up to God. Now, if one little lamb erased a wrong from your record, imagine how many a demon must clear. You'll be in the black in no time."

Too tired to respond, I rubbed my eyes with my palms.

"Sure you won't have a drink?" Czarnecki said.

"No drink," I said.

Czarnecki sipped his. "I don't understand why anybody'd want to live forever anyway," he said. "Not even in heaven. When I die, I want to sleep for a million years."

I was struck again by how frail he looks in repose. His hatred for the monsters he's hunted so long has dried him to brittle bones and leathery yellow flesh. In the right light, he looks dead already.

The refrigerator clattered, spooking me, and I used the momentum from the jolt to get to my feet. Czarnecki didn't say anything when I walked out, didn't look up.

Exhausted as I am, I was sure I'd drop off as soon as I hit the cot. My brain, though, keeps replaying what I saw in the shed, so I'm putting it down here—hoping, like a guilty criminal, that baring my soul will ease my mind. And now, God, let me sleep.

June 28, 1976, Bishop, California

After a long, rotten night I finally dozed off as the sky lightened and the first birds woke. When I sat up five hours later, weariness still clung to me like a spider's web, but my mind was clearer, and I felt like I could put one foot in front of the other without falling.

The banana in the cardboard box that serves as my pantry had gone black and gooey. Ants swarmed it, squeezing through a slit in the peel to get at the mush inside. The apple next to it was fine, so I cut that into quarters and ate it with spoonfuls of peanut butter and a cup of cold instant coffee.

The day warmed quickly, and it was soon too hot to be reading my Bible in the van. I set up my chair in the shade outside and settled there. My eyes kept wandering to the shed, my thoughts to the creature that'd been locked inside it for almost a decade. I snuffed a flicker of sympathy by imagining him hunched over Benny the same way he'd hunched over Czarnecki, drinking his blood.

I listened to two squirrels argue. I watched a thunderhead balloon on the horizon. I opened my Bible to a random page and dropped my finger to the text for guidance. The verse was no help. A list of names of the sons of Noah, the sons of Japheth, the sons of Gomer. All the while I kept expecting Czarnecki to step out of the cabin, snorting, spitting, and blowing smoke, but he never did.

About noon I walked over and called for him. There was no response. The cabin door was open, but the screen was closed. I climbed onto the porch and shouted again. Again, no answer. The flag hanging next to the door flapped once, loudly, like a whip cracking. A fat black horsefly circled and buzzed off toward the shed.

Cupping my eyes, I peered through the screen, nose pressed to the mesh. A patch of sunlight lay on the empty bed like a brilliant quilt. Another spilled off the table onto the floor. The bright spots only made the rest of the room darker. I had to squint to penetrate the gloom.

The first thing to come into focus was one of the chairs that'd been next to the table. It lay on its back in front of the fireplace now. The rack that held the fireplace tools had toppled, too, and the poker, shovel, and broom were strewn across the hearth. I raised my eyes higher, dread a dark fizz in my chest, and there was Czarnecki, two feet off the floor, dangling from a rope thrown over a roof beam.

I rushed into the cabin, but it was too late. The old man was dead, had been for some time. One end of the rope was tied to a steel hook screwed into the wall, the other had been twisted into a noose. It wasn't an easy death. His tongue was nearly chewed through.

"You sonofabitch," I said. He'd laid his burdens—the rovers, Mr. Otto's crusade, the kid—on me, and I doubted I was strong enough to bear them. I came close to walking out to the van and driving off, close to turning my back on the whole nightmare and returning home. But I'm not that kind of man, and I think you know it, baby. I hope you do, anyway.

It was too much to contemplate the big picture right then, so I focused on what was in front of me. Czarnecki's body had to be dealt with, and there'd be no police or coroners or funeral homes involved.

Grabbing a knife from the kitchen, I cut the rope and lowered the corpse. It weighed almost nothing. I pulled the sleeping bag off the bed and zipped the body into it, found a wheelbarrow in the yard, and used that to move the bundle. Wildflowers grew at the base of the pine tree where I dug the grave, shoveling through duff to packed earth. I kept digging until I was waist-deep in the hole, then rolled the body into it and recited what I could recall of the funeral prayer—earth to earth, ashes to ashes, dust to dust.

The sun was dropping fast by the time I'd refilled the grave and spread pine needles to cover my tracks. Back in the Econoline, I lay on my cot. I dreaded the internal battle I was sure was coming over what to do next, but got to sleep just like that and didn't wake until after dark.

The kid turned to look at me when I opened the door to the shed. I stepped inside, put on the light, and threw him the keys.

"Get up," I said, waving Czarnecki's .45.

"Where's the old man?" he said.

I wasn't in the mood to explain. I pointed the gun at him and said, "We're leaving. Get yourself out to the camper."

He detached his chain from the bolt, picked up his slop bucket, and shuffled to the truck. When he was sitting in the crate, I gave him a tuna sandwich.

"Thanks, boss," he said.

"Lie down," I said, and lowered the lid.

An hour later I was headed south on the 395, driving the pickup through the night. I don't know where I'm going yet, but it feels right to be on the move. I'm still not thinking too far ahead. I couldn't stay at Czarnecki's place, so I split. I couldn't leave the kid, so I swapped the Econoline for the old man's truck so I could bring him along. And that's where things stand now.

After a few hours I got off the highway at this truck stop in Bishop. I'm parked facing the Sierras, and the peaks are glowing even though there's no moon out, patches of snow bright white against the blue granite and black sky. I wish you could see how pretty it is.

I'll rest here in the cab, as I wouldn't be able to sleep in the camper beside the kid. He's my next problem, and I'll have to deal with him soon.

Good night, baby. I love you.

TODAY'S PASSAGE: Don't let fear hold you back from your destiny. Be a hero. Strap on your armor and charge. If you give it your all, there is victory even in failure.

—*Listen, Respond, Win: A New Path to Success*
by Dr. Christine Pellegrino

16

THE ONLY BOB LEFT COMES TO ON HIS BACK, THE NIGHT SKY snapping into focus. Half a second earlier he was ten years old and swimming in the East River with kids he grew up with, Tommy Boyle treading water and reciting a limerick.

> There was a young man of Leeds
> Who swallowed a packet of seeds
> Great tufts of grass
> Sprouted out of his ass
> And his balls were all covered with weeds.

But he's back in Arizona now, lying at the bottom of a mountain, a sharp rock poking his liver. The pain when he straightens his broken left arm with his good right one nearly makes him scream.

He knew when he jumped the fall wouldn't kill him, but he's pretty sure he got as close to dying as he ever has before. If the fuckers up top came after him now, it'd be all over. He wouldn't be able to fight back. He lifts his head to look around. Nothing but moon rocks and stunted cactus. He tries to hurry the healing by concentrating on where he hurts most.

Half an hour later his bones have knit enough that he can stand. He stomps to test his legs and sets off down the mountain. It's a little after midnight. Five hours until dawn. He picks up his pace. Town is a long way off.

He comes to a trail, follows that until it hits a Jeep track, and follows that to pavement, the road back to Phoenix. He walks on the shoulder, ducking when cars pass. Distances out here are deceptive. He sees the lights of a ranch up ahead and figures it'll take fifteen minutes to reach it. An hour later the lights are as far away as ever. His plan was to get back to the motel on his own, but he worries he might have miscalculated, might wind up in the open at sunrise, so when he comes to a crossroads, a four-way stop with a red signal blinking above it, he hides in the scrub and waits.

A pickup driving toward Phoenix approaches. Bob steps out in front of it, hands in the air. With his face smeared with dried blood, he's a nightmare come to life. Still, the truck stops.

"What's wrong?" the driver asks.

"I flipped my bike," Bob replies. He fakes a limp as he moves to the window. The driver is a kid with a flattop and thick glasses. He's wearing white pants and a white shirt with the words *Danziger Dairy* embroidered on it.

"Are you hurt?" the kid says.

"I'm banged up, but I'll live," Bob says. "My bike's trash, though. I could use a lift into town."

"I'm on my way to work," the kid says.

Bob pulls a twenty-dollar bill from his pocket. "Drop me at the first pay phone."

"Keep your money," the kid says. "Get in back."

Bob climbs over the tailgate. When he's settled against the cab, the kid hits the gas. The crossroads dwindles until all Bob can make out is the faint red throb of the signal. For the first time since the fight, he thinks of the other Bob. *Rest easy,* he tells him. *You will be avenged.*

The kid stops at a gas station. Bob hops out and walks up to thank him, but he's already pulling away. The station attendant is asleep in the office, head resting on folded arms. Bob goes to the phone booth, gets the number for the Apache Motel from the book, and puts a dime in the slot. The night clerk connects him to Antonia and Elijah's room. Antonia answers.

"Bob's dusted," Bob tells her.

"Dusted?" she says. She sounds like she thinks he's joking.

"We got ambushed, and he was killed."

"Ambushed by who? Where?"

"I'm not getting into that now."

"Are the rest of us in danger?"

"I have no fucking idea, but if you are, you'll be better off with me there, so hurry and send someone to pick me up."

Elijah and Pedro come for him. They ride back to the motel, and everyone gathers in Antonia and Elijah's room to hear what happened.

"We were at the spot where we were gonna feed," Bob begins. "A rover and an unturned girl tried to snatch the kid, but I caught them at it."

He goes on to tell how the dude stopped his ticker with a lucky poke and Bob brought him back, but he was still too late to save Bob from getting dusted. He tells how he fought the rover who killed Bob and another who was with him and was almost dusted himself before escaping by jumping off the mountain.

He calls for a smoke when he finishes. Johnny Kickapoo passes a pack of Lucky Strikes.

"What happened next?" Antonia says.

"I laid there until I healed, then made my way back here," he says.

"No sign of them on the way?"

"Not hide nor hair."

"Would you know them if you saw them again?"

"The motherfuckers who dusted my best friend and tried real hard to dust me? Yeah, I'd know them."

The Fiends are roiling, thirsty for revenge, ready to ride out and tear the city apart searching for the lowlifes who killed their compatriot, but it's already 4 a.m.—only an hour until daybreak.

"We'll come up with a plan and start hunting as soon as the sun sets tonight," Antonia says.

"I'm not waiting," Bob says. "Who'll lend me a bike?"

"Take mine," Johnny says.

"And I'll ride with you," Pedro says.

"No," Bob says. "I'm going alone."

He cruises the strip of seedy motels on East Van Buren, the ones that rent rooms by the hour and show dirty movies on the TVs. There's hardly anyone on the street. A jitterbugging speed freak swatting at imaginary insects, two alkies grappling under a neon cactus, a cop walking from his patrol car into a diner. No rovers.

A dark-haired skeleton wobbling down the sidewalk makes him ease off the throttle. She resembles the girl from the mountain. As he rolls slowly past, she yanks the neck of her T-shirt down to flash her tits, and he sees it's just some whore, some dope fiend. He feels like killing her anyway, feels like watching someone die. Problem is, the sun'll be up before he could do her and get rid of the body.

Even so, he pulls over and waits for her to catch up.

"Hey, Daddy," she says.

"Hey, beautiful," he says.

"You looking to party?"

"You looking to die?"

The whore recoils. "Get the fuck out of here, man, before I call a cop," she screeches.

Bob roars off, leaving her spewing curses.

He gets back to his room right before daybreak. As he lies down on the bed, the phone rings.

"Any luck?" Elijah says.

"Nope," he replies.

"We'll find them tonight, don't worry."

Elijah hangs up the phone and pulls the curtains tighter to keep out the rising sun. Antonia is reading on the bed. Her nose is always in a book, which delights Elijah. He views it as something special about her, as he's never in his life known anyone else who read for pleasure.

And a long life it's been. He's the oldest of the Fiends, born in 1757 in Madrid as Diego Mateo Casal. His father was a wealthy trader and confidant of the king, but all Elijah remembers about growing up is learning to hunt. Boar, deer, mouflon, pheasant. Until he turned, stalking game with a rifle was his greatest passion, and he still finds it funny that a man who once lived to hunt now hunts to live.

He eventually went to work for his father, who sent him to New Orleans and put him in charge of the family company's office there. He fell in with a crowd of dissipated expatriates, including a wild, troubled Creole girl, a rover, who introduced him to opium and persuaded him to turn.

She killed herself a year later, dashing, in the throes of a drug frenzy, out of their room and into the sun-blasted courtyard at high noon one day, and he fled New Orleans bereft, disowned, and under suspicion. He changed his name and roamed the growing towns, swelling cities, and endless wildernesses of the new country of America. He met Antonia in Boston in 1842. She was the smartest and most beautiful rover he'd ever encountered, and they've been inseparable ever since.

"Bob didn't find the men who attacked them," he says to her.

"Did you think he would?" she replies. "They probably left town right afterward."

"We have to search at least one night if we expect to keep him and the rest in line."

"They do love to go on and on about loyalty, don't they?" Antonia says. "One for all and all for one and how willing they are to die for the gang."

Elijah sits on the bed beside her. "You used to feel that way, too, when we started this thing," he says.

"And now most days I wouldn't be comfortable turning my back on a one of them."

"There's another reason we need to find the killers. If word spreads that we let someone get away with dusting one of ours, it'll make us look weak—weak enough that someone else will take a crack at us. We need to keep people scared. That's what keeps us strong."

"Nobody'd be scared of us if they knew how close the legendary Fiends were to coming apart these days, how little it takes to set us at each other's throats."

"Even so, now's not the time to walk away," Elijah says. "The least we owe them is to see this situation through. We've ridden together for a good while."

Antonia scoffs and shakes her head. "You know what your problem is?" she says. "You're tenderhearted."

Elijah tears the book out of her hands and climbs on top of her. He pins her wrists to the mattress and kisses her hard on the mouth. "Who are you calling tenderhearted?" he says.

17

Jesse stops for gas in Flagstaff. He'd like to push on and put more miles between him, Edgar, and Johona and the Fiends, but it's already 3 a.m. They could make Tuba City before sunrise but would be in trouble if no rooms were available. Better to play it safe and hole up here for the day.

"Do you know of a decent motel?" he asks the kid scrubbing bugs off the windshield of the Grand Prix.

"The Spur's down the road," the kid says around a wad of tobacco. "It's cheap and pretty clean."

Edgar and Johona return from the station's bathrooms. Edgar asks for change for the candy machine. Jesse tells him to get in the car. Johona yawns and stretches. She's calmed down over the past few hours, had time to think things through.

Jesse asks if she's tired.

"Bad dreams keep waking me up," she says.

"We'll stop here. You'll rest better in a bed."

They check into the motel and walk to a diner next door. It has a cowboy theme. Knotty-pine paneling, steer horns hanging behind the cash register. The breakfast special is called the Roundup. Jesse, Edgar, and Johona are the only customers.

"Out late or up early?" the waitress asks as she pours coffee.

"Driving at night to beat the heat," Jesse says.

"Good thinking. What can I get you?"

Eggs, pancakes, sausage, biscuits—Jesse and the others order more food than they can finish and eat it faster than they should. When Jesse runs out of steam, he sits back and looks out at the empty parking lot and deserted highway. He hates the orange streetlights that are replacing the old white ones. They suck the color out of everything and put him in mind of fire.

"How far are we from Denver?" Johona says.

"Ten, eleven hours," Jesse says. "We'll have to stop again, probably in Albuquerque."

"We'll be passing the rez," Johona says. "I've got family on it. My grandma and grandpa, *shimá sání* and *shicheii*. I should have you let me off. If any bikers show up out there, my cousins'll beat the shit out of them."

She wants to sound tough but is too tired to be convincing. Chewing her bottom lip, she drags her fork through a puddle of egg yolk. She looks most like Claudine when she's like this, unmasked, unselfconscious.

"You speak Navajo?" Jesse says.

"*Diné,*" she says. "The language is called *Diné*. My mom tried to teach me, but I wasn't into it. I took French instead."

"Say something in French, then," Jesse says, not sure he really wants her to, not sure he can handle it.

"*Je t'aime,*" she says, and he sees Claudine saying it.

"Do you know what that means?" Johona says.

"No," Jesse replies, lying.

"That's *I love you.*"

Edgar opens a jelly packet and slurps the jelly out of it.

"Quit," Jesse says, glad to have a distraction.

"It's good," Edgar says, sliding him a packet. "Try it."

"There's a lady present," Jesse says. "Act like a gentleman."

"Forgive me, Miss Johona," Edgar says with a courtly nod. He can't keep it up, starts giggling. "Convoy" comes on the radio behind the counter, and he sings along. "Breaker one nine, this here's the Rubber Duck…"

Outside, the stars are disappearing one by one. Jesse feels day creeping up.

Edgar and Johona get the beds, and Jesse stretches out on the floor with a blanket and pillow. The long night has taken its toll. He falls asleep as soon as he closes his eyes. As a reward for all he's been through, he finds himself walking his desert road again, dreaming his dream.

He watches a dust devil whirl, a lizard skitter. He kicks the pop can, chases it, kicks it again. A hawk circles in the sky this time, its shadow crossing and recrossing the road in front of him. *Jesse.* A voice calls his name. He looks around. *Jesse.*

The dream fades, and Johona's crouched beside him.

"I'm freaking out," she says. "Come talk to me for a while."

He's reluctant. His weakness for her has already led to this, to them running for their lives, and the last thing he needs is something to happen that'll complicate things even further. He has a plan, and he's sticking to it: Drop her at the bus station in Denver and forget her. But then she puts her lips to his ear and whispers, "Please," and his resolve sways and topples.

He checks on Edgar, who's snoring quietly, Abby between his legs, checks the door for the fifth time to make sure it's locked, and climbs onto the bed. He means to keep some space between them, but Johona pulls his arm around her and rests her head on his chest. The weight of her, the smell of her, the warmth triggers so many memories, he's not sure he can bear it.

"You're not lying, are you, about this rover jazz?" she says.

"You saw that man turn to dust," he replies.

"Maybe it was a trick."

A thin strip of sunlight blazes between the curtain and the window frame. "Look here," Jesse says, and Johona lifts her head to watch him stick his finger into the beam. Her body stiffens, and she wrinkles her nose at the stink of burning flesh. Jesse shows her the charred finger, and she stares wide-eyed as it heals. When it's good as new, she takes hold of it and examines it closely.

"That's so fucking weird," she says, reaching for her cigarettes. "So how old are you, really?"

"I was born August 30, 1876," Jesse says. "Edgar was born on the eighth of December, 1883."

"You've lived through so much stuff."

"I've been too busy looking after Edgar to pay much attention."

"It's been a hundred years. Everything's changed. There's cars, airplanes, TV."

"Yeah, but people are the same. Still lying, still thieving, still killing each other."

Johona strikes a match and puts it to a smoke. "There's a preacher who says the world is ending next year," she says.

"There's always a preacher saying that," Jesse says. "Don't listen."

"You're cynical. It's because you're a Virgo."

"Don't listen to that crap either."

Two men walk past the window, arguing about whether the liquor store is open yet and how much beer to buy. Edgar rolls over, and Abby climbs onto his back and licks a paw.

"What about Claudine?" Johona says.

Jesse tenses. "What about her?"

"Was she a rover too?"

"She was."

"And it's been how long since you last saw her?"

"Seventy-two years," Jesse says.

Someone flushes the toilet in the next room and falls back into bed. The headboard bangs the wall. Johona crosses her legs and balances an ashtray on her knee, sits there smoking and thinking things over.

"Do you know where she is now?" she says.

"She's dead," Jesse says.

He'd planned to leave it at that, but once he starts talking, he can't stop. He and Claudine hit the road after she turned him, and he saw more of the world than he ever dreamed he would. Along the way she taught him how to survive as a rover—how to hunt, who to feed on, when to hunker down, when to run. After four years together his love for her burned as hot as it had in the beginning. He never once regretted turning, never once pined for his old life.

In the summer of '04, short of money, they rejoined the carnival Claudine was with when they met. The owner's daughter was a rover, and the show was a refuge for her and others who'd turned. Claudine ran her fortune-telling racket, and Jesse worked as a roustabout.

They'd been with the caravan two months when it set up in Hot Springs, Arkansas. Claudine needed to feed but was trying to hold off until they got to a bigger town, where hunting would be easier and safer. Their second night in Hot Springs, though, potential prey caught her eye: a drunk in overalls and muddy boots who'd been bum-rushed from the hoochie-coochie tent for spitting at one of the dancers.

Claudine resolved to stalk this drunk and take him if the opportunity arose. Jesse told her it was too risky, but she wouldn't be swayed. She'd misjudged her hunger and couldn't wait any longer. All right then, Jesse said, but he was going with her.

They slipped away from the carnival and found the drunk pissing against a tree. He staggered and sang and argued with himself as they trailed him. The moon turned everything either bone white or blackest black. They'd walked about a mile when the drunk swerved off the main road onto a narrow, overgrown trail that sloped downward through a thick wood where the treetops meshed overhead to form a tunnel. Barely any moonlight penetrated this canopy, just enough to speckle the ground.

Jesse offered to bring the man down for Claudine, but she drew her knife and trotted off to make the kill herself. Swiftly, silently, she gained on the drunk, catching up to him in a small, bright clearing. Everything was going as it was supposed to until a branch snapped under her foot as she raised her knife and the man whirled and dodged her strike.

"Help," he bellowed. "Help!"

Claudine jumped onto his back, and his shout died in a gurgle when she cut his throat. She rode him to the ground and fastened her mouth to the spurting wound. He struggled, but in her bloodlust her strength more than matched his.

Footsteps approached from farther down the trail, and someone shouted, "Jim! Sing out, boy!" Three other men stepped into the clearing with lanterns and shotguns.

"What in the hell?"

"She's kilt Jim."

Claudine sprang to her feet, and a shotgun boomed. Jesse caught a glimpse of her in mid-air in the muzzle flash.

Buckshot tore through her, nearly cutting her in half. She dropped to the ground, and Jesse ran to her. The other men fired. One blast shredded Jesse's left arm, the other struck him full in the chest. After an instant of scalding pain, he lost consciousness.

He stops here, can go no further.

"I couldn't do anything to save her," he says.

"I'm sorry," Johona says. "I won't ask you about her again."

Jesse manages to get back to sleep, this time dreamlessly. He has no idea how long he's been out when the sound of the door being unlocked makes him sit up as awake as if he'd never closed his eyes. Johona is fumbling with the security chain. The sun is still shining.

"I'm gonna get something to eat," she says.

"We have to lay low," Jesse says. "The Fiends."

"I thought you said they can't be out in the daytime? I'm just going for Fritos and a Coke."

"There's candy on the table and some jerky."

"I need cigarettes too."

Jesse hesitates, unsure whether to push it.

"I'll be back in five seconds," Johona says. She opens the door and takes care to block the sun with her body as she squeezes through it.

As soon as she's gone Jesse kicks himself for letting her go, worried he's put too much trust in her. He paces the room, thinking of all the ways she might betray him. His anxiety turns to relief when she taps at the door ten minutes later and says, "It's me."

"I got you these," she says and hands him a pair of mirrored sunglasses.

"What do you expect I'm gonna do with them?" he says.

"Some people wear them at night."

He slips the glasses on.

"Check you out," Johona says. "Joe Cool."

"Joe Cool," Jesse says. "Okay, then."

They lie on the bed, and Johona tells him about growing up in Phoenix, chattering away until she dozes off in the middle of a story. He curls around her and buries his nose in her hair. He shouldn't have gone back to the bowling alley, shouldn't have taken her out afterward. Her resemblance to Claudine clouded his judgment, and now here they are in a world of trouble with the Fiends.

He recalls the threat the biker made before he jumped and the story of the stolen motorcycle and similar savage tales he's heard and knows that even if he puts Johona on a bus to Los Angeles, she'll never be completely safe. And neither will he and Edgar. They'll always be looking over their shoulders, worried the Fiends will catch up to them. And one night they will.

Maybe there's another way, though—an alternative to running and hiding that he's too scattered and too panicky to see. What he needs to do is talk to someone with a clearer head, someone who can look at the mess he's made and help him devise a plan to get out of it. What he needs to do is call Beaumont.

Monsieur Amadu Beaumont was born in Africa and turned there too. He claims to have met Jesus Christ, Attila the Hun, and William Shakespeare; to have lived in various countries that don't exist anymore; and to speak three forgotten languages. He's also acknowledged to be the oldest rover in existence, making him a respected figure among the turned. Hoping to benefit from his experience and wisdom, rovers seek him out for advice, regarding him as a mentor, judge, and sage.

Claudine introduced Jesse to him in St. Louis in 1903, a year before she died. She and Beaumont had traveled around Europe together before she came to the US, and after listening to the two of them wax rapturous about their adventures, Jesse suspected they'd been lovers. He asked Claudine if this was so, but all she did was make a joke, saying, "How dare you? Don't you know you're the first man I've ever been with?" What's true is that when Jesse next saw Beaumont, this time in New Orleans in 1920 or thereabouts, and informed him that Claudine had been dusted, the man wept like a child.

He and Edgar visited him on a couple of occasions after that, the last time being twenty years ago when passing through Las Vegas, where Beaumont had been living for a while. They met at a bar, and Beaumont spent the entire evening reminiscing about Claudine, bursting into tears once again as he described her dancing on a beach in Spain. His recollections kicked open the door to Jesse's own past, and for months afterward he was tormented by memories of Claudine. Unwilling to risk such anguish again, he hasn't contacted the man since.

Now, though, he needs his guidance.

He leaves the room at sundown, goes to the motel's pay phone, and dials the old number he has for the legendary rover. After three rings a deep, French-accented voice says, "Hello?"

Amadu Beaumont.

"How long's it been?" Beaumont asks when Jesse identifies himself.

"Twenty years," Jesse replies.

"Too, too long," Beaumont says. "To what do I owe the pleasure of hearing from you now?"

Jesse is awkward on the telephone, has never gotten the

hang of talking on it, so keeps the conversation short. He asks Beaumont if he knows of the Fiends.

"The motorcycle gang?" Beaumont says. "I've heard the stories."

Jesse tells him what happened in Phoenix and says he's calling in the hope he might have some ideas about how to handle the situation.

"This is serious business," Beaumont says. "I'll need to think on it. Where are you now?"

"Flagstaff," Jesse says.

"Come here, to Las Vegas. It's a good place to hide, and we can meet in person to discuss things."

"I'll call when we get there," Jesse says. "Thanks for trying to help."

"Thank Claudine," Beaumont says. "I'm only doing what she would have wanted."

Jesse hangs up and puts on the sunglasses Johona gave him. He's feeling better. Not good, but better. Vegas is only four hours away, and at least they're running *to* something now, instead of away.

18

JESSE'S CHANGED THE PLAN. WE'RE GOING TO LAS VEGAS TO see Monsieur Beaumont instead of Denver. Do you recall Monsieur Beaumont? Jesse asks me. Monsieur Beaumont's a friend of mine. He likes to hear me sing. We visited him in New Orleans and in Las Vegas. He had a parrot that could speak French.

He's gonna help Jesse figure out what to do about the Fiends. That's what Jesse tells Johona when we're eating at Denny's. What about me? Johona says. Jesse says Monsieur Beaumont's gonna try to help her too so she should come with us. However things turn out, he says, it'll be a shorter bus ride to L.A. for you. Johona pretends to mull this but I can see she's happy Jesse's keeping her around. Every time I look up she's touching him or he's touching her and neither pays me any mind.

I go to aping what they say. I do it louder and louder till Jesse tells me to leave off. I ain't your sweetheart, I say, I ain't the bad luck. Watch your mouth, Jesse says and Johona tells us to calm down.

We leave for Las Vegas. I ride shotgun with Abby on my lap and count broke-down cars. Johona asks Jesse to turn on the radio and he does. If it was me he'd have said no. Wolfman Jack plays Duke of Earl plays Honeycomb plays Maybe Baby by Buddy Holly.

Out of the blue Johona says, Why don't you let Edgar drive? Jesse says, I don't know about that. Johona says, There's hardly anybody on the road. She says, You want to drive don't you Edgar? She might be fooling so I say, It don't matter Jesse won't let me. Sure he will, Johona says. You gonna be careful? Jesse says. 10-4 good buddy, I say.

We come to Kingman and Jesse pulls into a filling station. He makes me check the oil. He makes me check the tires. Finally he says, She's all yours, and hands me the keys. I get in the driver seat and start the engine. Headlights on, I say and pull the knob, brake off. I step on the clutch pedal push the stick to 1 and ease onto the highway. I give it gas and push the stick to 2 then 3. No faster than sixty, Jesse says. Aye aye Captain, I say.

I drive all the way to Nevada and across the top of Hoover Dam. I go slow when I need to and fast when I need to. I keep the car between the lines even when it's narrow. Jesse has me turn into the parking lot of a casino by Lake Mead. He tells me and Johona to wait while he goes inside. Johona asks what he's doing. I tell her he's dipping. What's that? she says. Lifting wallets, I say, we need money. Oh, she says.

Jesse comes out and tells me move over he's driving now. We skirt the lake and the stars look like they're floating in it. Then there's Las Vegas. We drive real slow down the Strip. It's got lights in more colors than I know to name. They scamper like mice around signs and up the sides of buildings. Jesse puts the windows down and Johona sticks her head out and howls like Wolfman Jack.

Jesse stands by and lets me check us into the motel. I do it just right. He don't have to say nothing. When we get to the room he turns his pockets out and his take from the casino spills on the bed. Did you really steal that? Johona says. Who told you that? Jesse says, I won it. Johona knows he's lying but she don't care. He counts the bills. How much did you get? Johona says. Close to two hundred, Jesse says. So can we go out and have some fun? Johona says. Just to eat, Jesse says, we've got to be careful. I say hot dogs and Johona says pizza. Jesse says we'll get hot dogs tomorrow night. It's him and her against me.

The pizza place is full of noisy people. Jesse lets me play pinball and watch the man toss the dough. How I eat my slices is skin the cheese and lick the sauce off the crust. Jesse and Johona talk about Monsieur Beaumont. Jesse's meeting him tomorrow night. I told him about you, he says to Johona. He wants me to bring you along.

A boy at another table is staring. I make a scary face but he don't quit. I stick out my tongue and he shoots me the finger. I ain't having that. I pick up a knife and say, You best watch yourself I'll cut that fucking finger right off. His daddy wants to fight. Jesse pushes between us and says he's sorry says I'm simpleminded. The boy's daddy says I ought not to be out if I don't know how to behave.

Jesse tells me to get my ass to the car and keeps pushing me and saying how stupid I am. Johona tries to cool him off. It's no big deal, she says, the kid was a brat. I stop walking and start crying. I ain't stupid. I ain't simpleminded. I'll beat you black and blue if you don't get a move on, Jesse says. That's no way for brothers to talk, Johona says. We're standing by some slot machines. She holds out a handful of quarters. Feeling lucky? she says to me. Stop crying and you can have these.

She lets me pick the game. Star-Spangled Sevens. I put

in a quarter and pull the handle. A red seven comes up a white seven and nothing. You got to get three sevens to win anything. I put another quarter in and another and another and lose every time. I ain't lucky. I ain't never been lucky. I put my last quarter in and pull. Come on, Johona says, big winner.

Click click click. A red a white and a blue seven. The game goes to whooping and quarters rain into the tray. I'm hooting and Johona's hooting and even Jesse's got a smile. That's when darkness falls like a hood over my head like when I seen the wop in the mine. This time I see Jesse walking on a road as the sun rises. Walking and not worried about getting burned up. Quick as it came the picture goes.

I seen you in the desert, I say to Jesse. What are you talking about? he says. You remember the wop? I say. I just seen you walking in the daytime. Jesse looks at me strange. You were having some kind of dream, he says.

I know you got to be sleeping to dream but I let it lie. I scoop the quarters into a cup and Johona takes me to the money lady. She empties the cup into a counting machine and it adds up to ten dollars and twenty-five cents. I'm rich, I say but ten dollars ain't rich.

Jesse drops me and Johona at the motel and goes out again. We look at TV and play cards till he gets back. He's been dipping again. Las Vegas is the best town for it. Everybody's got money and everybody's drunk. Jesse scored big and he's brought Johona a green dress and me a plastic pirate sword. Johona puts the dress on. It matches your eyes, Jesse says. She gives him a kiss don't even care I'm watching. I poke Abby with the sword till she hisses. The sun's up when we go to bed. Jesse and Johona keep me awake with their whispering and giggling.

★   ★   ★

The circus man hanging upside down above us got a girl by the hands. He throws her to another man. All us watching go to clapping and whistling and the circus folks drop into a net and take a bow. A fella comes out with a pack of dogs. One in a top hat one in a dress. They commence to dancing on their hind legs jumping through hoops and pushing a pram.

I turn to tell Jesse we should get us a pup and catch him kissing Johona. She's wearing the new dress. The Little Devil gives me a kick and says, *I told you that bitch was trouble.* When the dogs is done the fancy man says, Ladies and gentlemen boys and girls that's our show for tonight. On behalf of Circus Circus and our performers I bid you good evening and wish you the best of luck.

I begged Jesse to bring me here and he said okay even though he's still worried about the Fiends seeing us. They got games upstairs. The one where you knock over milk bottles the one where you pop balloons the one where you toss rope rings. They're all gaffed but Jesse worked in a carnival so knows the tricks. Put some backspin on it, he says when I'm trying to throw baseballs into a peach basket but the balls still bounce out. Jesse steps up and—one two three—makes all his shots. He tells the lady to give me the rubber lizard I was playing for. Johona wants a stuffed bear. To get it, Jesse has to shoot a paper star with a machine gun. He does it his second try. Better'n Al Capone, I say.

We drive to Caesar's Palace. Monsieur Beaumont is waiting for us in a bar wearing a white suit. He's got six scars across his forehead. I asked him once did a lion get him over in Africa. He said the scars was a sign to show people what tribe he was in. I asked him did his tribe live in teepees and he said they got houses.

He shakes my hand and says, It's been a long time Monsieur Edgar. Do you still sing? I sure damn do, I say, want to hear something? He says maybe later. When he sees Johona his eyes get big and he presses his palms together like he's praying. You were right, he says to Jesse. It's incredible. She's the very image of Claudine. He takes Johona's hand and kisses her three times. It is a pleasure to meet you my dear, he says.

A lady's playing piano. Monsieur Beaumont pours some champagne for Jesse and Johona and Jesse says I can have some too. I ain't never had champagne before. It's got bubbles and smells like sour milk. Jesse asks Monsieur Beaumont if he's got any ideas for what to do about the Fiends. I've been asking around, Monsieur Beaumont says, and I may have found someone who can put me in touch with them. The first step is to see if they're willing to negotiate and perhaps accept some form of restitution in lieu of revenge. Will you do that for us? Jesse says. Monsieur Beaumont takes Johona's hand again and says, How can I say no after seeing this beautiful creature? She mustn't come to any harm. Thank you, Johona says.

The piano lady is singing that song about Moon River. Monsieur Beaumont comes out of his swoon and says to Jesse, Of course I can't guarantee anything. Stealing the infant, dusting one of their comrades. If it's even possible to arrange a settlement the price will be steep. Whatever it takes, Jesse says.

Monsieur Beaumont turns to me and Johona and says, Would you mind leaving us for a moment? We need to speak privately. Johona looks to Jesse. Everything's fine, he says.

Me and Johona go to the casino. She gets two paper rolls of quarters and we pick a couple slot machines. I put in half my quarters and don't win nothing. Then I get three oranges and the game goes to flashing and making noise but only a few coins come out. Johona keeps looking over to the bar. I tell her you got to pay attention if you want to win. A girl showing lots of leg asks do we want cocktails. I say to bring me a Coca-Cola with a cherry in it.

My quarters is about gone by the time Jesse and Monsieur Beaumont come over. Monsieur Beaumont kisses Johona again and says, Farewell for now. I hope to see you again when there's time to become better acquainted. Why you leaving so soon? I ask him, you didn't even hear me sing. Let's have a quick one, he says. How about Meet Me Tonight in Dreamland. I start right in: *Meet me tonight in dreamland under the silvery moon meet me tonight in dreamland where love's sweet roses bloom.* He claps when I finish and says, Bravo!

19

June 29, 1976, Las Vegas, Nevada

Time often slowed to a stagger this past year as I traced and retraced Benny's last steps, following the trail of postmarks on the cards he sent you. Five minutes in Eureka could seem like an hour, an hour in San Francisco like ten hours, a week in L.A. like an eternity.

The past few days, however, have flown by, full of enough tribulation for a lifetime. I feel like a meteor hurtling toward earth, falling faster and faster, growing hotter and hotter, about to explode.

I woke an hour before dawn yesterday, bought a couple of hamburgers from the truck stop's restaurant, and took them to the kid in the camper. He wolfed the first sandwich down, drank from a jug of water, belched, and started on the second.

"What's your name, man?" he asked me.

My coffee was kicking in, so I played along. "What's yours, man?"

"Sal," the kid said. "Cats call me Sally."

"Cats call me Charles."

"Cool," Sally said. His gold tooth flashed when he grinned. "Charles meet Sally, Sally meet Charles." He finished the burger and licked his fingers. "So the old man's dead?" he asked in an offhand way, like he was trying to trick me into answering.

"He is," I replied.

"And I'm working for you now."

"I'll be using you the same as he did," I said.

"Well, you're already a better bossman," Sally said. "I found rovers for him for ten years, and he never told me his name or asked for mine. It was nothing but, 'Get out of the box,' and, 'Get in the truck.'"

"Cross me, and you'll wish he was still around," I said.

"I know my place," Sally said. He grimaced and rolled his head as if his neck hurt. "You mind if I stand and stretch?"

I took Czarnecki's .45 from my pocket. Frail as the kid was, I wasn't too worried about him overpowering me, but I also wasn't taking any chances. He got to his feet, lifted his shackled arms as high as he could, and flexed his shackled legs.

"I used to be hell on the dance floor," he said. "Doubt I'd last one number now."

It was my first time conversing with a rover. I was curious. "How old are you?" I asked him.

"I was born in '27, in Nowheresville, Iowa, but took off for New York as soon as I could," he said.

"Is that where it happened?" I said. "Where you…" I was unsure how to put it.

"Where I became a creature of the night?" Sally said, joking. "Yeah, that's where."

"How?" I said. "Why?"

"The old man has a jar of peanut butter there in the cupboard," Sally said. "Let me at it, and I'll tell you what you want to know."

I took the jar down and gave it to him, along with a spoon I found in a drawer. He unscrewed the lid and dug in, scooping and licking while he talked.

"I met this cat in New York," he said. "A colored cat like you, a trumpet player. His name was Daniel Carson, but everybody called him DC. We started making the scene together. It was just kicks at first, a good time, but we ended up real tight. I knew he was a rover, but I didn't care. I thought it was kinda cool, kinda sexy. I even let him feed off me—got off on it, in fact.

"It was my idea he turn me. We had a good thing, and I wanted to keep it going. And it *was* good, for almost eight years. We bummed around, played gigs, got in trouble, got out of trouble, wore five-hundred-dollar suits, three-hundred-dollar shoes. It was a real gas. But then he got dusted."

He paused, overcome by emotion. When he tried to go on, he couldn't. "I'm done," he said. He handed me the peanut butter jar and lay back in the crate. "You're not gonna hold me being queer against me, are you?" he asked.

I was thinking of Benny, you know I was.

"No," I said. "I won't hold it against you."

I closed the lid and snapped the locks into place. As I was leaving the camper, stepping out into the new day blooming, he called to me again.

"Where we headed?"

"I haven't decided," I said.

"Vegas," he said. "If you're looking for rovers, that's where you should go."

The rising sun set the mountains on fire. I stood in the parking lot, marveling at the sight and wondering if it was a message from God, and if so, what it meant. I came up with nothing, which proves, I guess, that I don't have the imagination to be a prophet, so it's a good thing I've been called to be a killer.

Taking the kid's advice, I set off across the desert. Six hours of sand, rock, and sun, of ruler-straight stretches of shimmering asphalt and mountains as sharp and menacing as wolves' teeth. I stopped in Death Valley to top off the radiator and buy a cold drink. A thermometer at the service station read 116°. I had to squint in the glare, and the soles of my shoes stuck to the blacktop.

I took a bag of ice and a bottle of water out to Sally. Czarnecki would've said, "Fuck him," but I wanted the kid in decent shape, ready to hunt. The air inside the camper was so hot, it was hard to breathe. Sally was gasping when I opened the crate. He guzzled the water and laid the ice on his chest.

"You're a good man," he said.

"I'd do the same for a dog," I replied and locked him up again.

It was too hot to sleep in the truck once we got to Vegas, so I splurged on a motel just off the Strip. I closed the drapes, turned up the air conditioner, and took a cold shower. Lying on the bed afterward, I was snoring before my body dried.

I woke at dusk. Next to the phone was a menu for a Chinese restaurant that delivered. I called and ordered the works, the Emperor's Feast, for two. The food arrived, and when I'd had my fill, I decided to bring Sally in to eat his share rather than carrying everything out to him.

The sun was down, but it was still stifling in the camper. I unlocked the crate and said, "You can come inside for a while, but if you so much as twitch in a way that spooks me, I'll kill you."

"You got my word, boss," Sally said.

I covered him with the .45 as he climbed out of the box. I'd backed the truck into the space in front of the room, so all he had to do was cross the walkway. He sat at the table in his chains and ate out of the cartons. I sat on the bed, keeping the gun on him. He used chopsticks at first but changed to a fork, said his fingers weren't working right.

When he asked if I'd turn on the TV, I couldn't think of a reason not to. He finished his dinner watching a cop show and wanted to take a shower. I could smell him from across the room, so I tossed him the keys so he could undress. Though I'd seen him without clothes in Czarnecki's shed, he seemed even more pitiful now: skin stretched over bulging bones, muscles wasted away, toothpick legs. The butterfly tattoo on his chest and gold tooth were like diamond earrings and a tiara on a corpse. I let him bathe without cuffs. There was no danger of him slipping out through the tiny window in the bathroom.

He was steadier on his feet afterward, stood a little straighter. I gave him a T-shirt and a pair of pants from my duffel. They hung on him like he was a scarecrow, but at least they were clean. Then I told him to get back into his chains. We were going hunting.

He locked himself in next to me in the truck, and we drove up and down the Strip. When we passed the Sands, I recalled when you and I stayed there. That was a good time. We saw Redd Foxx and Wayne Newton, laid out by the pool, and ate steak and lobster two dinners in a row. I'll have different kinds of memories after this visit, terrible ones. That's how it is now: Everything good in my past is being swallowed by a rising tide of horror.

After an hour with no sign of a rover, I switched to Fremont Street downtown. Remember how it is there, casinos crammed together cheek by jowl, tourists overflowing the sidewalks? You said the lights and noise hypnotized them into throwing away their money. Sally and I crawled past the crowds with our windows down, and it was like bees buzzing in a sparkling hive.

The kid had been quiet since we left the motel. Czarnecki accused him of playing games, of not pointing out rovers when he spotted them, and I wondered if he might be doing me the same way. A block later, though, he whistled and said, "Bingo."

It was a white woman, tall, skinny, blond hair piled on top of her head. She looked to be in her thirties and was wearing a short dress and the kind of high heels meant to attract attention. I kept pace with her as she bopped down the sidewalk, but then she ducked into the Golden Nugget.

"Are you sure?" I asked Sally.

"I'm sure," he said.

I found a spot on the second floor of a parking garage and, as soon as the coast was clear, hustled Sally into his crate. My heart was pounding as I ran down the stairs and through the back entrance of the casino. The place was packed with gamblers hovering over blackjack tables and slouched in front of slots. A celebration broke out at a craps game, clapping and whistling and shouts of "Attaboy" and "Keep 'em coming," and waitresses dressed like Old West saloon girls chanted, "Cocktails, cocktails."

I squinted through the cigarette smoke for the blonde, found her posing at the bar. The bartender set a drink in front of her and she reached for her purse, but the guy sitting beside her, a balding, paunchy white man in a cheap suit, laid a hand on her arm. "Pretty ladies drink for free when Mark Arcamonte's around," he said. He and the woman began to flirt.

I sat at a nearby slot machine and eavesdropped on the man's life story, or at least the version he told women he met in bars: Illinois, insurance, top salesman, only the best for him. He took out his wallet and showed the blonde photos of his car and his boat. When he flipped to a picture of his kids, he kept his thumb over the face of his ex-wife, who was also in the shot. "You don't want to look at her," he said. "You'll turn to stone."

The blonde laughed when she was supposed to, offered sympathy when Arcamonte asked for it, and thanked him for the free drinks with cheek kisses and cuddles. Finally, though, it was time to close the deal.

"This has been fun and all, but you know I'm on the clock, right?" she said.

"Sure, sure, I get that," Arcamonte replied.

"So what now?"

"Let's get the hell out of here."

I tailed them as they walked out of the casino and east on Fremont. The crowds disappeared after a few blocks, casinos giving way to liquor stores, pawnshops, and budget motels. The blonde and Arcamonte turned into the parking lot of a low-slung dump called the Sky Harbor Inn. I caught up in time to see them step into Room 104 on the ground floor.

It hit me that Arcamonte might be the blonde's next victim instead of a customer. I crossed the street, sat on the curb, and pictured her talking dirty to him, nuzzling his ear, then pulling a knife to cut his throat. God was kind to the man, however: An hour after he went into the room with the blonde, he left alone and slunk back toward Glitter Gulch.

Fifteen minutes later the blonde came out. She walked two

doors down, to Room 106, and used a key to let herself in. It was 2 a.m. I kept watch until 5, but she never reappeared.

I was wide-awake as day broke, buzzing with nervous energy. Knowing the blonde would have to stay put, I hurried back to the truck and grabbed Czarnecki's duffel bag, the one he carried into the Mexican's room in Reno. It held everything I'd need. Then it was back to the motel.

Fremont was deserted now, except for one crazy drunk shadowboxing in the window of a casino. The slot parlors' recorded spiels echoed down the empty street, and daylight dimmed the neon to almost nothing.

Nobody was stirring at the Sky Harbor, either. My chest was tight as I approached Room 106, my hands shook when I took the crowbar from the bag and wedged it into place, and I was going on pure instinct when I forced the door open.

The blonde, wearing only a bathrobe, flew at me from the bed. She went for my eyes, but I backed her off with the crowbar. Her skin smoked when she stumbled into the sunlight streaming through the doorway. She kicked the door shut and charged again.

I swung the crowbar and caught her in the head. Blond wig askew, she fell onto the bed, bleeding from a gash on her scalp. I pulled out the ice pick I'd slipped into the pocket of my coat and dove at her. As I straddled her, ready to stab her in the heart, a child's voice rang out.

"Mommy!"

I glanced over to see a girl of seven or so, dressed in Raggedy Ann pajamas, cowering near the bathroom. My pause gave the blonde time to recover. She bucked me off, and we wrestled for the pick. "Please don't kill my daughter," she said. This was something I hadn't planned on, something I hadn't even imagined. "Do what you want to me, but don't kill her."

I got on top of her again and drew back the pick. The child was crying now. The blonde lifted her hands, fingers laced together. "Please," she said, then punched me in the nose with both fists. Blinded by pain, I stabbed wildly.

The child jumped onto the bed and grabbed me around the throat from behind. She bit my ear, digging her teeth in and shaking her head until I fell back on top of her.

"Kill him!" she yelled.

The blonde came up with a knife, rolled over, and brought the blade down. I blocked her arm and stuck the ice pick in her neck. Blood spraying out of her mouth spattered my face. I yanked the pick free and jammed it into her chest. She stopped coughing and went limp.

I pried the child's fingers from my throat, bending them until some broke, then picked her up and flung her across the room. She bounced off the wall and lay moaning on the floor. I grabbed the crowbar.

"You motherfucker," the child hissed. "You piece of shit."

I brought the bar down on her head. That shut her up.

I didn't bother carrying the bodies into the bathroom. I used the hacksaw to turn them to ash where they lay, the blonde on the bed, the child on the floor.

After catching my breath, I put the ice pick and crowbar in the bag and took a winding route—side streets and alleys—back to the truck, stopping often to make sure nobody was following. I didn't notice I had blood on my hands until I pulled into the parking lot of my motel.

Even though I was in the blonde's room for less than five minutes, I feel like I was transformed there, like I burst and shed my old skin. What I fear is that I'm now more akin to one of the monsters than to a man, and farther away from home than ever. Pray for me.

June 30, 1976, Las Vegas

I took water to Sally in the hottest part of the day yesterday and brought him in to finish the Chinese food when the sun went down. He looked even steadier and more clear-eyed, and I thought of Czarnecki's warning about keeping him weak.

"Did you get the woman?" he asked as he broke open a fortune cookie.

"None of your business," I replied.

"You don't seem too happy about it," he said. "The old man, shit, he'd celebrate afterward, get drunk, fry up a steak, play his cowboy records. You look like someone kicked you in the balls."

"I don't take joy in killing, even if it's monsters," I said.

"So you're in the wrong line of work then," Sally said. "You want my advice? If it doesn't sit right with you, don't do it. Walk away. Cut me loose, and walk away."

"I've got a score to settle."

The kid picked up a chopstick and sighted down it like you would a pool cue to check if it was bowed.

"A rover took someone you knew?" he said.

"My son," I said. I've grown so used to talking about Benny's death with strangers that it slipped out before I could stop it.

"And how many rovers are you gonna have to kill to get even?" Sally said.

I wasn't in the mood for a philosophical discussion, especially not with someone who'd say anything to regain his freedom.

"Shut your mouth or it's back in the box," I said.

"I wasn't trying to upset you."

"Shut your mouth," I said again, this time acting like I was about to get up and do him harm.

"It's cool," Sally said. "Everything's cool." He turned to watch television. A news program was on, something about preparations for the Fourth around the country.

I stared at the set too, thinking about Sally's question regarding getting even. I wondered at what point the thirst for vengeance becomes a sin of pride. I remembered God's warning against lashing out at those who've wronged you, Him saying, "It is mine to avenge, I will repay." And then I questioned whether all that wasn't just me looking for an excuse to cut and run after getting a real taste of what my life will be like if I take up Czarnecki's crusade.

After a while, Sally said, "What's going on in Vietnam?"

"What do you mean?" I said.

"I've been in a hole for ten years, man. I don't know anything."

"The war's over," I said. "They say we lost."

"How about the Yankees? How are they doing?"

"Looking good this year. Might go all the way."

"Who's dead? Who's alive? Louis Armstrong?"

"He's dead," I said.

"Coltrane?"

"Dead."

"I bet fucking Sinatra's still kicking though. Fucking Bing Crosby."

"Both alive," I said.

"Figures."

Sally quieted down again, then said, "I've got a score to settle too."

"With who?" I said.

"DC? My pal?" Sally said. "You know who dusted him?

Rovers. Three nigger-hating rovers." He started to fidget. "We were in Memphis," he continued. "Him and this kid were walking back to our hotel from Beale Street where he was playing, and these rednecks jumped them. They said they didn't need another rover in Memphis, especially not a black one, and tied DC and the kid up and drove them out to the sticks.

"The kid got away but hid close by and came to me later and told me what happened. He said the hicks beat DC until all his bones were broken. He said one of them blew on DC's horn while the others took turns stabbing him. After that they put a noose around his neck and threw him off a bridge. Dumb as they were, they didn't think about the drop. When the rope snapped taut, it tore DC's head right off. He was dust before his shoes hit the river."

Sally bent double in the chair and went silent for a while, then suddenly sat up and said, "I loved that man. I still can't think about what happened to him without wanting to die myself."

"I loved my son," I said.

"So you understand," Sally said. "You understand that even though being locked up in that shed has been hell, I figure at least I've gotten a little payback for DC by leading the old man to rovers."

I was tired of listening to him, tired of having to think about things from his point of view. What I needed was clarity, not someone muddying the water even more. He stacked the empty takeout boxes one inside the other.

"What if I gave you someone special?" he said.

"What's that mean?" I said.

"A special rover, one more important than the rest, one who's like royalty to them. A rover who could lead you to a hundred others. If I gave you someone like that, could we make a deal?"

"A deal?" I said.

"I take you to this cat and you let me go."

"No way," I said.

"I didn't kill your son."

"You killed someone's."

Sally drummed his fingers on the table. "How about this then," he said. "How about you catch this cat, put *him* in the box, and dust me?"

20

NONE OF THE FIENDS SLEEP WELL AFTER BOB 1 IS DUSTED.
Pedro and Johnny toss and turn and jump at every little sound.
Yuma and Real Deal argue over nothing. Bob 2 smokes a
joint, drinks a bottle of whiskey, and stares at the TV, trying
to ignore the empty bed beside him as the day drags on,
never-ending.

When night finally smothers the sun and makes the world
safe for her bastards, the gang emerge from their rooms and
gather by the pool. Antonia and Elijah bring everyone foam
cups of lobby coffee, and Pedro passes a pint of VO to
sweeten it. They drink a toast to the dead Bob and get down
to business.

Antonia has a map of Phoenix. She's divided it into three
sections. She and Elijah will take one, Real Deal and Yuma
another, Bob and Johnny and Pedro the third. They'll criss-
cross the city, searching for the pair who dusted Bob and stole
the baby. It was a young man and an old one, but Antonia tells
them to grab anyone turned and put the screws to them.

Bob's not happy with the section he and Pedro and Johnny
have been assigned. It's mostly sleepy housing tracts and

farmland that'll soon be sleepy housing tracts. No dive bars, no whore strolls, no strip clubs or dirty bookstores—nowhere they're likely to find a rover on the hunt.

Hopped up on bathtub crank, he's riding bitch behind Pedro. They pull over and check a miniature golf course, walk through a supermarket, and sit in front of a movie theater as the show lets out. Nothing but clean-cut squares and their clean-cut wives and kids.

Eventually they come upon a discotheque glowing pink and purple at the edge of civilization. Next to it is a freshly uprooted orchard with a sign planted on it that reads FUTURE SITE OF SUNSET ESTATES. AFFORDABLE LUXURY. The disco is no massage parlor or dime-a-dance cantina, but the parking lot is full, so they decide to have a look inside.

Two men guard the door. One is wearing a denim suit and a white polyester shirt unbuttoned to display the gold chains around his neck. The other is a big Indian bruiser in a tank top and tight jeans.

"*Ho,*" Johnny says to the Indian. It's the only Kickapoo he knows. *Hello.* The Indian ignores him.

Gold Chains says there's a five-dollar charge to get into the club.

"What do you get for that?" Johnny asks. "A titty show?"

The flashing lights make the gold chain guy's mustache look like it's bouncing on his upper lip. "This ain't that kind of place, if that's the kind of place you're looking for," he says.

"Nah, nah," Johnny says. "This is the kind of place we want."

"You sure?"

"There's chicks in there, right? Music? Beer?"

"You dudes looking to dance?"

"Hell, yeah," Johnny says. "We're dancing fools."

The music punches the Fiends in the chest when they

step inside, the bass hitting like a steady jab. Swiveling lights, synched to the beat, disorient them, and the club is as hot and humid as a Florida swamp. They muscle their way through the crowd to the bar, a black schooner parting a churning sea.

Johnny orders for them, three beers. The girl behind the bar frowns at the grubby five he drops as payment. She straightens the bill gingerly, using her long red fingernails, puts it in the till, and walks away.

The Fiends find a wall to lean against. They sip their beers and watch the action on the dance floor. Everyone spins and claps in unison, the men shaking their asses as much as the women.

"I knew a pimp who had a getup like that," Johnny shouts in Pedro's ear, pointing at one of the dancing men.

After half an hour, the music and lights have given Bob a headache. He feels like he's trapped on a carnival ride. He's about to tell Johnny and Pedro "Let's get the fuck out of here" when a tall, thin dude surrounded by a black aura enters the club with an unturned chick on his arm. He's not one of the rovers that dusted Bob 2, but beggars can't be choosers.

The Fiends duck into the hallway leading to the bathrooms to avoid being spotted. Bob peeks around the corner to watch the rover and the chick dance their way to the bar. He and the others make their move while the guy's flagging down a bartender, surrounding him. He starts to bitch about being crowded but freezes when he sees it's rovers.

"What's your name, brother?" Bob says.

"Darren," the rover replies. He's wearing white pants and a lime-green shirt.

"We need to talk to you, Darren."

The rover looks from Bob to Johnny to Pedro, contemplating running. Bob wraps an arm around him. "Order me a scotch and soda," Darren tells the girl, a little blonde in a sequined dress that barely covers her ass. "I'll be right back."

The Fiends hustle him to the door and walk him out to the future site of Sunset Estates. Bob releases him when they're beyond the reach of the disco's lights. Darren straightens his clothes and smooths his hair, figures cocky's how he'll play this.

"Fiends," he says. "I've heard of you."

"We haven't heard of you," Bob says.

"I'm a city mouse. New York, Philly, Boston. And I keep to myself."

"What are you doing here, city mouse?"

"I'm on my way to San Diego to see a pal."

"And the chick?"

"Some local chippie."

Darren takes some Doublemint out of his pocket, pulls a stick for himself, and holds the pack out to the Fiends. Johnny pinches a piece.

"How long you been in town?" Bob says.

Darren unwraps the gum and sticks it in his mouth. "This is my third night."

"Seen any other rovers?"

"Nope."

"You sure? Nobody's traveling with you?"

"I told you, I keep to myself."

The Fiends exchange heavy glances.

"You said you heard of us," Bob says.

"This and that," Darren says.

"Like what?"

"Like steer clear of you."

"Good advice."

Pedro has slipped behind Darren. He slaps a hand over his

mouth, and Bob stabs him in the heart. They've dusted him ten seconds after he hits the ground. Johnny paws through the ash, retrieving the guy's wallet and puka-shell necklace.

"We going back in?" he says.

"Fuck it," Bob says. "Let's see what other shitholes we can find."

Antonia and Elijah have passed through Phoenix once or twice a year since before Arizona was a state. The first time they visited, they rode in on horseback. They've watched the city grow from a dusty cluster of saloons, dance halls, and assay offices into a sprawl of suburbs that's filled the valley with shopping malls, golf courses, and housing developments.

And now the powers that be are pulling down old Phoenix. Every time Antonia and Elijah return, more downtown landmarks have been demolished and replaced with smoked-glass-and-concrete high-rises. The Fox Theater is now a bus terminal, the cheap hotel where they used to stay is a gleaming Hyatt, and their favorite chop suey joint lies buried beneath a new convention center.

The area used to be prime hunting ground: the whores working the Paris Alley brothels, the sots pickling themselves in the dives lining the streets of the Deuce, and the assorted other lost souls who haunted the gambling dens, topless grinds, and all-night movie theaters. Ragged men and women still drink, fight, and fuck here, but now it's right out in the open, and when they crash, it's not in dollar flops or cots at the mission, it's on the sidewalk, curled in cardboard boxes in the shadow of the new buildings.

Elijah laments the changes, but Antonia couldn't care less. Nostalgia's a weakness as far as she's concerned. When something's gone, it's gone. Cut it loose and move on. She's lost so much in her two hundred years, she'd drown in tears if she mourned it all.

They're cruising the same streets for the third time. It's close to midnight, and nobody's out. Elijah taps his horn to get Antonia's attention and points to the Torch, a bar they know. They circle the block and park in front of the place.

"Let's grab a quick one," Elijah says. "Might be our last chance."

Antonia's reluctant. Three years ago she fed off an old man she picked up here. "I don't got a person who gives a shit about me," he told her. "Everyone I know is dead." She lured him to an abandoned produce warehouse on the promise of a hand job, drained him, and got rid of the corpse in the desert.

"Nobody'll remember you," Elijah says. "They won't even remember him."

They step over a kid passed out on the sidewalk to enter the bar. His girlfriend is messed up, too, sitting on the curb and chanting, "Greg! Greg! Greg!" The bar is bright as day inside. Four gargoyles are hunched over the stick, a few more in the booths. Something by the Doors wheezes out of the jukebox.

The bartender is a leathery redheaded woman wearing a cardboard red, white, and blue top hat. More star-spangled crap is hanging on the walls in anticipation of the Fourth. The woman takes Elijah's order for two draft A-1s and says, "Those junkies still out front?"

"They are," Elijah says.

"Call the fucking police, Sarah, will ya?" one of the gargoyles croaks.

"I don't need Phoenix PD in here," the bartender says.

"I should go out there and shoot them myself."

"You ain't gonna shoot nobody," the bartender says, rolling her eyes at Antonia and Elijah. "He ain't even got a gun," she says out of the side of her mouth.

The junkies are still on the sidewalk when the Fiends leave. Elijah doesn't feel like getting back on his bike yet. There's a porno theater next to the bar. THREE TRIPLE X FEATURES.

"You want to see a movie?" he asks Antonia.

"If you need to get your ashes hauled, we'll go to the motel," she says.

"Come on. We'll watch until the bars close."

They pay their admission to a zitty kid behind the candy counter. The only snacks for sale are warm sodas and stale popcorn. Elijah gooses Antonia while they wait at the back of the theater for their eyes to adjust. "Don't you touch me," she says. Someone's fucking someone on-screen. The moans aren't synched to the action, and the print is so bad, it's like watching a catfish flap its gills through the glass of a filthy aquarium, rhythmic flailing in greenish murk. They sit as far from the other patrons as possible, but even so, one of the sewer rats pops up to leer at Antonia. A hard look from Elijah sends him back into his hole.

Elijah tries to follow the movie, but there's not much story to keep track of. Squinting at the screen, he wonders if this is what it's like to be a ghost, if after you die, you're doomed to peer from the dark into the light, the living world just out of focus, a smear of writhing bodies, speeding cars, and ringing telephones. He leans over to whisper this thought to Antonia, but she's fast asleep.

The Fiends reconvene by the pool near dawn.

"Nothing?" Antonia says.

"We drove our section five times," Real Deal says.

"We got something," Bob says, and tells everybody about Darren. "Maybe the next one we find'll know something about those that dusted Bob."

"And maybe not," Real Deal says. "Maybe they've already hit the road. Maybe we ought to hit the road too."

Bob bristles. "We're not giving up," he says. "Not after one fucking night."

"I'm not talking about giving up," Real Deal says. "I'm talking about looking for them someplace else."

Antonia just wants to get to bed. "We'll go out again tomorrow," she says, "switch routes and put fresh eyes on everything."

"However you want to do it," Bob says, "but we're not giving up."

Johnny hands him a can of beer. He presses it to the back of his neck, trying to cool off.

After another restless day, the Fiends set out for a second night of searching. Bob rides with Pedro and Johnny again. They're covering downtown this evening. Lots more people on the street, lots more places you might find a rover.

They take a break at a hamburger stand. An old alky trying to place an order at the window can't keep his pants up. They're too big for him—probably pulled out of a trash can—but he keeps forgetting and letting go of the belt loops, whereupon the trousers drop to his ankles, exposing his skinny legs and bare ass until he squats to yank them up again.

"Be a good boy and give your dad your belt," Bob says to Johnny.

"He looks like a jack-in-the-box, don't he?" Johnny says. He kicks Pedro, who's crouched next to his bike. "What do you think? Is he just a weenie wagger putting on a show?"

Pedro doesn't respond. His head is down, and he's gasping for air. Johnny kneels beside him.

"What's wrong?"

Pedro wipes away a strand of drool and swallows hard. "Help me up," he says.

Johnny and Bob walk him around the parking lot until he's breathing normally and able to stand on his own.

"I've gone too long without feeding," he says. "It snuck up on me."

"How bad are you?" Johnny says.

"I'm gonna have to hunt tonight."

"So we're calling off the search?" Bob says, anger in his voice.

"I'll be fine on my own," Pedro says. "You two keep looking." He gets on his bike and starts it. "I'll catch you back at the motel," he says before riding off.

"*Cuidado,*" Johnny calls after him.

Real Deal and Yuma start by riding every street in their sector twice. The problem is, nobody walks in this town, so pretty much their only hope of spotting a rover without getting off their bikes and going into every goddamn place is to catch one entering or exiting a bar or 7-Eleven. And what are the odds of that?

Yuma signals Real Deal to turn into the parking lot of a strip mall with a twenty-four-hour laundromat. The place is empty, and all the other businesses in the mall are closed for the night.

"You see something?" Real Deal says.

"I'm bored," Yuma says.

She steps off her Harley and pulls a screwdriver out of one of her saddlebags. Walking into the laundromat, she goes to the soap vending machine, uses the screwdriver to bust the lock, and pockets the money she finds there.

"Feel better?" Real Deal says when she comes out and gets on her bike.

"Still bored," she says.

The two of them have been together for nine years. They met in Dallas and fell in love fast and hard. She's on-and-off crazy, so's he, and they accept this in each other. So far, whenever she's lost it, he's been right enough in the head to stop her from getting in too much trouble, and she's done the same for him. Riding with the Fiends for the past five years has helped too. The discipline imposed by Antonia keeps them on track most of the time.

Real Deal's not sure what flipped Yuma's switch tonight—Bob getting dusted, the other Bob acting like an asshole, losing out on the baby—but he knows he's got his hands full. Her next stop is a closed gas station. He waits while she jimmies the Coke machine. A few minutes later she tries to smash her way into a parking meter with a hammer.

"If you need money, all you got to do is ask," Real Deal says, joking.

"I don't need your fucking money," she replies.

She gets back on her bike and rides until she comes to a liquor store in a Mexican neighborhood. Real Deal follows her into the parking lot and turns off his engine when she does. Three men leaving a bar next to the store stop to admire her Harley.

"How much you pay?" one of them asks her.

"A million dollars," she says. "Two million."

The guy makes a face and repeats what she said in Spanish to his buddies. They scoff too. "No two million dollars," the guy says to her. "Two million *pesos.*" His buddies laugh, and all three climb into a pickup bristling with gardening tools and drive away.

Real Deal runs a hand over his closely cropped afro. It comes away sweaty.

"What are you up to now?" he says.

Yuma walks into the store without answering. He follows. An old Mexican couple is behind the counter. The wife's sitting on a milk crate, watching a soap opera on a tiny TV; the husband's at the register, a cigar stub wedged in the corner of his mouth.

The store shelves are overflowing with merchandise. The place sells groceries in addition to booze—cans of beans and hominy and menudo, sacks of rice, wilted vegetables—and also odds and ends like toilet plungers and tamale pots. Dramatic music plays on the TV as Yuma goes to the beer cooler without so much as a nod to the old man. Real Deal tries to be friendly, saying "*Buenas noches*" and pretending to be interested in a display of car deodorizers—pine trees, Playboy bunnies, Mexican flags. The old man ignores him. He's watching Yuma in a round mirror mounted on the ceiling.

Yuma grabs a six-pack of Coors tall boys and lets the cooler door slam. She asks the old man for a pint of Cuervo. When he turns to get it off one of the shelves behind him, she shoves a fistful of Slim Jims into the pocket of her jacket. The old man sets the bottle on the counter and rings it up. His wife's standing now too, staring at Yuma.

Yuma grabs the beer and tequila and walks out without paying.

"Hey!" the old man shouts, all of a sudden holding a pistol. The old woman has a machete in her hand.

"It's cool," Real Deal says. "I got it."

He lays a twenty on the counter and backs out of the store.

Yuma cracks one of the beers in the parking lot and downs half of it. Real Deal finishes it while she loads the rest of the stuff into one of her saddlebags. She throws her leg over her bike and starts it. Real Deal puts his hand on hers to stop her from revving the engine. She glares at him, something wild thrashing behind her eyes.

"You see me, right?" he says. "I'm here for you."

"But you weren't always," she says. She puts her bike in gear and takes off.

Pedro keeps a string of boxcars between him and the hobo jungle at the edge of the train yard. The track bed is elevated enough that if he crouches, he can see under the cars to the camp beyond. He makes his way toward it stealthily, avoiding the noisy crushed-rock ballast covering the embankment.

The jungle is nestled in a grove of willows. A small fire flickers there, and Pedro hears someone speaking Spanish. He climbs on top of a car and lies on his stomach, giving him a clear view of four men gathered around scrap wood burning in a ring of stones. They're *indios*, like the ones who did all the shit work in Huamantla, the town in Mexico where he grew up. Short, stocky, and dark.

Two of them are playing cards on an apple crate. The other two are lying on the ground, staring at the flames. A gallon of Gallo is making the rounds. The men in these camps are wanderers and vagrants, runaways and fugitives. The kind of men who disappear. The kind of men nobody misses. Pedro's knee trembles. He'll be feeding tonight, he's sure of it.

"I was in a game in Salinas once, a guy bet his truck."

"I was in a game where a guy bet his house. And I won it."

"You never won anything in your life."

"A woman carrying a baby gets on a bus."

"No jokes! No jokes!"

"Pass me the bottle."

"It's empty."

The *indios* are drunk. Pedro can hear it in their voices. He reaches into his pocket for his knife. A train blows its horn somewhere behind him.

"Go for another."

"The market's closed."

"It's open till midnight."

"*Pendejos.*"

One of the card players staggers up the path leading from the jungle to the rail yard. Pedro drops from the top of the boxcar. The only light comes from a few weak bulbs mounted on poles widely spaced around the yard.

The *indio* crosses two sets of tracks and approaches the string Pedro's hiding behind. Three cars up from his, the man crawls under the train, emerging on the same side as Pedro. Pedro lies flat on the ground, but the *indio* is focused on his mission. He sets off across the yard toward a road leading to a small store.

Pedro follows, closing the distance between them. Another string of cars blocks their way. When the *indio* ducks to pass beneath it, Pedro scrambles under the car right on his heels. He grabs the man's arm, flips him onto his back, and presses a hand to his mouth. Lying on top of him, he uses the tip of his knife to poke a hole in his jugular.

The *indio* struggles, but there's no chance of him squirming out from under Pedro's bulk. Pedro fixes his lips to his neck. He smells cheap wine. The man eventually settles, and Pedro repositions him to keep the blood flowing. When the well runs dry, he keeps sucking, enjoying the warmth creeping through his body and the calm enveloping his brain after days of feeling antsy.

The yard bull plays his flashlight over a string of cars a

couple of tracks away. Pedro waits until he's gone before dragging the *indio's* body from under the car and slinging it over his shoulder. He carries it to the other side of the yard, where another trail leads to a reservoir ringed by cottonwoods.

Once at the reservoir, he lays the body next to the water and removes its clothes. By the light of a fingernail moon he cuts open the belly of the corpse and scoops out the innards, tossing them into tall grass. Coyotes will eat them before dawn. The buzzing of a million cicadas in his ears, he gathers the biggest rocks he can find and fills the *indio's* stomach cavity with them.

The water is warm as he walks out into the reservoir, towing the corpse behind him. The muddy bottom slopes quickly downward, and he lifts the body to keep it from sinking, carries it in his arms. When the water reaches his chin, he pushes off and keeps going, swimming now, kicking hard while bearing the dead man.

In the middle of the reservoir, he lets the body drag him down. When his toes touch mud, he looks up toward the tarnished silver shimmer of the surface. The water is ten feet deep here, deep enough nobody will ever find the *indio*. He releases the corpse. It sinks to the bottom, and he rockets back to the surface and swims to shore.

Back on the bank, Pedro dresses and turns for a last look at the reservoir. The water is calm again, faintly reflecting the moon, the stars, and the overarching trees. It's not so bad. There are worse spots the *indio* could have ended up.

The fireworks stand, a trailer parked in an empty lot, is locked up for the night. Yuma and Real Deal park across the road. Yuma fetches her screwdriver, and Real Deal doesn't bother to tell her what a stupid idea this is. She's drunk now, which only makes her more stubborn. He gets off his bike and follows her to the trailer.

She walks around to the door in back. Unable to get a good angle on the padlock with the screwdriver, she pries the hasp off the wall instead. When she gets the door open, she steps inside.

Real Deal pokes his head in as she thumbs her Zippo. Red Dawn, Devil's Gold, Thunder King, Big Mama, Titan. The glow from the lighter reveals floor-to-ceiling shelves filled with boxes of rockets, crackers, and Roman candles. The air is spiced with the tang of black powder, and signs warn NO SMOKING.

"Christ almighty, be careful," Real Deal says.

Yuma pokes around for a cash box but comes up empty-handed. Approaching headlights send Real Deal into the trailer too. He pulls the door shut and hisses at Yuma to douse the flame. They stand silently in the dark, so close together they feel the heat coming off each other.

The one-two punch of tension and relief when the car passes does something to Yuma. She's suddenly tingling in all the right spots and has an idea of what might calm the whirlwind that's been spinning inside her all night. She grabs Real Deal's hand and puts it on her pussy. Real Deal protests, something about too risky. "Shut up," Yuma says and goes to undoing his belt while he works on hers. They do it standing up, her bent over the counter, him coming from behind. She gets off in only a couple minutes, and he pops right after.

Real Deal makes himself presentable and steps outside. The road is empty in both directions, the body shops, retread-tire outlets, and used-car lots scattered along it snoozing away. Real Deal adjusts his pecker and smiles to himself. What a trip. He smells something acrid, and Yuma dashes out of the trailer. A fusillade of ear-splitting screeches, whistles, and bangs shatters the quiet, and a ball of fire shoots from the trailer's door and blossoms into a spray of hissing sparks.

Yuma, waiting at the edge of the lot, laughs at the terror on Real Deal's face as he runs to join her.

"Happy Bicentennial," she says.

The din increases in volume, boom upon boom, screech upon screech, and the geyser of sparks shooting out the door is so intense, it resembles the tail of a captured comet. A huge explosion makes the Fiends flinch, and part of the trailer rises on a mushroom cloud of green and silver glitter and spins end over end to crash to the ground twenty feet from them.

They sprint across the road, hop on their bikes, and speed away. Yuma's calmer now, thanks to either the fuck or the fireworks show. Real Deal would like to be angry with her, but he remembers a few years back when he went on a three-day binge and she stayed by his side the whole time, somehow getting him out of every bit of trouble he got himself into. Afterward, he asked why. "I've got all my chips on you," she said, and that's been their motto ever since.

Antonia and Elijah are parked outside a bar that's closing for the night. The drinkers turned out of the tavern stand stunned on the sidewalk like people whose houses have been whirled away by a tornado, but there's not a rover among them.

The Fiends' next stop is a coffee shop called Helsing's. They intended to step inside briefly to check out the customers but end up at the counter with menus in front of them.

"It's time to move on," Antonia says.

"New Orleans?" Elijah says.

"We'll take it slow, search all the towns we pass through on the way."

"Think the others will go for that?"

"They know it's silly to keep riding around here night after night when the fuckers who dusted Bob are probably long gone. Bob will kick, but he'll either accept it or be on his own."

"I take it you wouldn't be sorry to see him go."

Antonia lets a shrug be her answer, sips her coffee. "They eat raw fish in Japan," she says. "It's supposed to be healthy for you." She peruses the menu. "And we've got hotcakes. I'm so fucking sick of hotcakes."

"I met a man who swore by potatoes and vinegar," Elijah says. "That's all he ate, and he claimed never to have been sick a day in his life. Claimed, in fact, that he survived the plague in Istanbul."

"Remember that girl in Seattle?" Antonia says. "Dutch Charlie had turned her?"

"Dutch Charlie," Elijah says. "I haven't thought of him in forever."

"He had that girl who took arsenic to stay skinny, a drop in her tea every evening."

"Your memory is a marvel," Elijah says.

Antonia appreciates the compliment but doesn't acknowledge it, being shy that way. She goes back to griping about hotcakes instead.

She and Elijah continue to ride the streets after their meal but with no more success than before. At 3:30 they return to the motel, the first ones back. A red light is blinking on the telephone when they get to their room. Antonia calls the office, and the night man answers.

"A Mr. Beaumont called," he says. "Wanted me to tell you it's urgent."

21

WHAT DID BEAUMONT SAY IT WOULD TAKE TO MAKE PEACE WITH the Fiends?"

The question from Johona comes out of nowhere. Jesse had thought she was asleep beside him, thought he was the only one lying awake, mind racing. She's under the sheet, in a T-shirt and panties, and he's on top of it fully clothed. For the first time he notices a splash of freckles on her nose, something Claudine didn't have. He likes them.

Would you bring them another baby to replace the one you stole? Beaumont asked him.

I would, Jesse replied. I'd bring them two.

Would you give up the girl to them?

No.

Your brother?

"He thinks they might settle for money," Jesse says to Johona.

"How much money?"

"He didn't know. However much it is, though, I'll get it."

"How? Not picking pockets."

"Didn't you tell me you wanted to go out with a bank robber?"

Edgar turns on the television. So he's awake too. He flips

through the channels until he finds a cartoon. It's only 2 p.m., a long time until sundown. Johona's stomach growls. Jesse puts his ear to it. "You got a bear in there?" he says.

"A hungry one," Johona replies.

"There's peanut butter, bread, some of that deviled ham. You want me to make you a sandwich?"

"I only like peanut butter with milk."

"Me too," Edgar says. "Only with milk."

"Since when?" Jesse says.

"I'll go out and get some," Johona says. She picks up her jeans from the floor and pulls them on under the sheet.

Jesse feels a pinch of worry as she slips out the door. It's daytime, and only Beaumont knows they're here, but he'd still rather she didn't wander. He sits at the table and makes the sandwiches.

"I'm feeling lucky," Edgar says. "I bet I hit a super damn jackpot soon."

"Okay, Big Time," Jesse says. "What'll you do with your winnings?"

"Get me a sweetheart too."

"Johona's not my sweetheart. She's just traveling with us for a while. We're looking out for her."

"You're a liar. I saw you kissing her. You was probably feeling on her titties and her cunny too."

"What would Mama think if she heard you talking like that?"

"Mama's dead," Edgar says. "She can't hear nothing."

Jesse is surprised by this. Edgar normally backs right down when their mother is invoked. Jesse fears he's given him too much rein lately. The best way to keep him safe has always been to keep him cowed.

Johona returns, and the three of them watch Bugs Bunny while they eat. Edgar fills Johona in on the local kid shows.

"This here's channel 8," he says. "They used to have Commander Lee and *Bostwick's Western Corral,* then they had Miss Cinderella."

The telephone rings. Edgar jumps up and says, "I'll answer," but Jesse grabs the receiver before he can get to it.

"I'm still trying to make contact with the Fiends," Beaumont says. "They're a difficult bunch to track down."

"Thanks again," Jesse says. "Let me know as soon as you hear anything."

"Of course," Beaumont says. "In the meantime, I'd like to invite you to dinner. You and Edgar and Johona."

"You don't have to do that."

"It's been twenty years since we last got together. That's too long for old friends like us. We have catching up to do."

Jesse is in no mood to socialize but wants to make sure he stays in Beaumont's good graces.

"As long as you don't go to any trouble," he says.

"Splendid," Beaumont says. "I'll be looking forward to it. I haven't entertained in ages. I'll expect you tomorrow at midnight. Take down the address."

Edgar is thrilled by the invitation. "He still got that piano that plays itself?" he asks, recalling a visit they made to Beaumont when he was living in New Orleans. "He still got that parrot?"

That night, at Johona's insistence, they take in a magic show at the Desert Inn. It's a big production. Showgirls high-kick across the stage, a tiger appears out of thin air, and Buddy Hackett stops by to help out on a card trick.

Jesse's having a fine time until the magician brings out a rope and ties his assistant to a post, telling a story about how they used to burn witches at the stake. *Witch.* That's what the men in Hot Springs called Claudine. The magician douses his assistant with liquid from a gas can, strikes a match, and tosses it at the girl's feet.

Flames shoot up around her, and Jesse's suddenly back in that Arkansas clearing, coming to in agony but healing quickly after being shot to pieces by the friends of the drunk Claudine fed on. The men are standing over the drunk.

"Poor Jim."

"Gone, is he?"

"Gone."

Jesse plays dead as the men approach him and Claudine.

"Who are these two?"

"The bitch was drinking Jim's blood."

"Some kind of witch then, and him the devil that rides with her."

One of the men brings a lantern close to Claudine. "Would you look at that," he says.

Claudine's bones are knitting, her flesh mending.

"She's putting herself back together," the man with the lantern says.

"We got to burn them," another says. "We got to burn the both of them." He runs down the trail to a shack.

Jesse tries to roll over but is still too busted up. One of the men sees him struggling and slams the butt of his shotgun into his head, dazing him. The man who went to the cabin returns with a five-gallon can of kerosene. He soaks Claudine and Jesse with the fuel, and they howl as it seeps into their wounds. The man tries to strike a match but fumbles.

"Stop," Jesse shouts. "Stop!"

Another of the men pulls a match and sparks it. He drops it on Claudine, and she's immediately enveloped, screaming and writhing, in a cocoon of fire. The trees pulse red. Smoke bubbles into the sky. The men turn to Jesse, but before they can light him up, too, Claudine springs to her feet and lurches at them, a wailing human torch. One of them runs, but another lifts his shotgun and pulls the trigger. The blast knocks Claudine back to the ground, where she lies burning, silent and still again.

Jesse realizes he can move his legs, and, marshaling every ounce of his strength, he staggers to his feet and sprints for the dark woods. A shotgun booms and buckshot burrows into his back, but desperation keeps him going. He plunges into a thicket. Nettles lash at him, thorns threaten to hang him up. The men pause at the edge of the tangle to argue about who's going after him.

He thrashes on until the ground disappears from beneath his feet and he plummets through darkness to land in a cold, black river. An electric shock shoots through him when he hits bottom. His legs are broken, both of them. The current takes hold of him and whisks him off.

He managed to get to shore, managed to find a riverbank cave to shelter in for the day. As soon as the sun set he returned to the clearing. All that was left of Claudine was a mound of ashes and a patch of scorched grass. He heard a noise on the trail leading to the men's shack and fled, an act of cowardice he's regretted ever since. It would've been better to have been dusted while trying to get revenge that night than to plod on as he has all the years since under ten tons of guilt and grief.

He held his life cheap afterward, came close to dying many times—tried to, in fact. It wasn't until he started looking after Edgar in the wake of their mother's death that he finally turned away from the grave.

The flames die down, and the audience gasps. The girl has

vanished. The magician feigns confusion. Knocking comes from inside a wooden crate on the stage. The magician prances over and opens it, and the girl steps out unscathed.

They go for ice cream after the show, and Jesse lets Edgar play another slot machine. He feeds it a roll of quarters without getting anything back and insists the machine is broken, tries to reach inside it through the tray.

Back at the motel Jesse gets him interested in a Frankenstein movie on TV so he and Johona can sit by themselves on the walkway in front of the room. A couple of kids are splashing in the pool. Johona lights a cigarette and picks up the ashtray.

"Is it stealing to take this with you?" she asks.

"They must mean for you to," Jesse says. "With the name of the place and the telephone number and everything on it."

"The Holiday Motel," Johona reads off the ashtray.

"Will your folks be worried about you?" Jesse says.

"They live in Santa Fe. They won't even know I'm gone until you make me leave and I call them for the money to get to California."

"You should be glad to be moving on."

"Will you be glad to get rid of me?"

No, he wants to say, but doesn't. "You wouldn't want to live the life me and Edgar have. Believe me."

"Maybe me being around would make things easier for you," she says. "I could run errands during the day, keep you company at night, help with Edgar."

More and more it's her Jesse sees when he looks at her, not Claudine. More and more it's her that makes him smile, not memories. But it's cruel to even flirt with the notion of keeping her with him.

What are you going to do when you find out the truth? he thinks.

The first time I bring a girl back and cut her throat so Edgar'll stop moaning about his Little Devil? Or maybe you're thinking you'd like me to turn you, make you into a monster too.

"As soon as Beaumont sounds out the Fiends and sees where they stand, you'll be on your way," he says. "Even if this mess gets settled, you're going. That's the way it has to be."

Johona takes a puff off her cigarette and watches the kids in the pool. "You're the boss," she says.

He heads out again to go dipping. Johona's right, he'll never pull together enough money to pay off the Fiends by lifting wallets, but he's got to start somewhere. And he wasn't joking about robbing banks. He's considered it before but always felt it was too risky. Now, if that's what it takes to save Johona and Edgar, he'll rob ten of them. It's something else to talk to Beaumont about.

He can only hope that any heists he plans go as well as dipping does. He hits two casinos, and people are practically handing him their wallets. He scores a thousand dollars in only three hours.

He returns to the motel at dawn. Edgar's out cold, but Johona sits up when he comes in. They eat Pop-Tarts, and he tells her about his luck. They fall asleep lying side by side, but he comes awake later to find her on top of him. She presses her body against his and kisses him deeply.

They undress without a word, and before he can stop himself, he's inside her. It's been a long time. There were a few animalistic couplings in the years between Claudine's death and him taking charge of Edgar, but they left him so soul-sick and regretful, he hasn't been tempted since. This time, with Johona, it's like a balm, a soothing salve that makes him think his sorrow might not be permanent after all.

Afterward, they're both on their backs, looking at the

ceiling. Sunlight beams through a hole in the blackout curtain, and music's playing somewhere.

"Thank you for that," Jesse says.

"I shouldn't have done it," Johona says. "I wasn't thinking."

"It was a gift," Jesse says.

Johona rolls away from him. "Stop," she says. "Please."

Whatever it takes to save her. Whatever it takes.

He rolls over in the other direction, toward Edgar's bed, and his brother's eyes are wide open, glaring at him.

He lets Edgar mess around in the pool for half an hour after the sun goes down. He's tried a hundred times to teach him to swim, but Edgar can't move his arms and legs in unison and won't put his face underwater. His idea of fun is walking out into the deep end until only his head's showing, then bouncing back to the shallow end.

"Bring me my cars," he calls to Jesse. "I'm gonna wash 'em."

"Time to go," Jesse says.

He stands and stretches while Edgar lollygags to the ladder. Something sharp digs into his heel. He dislodges a sliver of glass embedded there with his fingernail and wipes away the drop of blood that wells before the puncture closes.

Johona is in a good mood as they get ready to go to supper at Beaumont's. Jesse's happy to see it. She turns on the radio and dances while brushing her hair. Twirling in the green dress Jesse bought her, she asks, "Is this fancy enough for Monsieur Beaumont?" hamming a French accent.

"Fancy enough for anyone, if you're wearing it," Jesse says.

Edgar's locked in the bathroom. Jesse knocks on the door.

"Hold your horses."

"Let me in."

The door opens, and Edgar's standing there with Jesse's razor in his hand and a big grin on his face.

"What the hell did you do?" Jesse says.

"Shaved myself," Edgar says. "What do you think?"

Jesse's been shaving his brother as long as he's been looking after him, Edgar afraid to do it himself after trying and winding up nicked from cheek to chin. He got himself in a couple spots this time, too, but that didn't stop him. Jesse takes hold of his jaw and twists his head from side to side.

"Smooth as a china teacup," he says.

Emboldened by this success, Edgar demands to drive to Beaumont's when they go out to the Grand Prix and gets pissy when Jesse refuses. Johona distracts him with a game.

"I spy, with my little eye, something yellow," she says.

"Is it a banana?"

"Man, where's there a banana around here?"

Beaumont lives beyond the edge of the city. His house, which resembles a concrete bunker fortified against the hot sun and scouring winds of the desert, is perched on a rise with a view of the Strip, the yard landscaped with cacti and boulders lit from below. Jesse parks on the driveway next to a white Cadillac.

Beaumont answers the door dressed in a bright-red disco suit. He shakes Jesse and Edgar's hands, kisses Johona's. "You look lovely," he says.

The furnishings of the house are modern, chrome and black leather, the carpet spotless white shag. Nothing—not the abstract paintings on the walls, the enormous television, the hi-fi system—hints that the man living here is 2,000 years old.

Beaumont leads them into the sunken living room, where they share a long couch while Beaumont relaxes in a swivel chair on the other side of the glass coffee table.

"Champagne, Tommy," he says, and a young man dressed in old-time livery brings in a tray with four glasses on it.

"This place is something," Jesse says.

"I designed it myself," Beaumont replies. Jesse once asked Claudine where the man got his money. "He married well," she said. "Many times."

"You don't got that parrot anymore?" Edgar says.

"Gigi?" Beaumont says.

"The one could speak French."

The man in the servant getup returns, this time offering shrimp and little meatballs on toothpicks.

"Gigi passed away some time ago at the ripe old age of eighty," Beaumont says. "I was devastated."

Edgar licks a meatball and pops it into his mouth. "You should get you another," he says. "Teach it to talk Chinese."

"I'm afraid I don't speak Chinese," Beaumont says.

"I do," Edgar says. "Ching chong ching chong ching chong."

"I have something you'll like even more than Gigi," Beaumont says.

He takes Edgar over to the hi-fi and hands him a microphone. "Sing something."

Edgar belts out "Take Me Home, Country Roads," and Beaumont flips a switch when he finishes, playing back a recording of the performance. Edgar is thrilled.

"I could be on the radio," he says.

"After dinner you can do another, an old one for me," Beaumont says.

Sliding glass doors in nearly every room of the house open onto an interior courtyard. Dinner is served there, at a table set with a white cloth, black plates, and candelabras that look like silver snakes strangling one another. Tommy pours wine. The soup has lobster in it.

"So fancy," Johona says.

"I don't have many guests, so when I do, I go all out," says Beaumont.

"You live here by yourself?"

"Tommy stays in the guest quarters and runs the house, but it's still a lonely life. In fact, your visit, Johona, is the most exciting thing to happen to me in a long time."

Johona blushes and says, "I doubt that."

"You're from Phoenix. How do you find it there?"

"It's fine, but I'm on my way to L.A. now."

"Los Angeles is a wonderful city. I lived in Hollywood for a time. Are you hoping to get into the movies?"

"Now you're being funny."

"You're certainly pretty enough," Beaumont says. "Isn't she, Jesse?"

"Sure," Jesse says.

"I always told Claudine that, under different circumstances, she could have been a star on the stage, and you're as beautiful as she was."

"She sounds like she was a special person," Johona says. "Jesse speaks highly of her."

"He hardly knew her," Beaumont says, the sudden scorn in his voice making Jesse uneasy. "She and I traveled together for twenty years, the best twenty years of my life. She was a jewel, a rare jewel too valuable to be entrusted to the likes of Jesse. He was much too stupid to appreciate her."

"I told you what happened," Jesse says. "There was nothing I could do."

"I grieve her still," Beaumont says to Johona. "But now, look, you've come along, and though you're not the original, there is value in an almost-perfect copy."

The doors surrounding the patio all slide open at once, and

big men and hard women in leather and denim step through them. The Fiends. Jesse stands, on the verge of panic. The rover he fought, the one who jumped off the cliff, slips behind Johona and lays a knife to her throat.

"Down, motherfucker," he says to Jesse.

Jesse collapses more than sits, legs gone numb, and a short-haired blond woman puts a gun to his head. There are seven Fiends in total, guarding him, guarding Edgar. They check them for weapons, running their hands over their chests, around their waists, up and down their legs.

"Jesse?" Johona says, eyes wide with fear.

"It'll be okay," Jesse says. He turns to Beaumont. "You set me up?"

"I've put things right," Beaumont says. "I thought of taking revenge for Claudine every time I've seen you since her death, but either my courage wavered or the circumstances were against it. I've lived long enough, however, to understand the power of patience, and I knew an opportunity to punish you for your carelessness would eventually present itself. When you called the other day, everything finally fell into place."

The ancient rover sips his wine and gestures with the glass at Johona. "The girl was something I hadn't anticipated, but something that pleases me greatly," he continues. "Partial compensation for my years of mourning Claudine." He stands and holds out his hand. "Come with me now, and you'll not be harmed," he says to Johona. "You'll live a life beyond your wildest dreams."

"I...I...I...," Johona stammers.

"Go with him," Jesse says.

"What's your hurry, Beaumont?" the short, burly Fiend holding the knife to Johona's throat says.

"We agreed—"

"Sit down."

Beaumont sinks into his chair.

Jesse addresses the Fiends, though he knows it's futile. "I can get money," he says. "I can get another baby. Whatever you want me to do to make up for what happened, I'll do it."

The Fiend holding the knife on Johona says, "Money's not gonna even things up. Neither is another baby."

"Fine," Jesse says. "But let my brother and the girl go. He's a half-wit, and she stumbled into this."

The Fiend with the knife walks over to Edgar and bends to peer into his face.

"Is that true?" he says. "Are you a half-wit?"

Edgar starts to cry.

22

I GOT A SACK OF SALTWATER TAFFY FROM VIRGINIA BEACH. I GOT a Mickey Mouse shirt and a Superman shirt. I got a Sunday school medal for memorizing verses. And when I passed by thee and saw thee polluted in thine own blood I said unto thee when thou wast in thy blood Live. Yea I said unto thee when thou wast in thy blood Live.

I knew what Jesse and Johona were up to under the covers at the motel. He had his pecker in her. And all the while the Little Devil hissed how I should do something about her. He didn't believe she'd be shoving off soon. He said her and Jesse was gulling me. In the swimming pool I played I was a giant in the ocean. I scooped up a drowned moth. They're the same as butterflies but come at night. Their wings are made of powder and if you touch them turn to dust.

I shaved myself. There's an extra two bits in it for ya if you don't draw blood. Down on the cheeks up on the neck easy does it under the nose. Monsieur Beaumont lived in a big white house in New Orleans. Now he lives in the desert. Jesse made me comb my hair before he knocked on the door. We sat down to supper. The soldier brought wine and I did a toast. Here's to Monsieur Beaumont here's to Miss Johona here's to Mr. Jesse and here's to me.

The Fiend from the mountain put his face in front of mine and the way he looked made me cry. Hold him, he said and went to sawing at my ear with his knife. Leave him be, Jesse yelled but that didn't stop him. Wasn't nobody gonna do me like that though. I stood and shrugged off the bastards holding me down. They went to stabbing me, but I kept swinging. Jesse broke away too and we gave them a fight until the Fiend from the mountain yelled, Hey!

He was behind Johona again using her hair to pull her head back had his knife at her throat again. His men shoved me into my chair and Jesse into his. I was cut so bad I couldn't breathe. The Fiend from the mountain said, My partner's name was Bob and he was worth ten of this cunt. Stop! Beaumont yelled, but the Fiend ignored him and cut Johona's throat just like that. Her heart pumped her blood through the gash beat by beat and it sprayed across the tablecloth. She tried to pull in air but couldn't and her face got the same scared look they all get when they know they're dying. Don't fight it, Jesse yelled, let go. She blinked like someone trying to stay awake. She started to shiver. Then she was gone.

Mama's making biscuits. Flour baking powder baking soda salt lard milk. She folds the dough and presses it flat and lets me cut circles with an empty soup can. You got to press straight down without twisting and got to be careful when you take them out of the oven. If you drop one you'll have uninvited company.

When the flow was down to a trickle the Fiend stuck his finger in the cut showed the blood to Jesse then licked it off. He let Johona's head drop and come at me again. Now you big boy, he said, let's see what you look like without a nose.

I yanked a hand free and grabbed him by the throat. Something cracked and he went to gagging. The others swarmed me like wild dogs punching kicking stabbing. For every one I slung off two more jumped on. Jesse was up again too. He slammed a blond girl's head into the table took her gun and shot a man.

Monsieur Beaumont was against a wall looking like he was gonna be sick. It was all his doing and I meant to kill him but was having trouble walking. Someone stabbed me in the back. The blade was cold as an icicle going in hot as a freshly forged spike coming out. A redhead raised a pistol and shot me in the chest. I fell fast down into the dark.

The Little Devil laughs and shows his teeth. I'm dead, I tell him, leave me be. *I ain't done with you yet,* he says. Popeye eats spinach to get strong. Sinbad the sailor cinches his belt. Underdog's got him a pill. I chew a red M&M and lift a chair over my head till Jesse makes me stop. Where you at Jesse? I ain't mad at you no more. Come get me. Come bring a light and I promise to toe the line.

23

June 30, 1976, Las Vegas (cont.)

YOU WANT ME TO KILL YOU?" I SAID, NOT SURE I'D HEARD
Sally right.

"If you won't let me go, yeah," he said. "I'll take you to Beaumont, you catch him and lock him in your box and dust me."

I was standing in a heartless motel room in a heartless
city, clutching a dead man's pistol and listening to a monster
try to convince me to end his life. The grotesqueness of the
situation stalled me for a second.

"What do you say?" Sally asked.

There was no way I could give him an answer right then,
so I marched him out to the camper and locked him in the
crate. Back in the room the television blared. I turned off the
set, but the silence was even worse. I put on a clean shirt and
walked the two blocks to the Strip.

A band was playing your favorite song, "Misty," in the lounge
of the first casino I came to. It was pearls before swine. Three
white girls in bouffants and minidresses cackled over mai tais,
a table of cowboys talked baseball at the top of their lungs,
and the bartender's corny jokes drowned out the singer.

A man sitting at the corner of the bar struck me as strange
as I sipped my beer. His blond hair was neatly combed and

parted, and he wore a nice sport shirt and pressed slacks, but there was something mocking, something sinister, about his smile. He turned his colorless gaze my way and lifted a long, thin cigarette to his too-red lips.

A rover, I thought.

He got up quickly and left the bar, and I wondered if in the same way they recognize each other, the monsters are able to sniff out someone who's killed their kind. Was there something in the blood of the woman and child from last night that clung to me and marked me as a hunter? Or was the man just another tourist and my imagination running wild?

I worry that part of my fate is to live life choked by that kind of fear and paranoia. I imagine it's how Adam felt after eating the fruit of the tree of knowledge, when all the evil he'd been ignorant of was suddenly revealed. Did he, like me, mourn his loss of innocence? Did he, like me, question whether the knowledge was worth it?

TODAY'S PASSAGE: Have pity upon me, have pity upon me, o ye my friends; for the hand of God hath touched me.

—Job 19:21

July 1, 1976, Las Vegas

I felt better this morning after last night's hysterics. Sleep had recharged my batteries, and I spent an hour with the Good Book to fortify my soul. I decided this Beaumont, this rover royalty, was someone I should look into, so when the sun went down I brought Sally in and asked where I could find him.

"He lives here in Vegas," Sally said. "At least he did fifteen years ago, when I last saw him. I remember where his house is. We can drive out there right now."

I didn't have a better idea, so I walked him to the truck, locked him to the bolt in the cab, and we were on our way.

His directions took us out of the city and into the desert, to a neighborhood where the houses were widely spaced and set far off the road. We meandered for an hour, making U-turn after U-turn and driving the same streets again and again. When we came to our tenth dead-end, asphalt giving way to sand and tumbleweeds, I'd had enough.

"You don't have any idea where you're going, do you?" I said.

"We're close, I feel it," Sally said.

"And I feel like you're wasting my gas and my time."

"Whip around and go back to that last intersection."

We came to a street sign we'd missed before, for Red Rock Road. I turned there, and Sally rolled down his window and stuck out his head to see better. We'd gone half a mile, passing five or six driveways, when he pointed to a house.

"What makes you sure?" I said. "They all look alike in the dark."

"I told you, man, I remember."

I parked far enough up the road that someone turning into the home's drive wouldn't notice the truck. After unlocking Sally, I grabbed a pair of binoculars out of the glove box, and we walked a short distance into the desert, the kid's chains rattling with each step, then turned toward the house. We eventually topped a low rise capped by a stunted tree, a lucky bit of cover. Crouched there, we had a clear view of the driveway and front door fifty yards away.

The house was a concrete box built around a patio and had

a guest cottage out back. The few windows were small and set high on the walls. There was no car in the drive, and the only lights were colored spots scattered around the yard.

"Looks like nobody's home," I said. "Or maybe he's gone to bed."

"Before daybreak?" Sally said. "Not Beaumont."

"Let's get closer," I said.

We ended up walking all the way down to the house and circling it. A door in back had a window in it. I looked through it into a storage room that opened onto the dark kitchen. Beyond that was the patio on the other side of a sliding glass door. There were no signs of life.

We returned to the rise, and I told Sally I was going to wait another hour, see if anybody showed.

"Fine with me," Sally said. "I'm enjoying the fresh air." He sprawled on the sand.

The night was warm and windless, and the stars outshined the Strip in the distance. Sally pointed out airplanes passing overhead and traced the paths of satellites. A coyote yipped, another chimed in, and soon a chorus howled. Sally peered into the darkness.

"You got that gun?" he said, making me uneasy too.

He talked about his childhood. I wasn't interested, only half-listened while watching the house.

"My old man got it into his head he was gonna raise rabbits for extra money," he said. "Since it was summer, and school was out, taking care of them was my responsibility. I didn't want the job, but that didn't matter. The old man's word was law.

"It was three does and a buck. There wasn't much to looking after them besides feeding and watering. Those rabbits had it better than we did. When it got hot I soaked burlap sacks and spread them over the hutches to cool them while we suffered with a swamp cooler. I was only ten years old but already knew I couldn't live like that."

I dropped to my belly when a car came down the road and hissed for Sally to do the same. The white Cadillac turned into the driveway of the house, the garage door rose, and a light went on. While the driver, a white boy, waited to pull into the garage, a tall, bald black man got out of the back seat and walked to the front door of the house. He had those scars on his forehead, the kind you sometimes see on African brothers. I passed the binoculars to Sally.

"That's him," he said.

Beaumont went inside, and the garage door clanked down behind the car.

I'd learned enough for one night, didn't want to push my luck. Sally and I crept to the truck and came back to the motel. He kept at me the whole way, asking when I was going to make my move on Beaumont. I told him I hadn't worked out yet whether making a move was worth my while. It wasn't what he wanted to hear, and I had to lock him in the box so I could get some peace.

That was an hour ago. I'm going to hit my knees here before I go to sleep and ask God for guidance, and hopefully my prayers won't be snatched out of the air by any devils working to defeat me.

TODAY'S PASSAGE: To *expect* the worst is to set yourself up for failure. *Prepare* for the worst. Expectation is passive. Preparation is active. Always be active.

—*Listen, Respond, Win: A New Path to Success*
by Dr. Christine Pellegrino

July 2, 1976, Las Vegas

I got no direction last night, no revelations or commandments. Whether or not I was going after Beaumont, though, my arsenal needed beefing up. So, after a banana and a cup of instant coffee, I went to a sporting-goods store and bought a twelve-gauge shotgun and shells; more rounds, an extra magazine, and a shoulder holster for the .45; and a hunting knife with an ankle sheath.

Back at the motel I loaded the magazines and put one in the .45. The holster was invisible under my jacket, and after a little practice my draw was pretty smooth. I'll never again be overwhelmed like I was by the woman and child. Whenever I hunt from now on, I'll be armed to the teeth and loaded for bear.

I brought Sally in at sundown and fed him some Kentucky Fried Chicken. The Dodgers were playing the Padres, and I let him watch the game. By the time it was over, I'd resolved to drive out to Beaumont's again. I locked Sally in the crate for this trip, tired of his constant jabber and wanting to see if I could find my own way. I remembered the route fairly well, made only a couple of wrong turns. Parking in the same spot as last night, I walked up the rise alone. This evening there were lights on in the house, and music played faintly, something classical.

I started thinking I should go in after Beaumont right then. The .45 was under my arm, the knife strapped to my leg, and Czarnecki's bag, in the camper, had everything else I'd need. I talked myself out of the notion pretty quickly. I didn't know the layout of the house and wouldn't have the advantage of daylight. And what if someone else was with him?

I watched a while longer but learned nothing new. I won't

say the trip was a waste of time, but I don't feel the need for any more scouting. If I'm going to do this, I've got to do it. And tomorrow's the day. I'll storm the house at noon, and if I can't capture Beaumont, I'll kill him. Sally will be disappointed if that's how it goes down, but what are a monster's tears to me?

July 4, 1976, Las Vegas

A blunder, a battle, a deal with the devil. I'm taking advantage of a quiet moment to set down what happened over the past twenty-four hours, and they may well be the last words I ever write.

As I'd planned, I parked up the road from Beaumont's house at noon yesterday, guns loaded, knife ready, crowbar in hand. I left Sally chained inside the crate, and snuck to the top of the rise. Lying beside the little tree, I scanned the house through the binoculars. The drapes were drawn, but I was sure Beaumont was inside.

I said a prayer to steel myself. *Dear Lord, you are my refuge and fortress, you are my sword and my shield. Fill me with bravery and strength as I prepare to confront evil.*

Then...nothing. I lay on my belly in the dirt. The fire I'd been stoking all morning had gone out. Five minutes passed, ten, as I tried to will my body to stand and approach the house. I pleaded with myself, reasoned with myself, slapped my face until my cheek throbbed, but it was no use.

All the way back to the motel I invented fresh excuses: I needed more time to think the plan through. I hadn't slept well the night before. My back was giving me trouble. The truth is, I'd simply lost my nerve. Beaumont wasn't drunk like the Mexican in Reno. He wasn't a woman or a child. According to Sally, he was a powerful figure, king of the rovers, and contemplating that had unstrung me.

Nervous energy and dumb luck had gotten me through my first encounters with the monsters, but that wouldn't be enough in the long run. I spent the rest of the day questioning whether I was cut out to follow in Czarnecki's footsteps. It seemed I lacked the courage to confront evil face-to-face and the savagery to dispatch it with no qualms, and without iron resolve and a killer's cold heart, I was doomed.

By nightfall I was exhausted. It was a relief to bring Sally in for dinner and listen to his story about a thief who got caught because he couldn't stay away from his favorite Times Square dive. He asked for a beer. I said no but made him a second ham sandwich. It was right about then I decided I'd rather spend the night watching Beaumont's house than torturing myself in the room. Maybe this would be the time I'd discover some weakness that'd give me an advantage.

I drove out and parked by the side of the road. Sally begged to join me when I went back to the camper for the .45, said four eyes would be better than two. I gave in and let him out of the crate, hoping his chatter would drown out the bickering in my head.

The first thing I noticed when we got onto the rise was a second car in the driveway, a Grand Prix. Then the sound of someone singing inside the house reached my ears, followed by laughter and applause. It got quiet after that. My eyes were pressed to the binoculars, but there was nothing to see. I was considering sneaking down to peek through the window in the back door when Sally moaned.

"What is it?" I said.

"The cuffs are pinching," he replied.

I crouched beside him. "Show me."

I caught a glimpse of the rock in his hand right before he slammed it into my head. The first blow stunned me, the next laid me out.

I came to in a world of pain. My brain wobbled when I sat up, and I had to wipe blood out of my eyes. I don't know how long I was down, but Sally had almost reached the house, going as fast as he could in his shackles. I drew the .45 and set off after him.

A commotion—yelling and gunshots—erupted inside the house. This didn't slow Sally. He pounded on the front door, shouting for Beaumont and saying, "It's Sally Spiotto! I need help!" I didn't slow down either. Mad as hell, I crossed the driveway as Beaumont ran out the door. He pushed past Sally but pulled up short when he saw me. Without thinking, I shot him in the chest, and he dropped to the ground.

Sally dashed inside and tried to close the door on me. I put my shoulder to it, forced it open, and stepped into a slaughterhouse, blood everywhere. Sally ran off, but my way was blocked by a body on the floor and a black biker with a short natural and a goatee bent over it with a knife. A redheaded white girl pointed a pistol at me. My hands are shaking now, recalling the scene, but in that instant I fired the .45 with no hesitation and got her in the head. Then the brother charged, and I shot him, too.

Another biker, a big Mexican, ran at me out of the shadows, and I fired once more, hitting him in the arm. He dropped the knife he was carrying but kept coming. I lost the .45 when he tackled me. He hooked his good arm around my neck, but I grabbed his hair, shifted my weight, and was able to flip him so we were both lying on our backs, me on top. I hammered him with my elbows, then grabbed for the knife sheathed on my leg. He got hold of it before I did and slipped out from under me. Sitting on my chest, he punched me in the face again and again and raised the blade.

Before he could finish me off, a gunshot sounded and a geyser of blood spouted from his forehead. He fell on me, dead weight, and when I pushed him off, I found myself looking down the barrel of a pistol held by a young white man, maybe twenty-two, twenty-three, with dark hair and eyes.

"Who are you?" he said.

"I came for Beaumont," I told him.

"Where is he?"

"Out front. I shot him."

"If you want to get out of here alive, we have to work together," the kid said.

"I want to get out of here alive," I said.

The young man—Jesse is his name, I know now—picked up my knife and said, "Stick this in Beaumont's heart and bring him inside."

Still rattled by the fact that I'd just killed two people and dazed by the beating I'd taken, I was happy someone else had a plan, happy to do as I was told. I grabbed the .45 too, and walked to the front door. Beaumont was already trying to crawl away.

"Wait," he said, raising his hand.

I kicked him onto his back and jammed the knife into his chest. Leaving the blade inside him, I dragged him into the house.

Jesse was kneeling next to the man I'd almost tripped over when I came in the first time. He helped him—his brother, Edgar—sit up, saying, "Take it easy. You'll be good as new soon enough."

The redhead I'd shot groaned, coming back to life. Jesse

found a knife on the floor and stabbed her with it, then hacked at her neck until her head came off and she turned to ash.

"Rovers?" I said. "All of them?"

"You didn't know?" Jesse said.

My relief—I'd killed monsters, not humans!—was short-lived. I knew I was still in danger.

"We've got to dust them," Jesse said. "You take care of these two"—he gestured at the bikers on the floor, the Mexican and the black one—"and I'll do the ones on the patio."

I picked up the knife the Mexican had dropped and went to work on him. The wound in his forehead was already smaller than it had been moments before. He opened his eyes and screamed a silent scream, but I kept cutting until he crumbled.

I was about to do the same to the brother when a glass door shattered, and Jesse backpedaled into the house, firing his pistol. He ran past me and pulled Edgar behind a couch. I scurried to an open door and found myself in a hallway. A blood-spattered blonde and a limping biker came in from the patio, headed for a door on the other side of the living room. A third biker, a short white man, followed, waving a pistol.

"Any of you still walking, we're getting out of here," the blonde shouted.

Jesse popped up from behind the couch and squeezed off a shot. The short biker fired back. All of a sudden the black one got to his feet and staggered toward the others. I fired at him and missed, but Jesse put a round in his leg. He kept going, the short biker helping him along while pinning Jesse and me down with random shots.

The gang scrambled through the door and slammed it shut. Over the ringing in my ears I heard motorcycles start up. Jesse ran outside as three Harleys exploded out of the garage and fired after them until his gun was empty. When the sound of the engines had faded, he came back into the house and went to his brother, who was cowering next to the couch.

I found Sally hiding in a closet in one of the bedrooms. He didn't struggle when I hauled him out and threw him on the bed.

"I had to try," he said.

"I guess," I replied.

I slipped the biker's knife between his ribs. He grimaced, moaned, and went limp. I cut off his head, shook his ashes from his shackles, and carried them to the living room.

Edgar was lying on the couch. He sat up when I came in. He was a big man, bigger than Jesse, and looked old enough to be his father. He asked me who I was.

"None of your business," I replied.

"He's simple," Jesse said. "Ignore him."

"You're rovers too?" I said.

"I'm the man that saved your life," Jesse said, "and this is my brother."

He bent and pulled my knife out of Beaumont. I asked what he was up to.

"He double-crossed me," Jesse said. "I want him to see my face before I dust him."

"I can't let you kill him," I said.

"Try and stop me."

I pointed the .45.

"I'm taking him with me," I said.

"What for?"

"To hunt with."

"Hunt?"

"Rovers."

Jesse smirked. "And I should let you?" he said.

"You owe me," I said. "Your brother'd be dead if I hadn't shot those two when I came in."

Jesse thought this over, then dropped my knife. "Go on," he said.

I told him I'd need help getting the man to my truck.

"You'll have to haul me up," he said. "I took a bullet to the gut, and I'm not quite right yet."

He grabbed my arm when I reached out, yanked me off balance, and snatched the .45 out of my hand. Pointing it at me, he stood on his own and said, "Any other weapons you've got, drop them too."

"I don't have anything else," I said, feeling like a fool for letting him get the jump on me.

"I'll make you a deal," he said. "I mean to wipe out the rest of those bastards. I can do it myself, but it'd be quicker and easier with two. Fight with me, and you can have Beaumont once they're dusted."

"How much help do you think I'd be?" I said. "It took you all of two seconds to get my gun off me."

"You handled yourself okay up to then."

"And if I say no?"

"I'll kill you and Beaumont right now."

I'd lost a lot of blood from the cut on my head, and the adrenaline was wearing off, so, truthfully, at that moment I didn't give a damn about Beaumont. I was only thinking about getting out of that house alive.

"What do you want me to do?" I said.

Jesse pointed at Sally's chains. "Put those on Beaumont before he comes to."

I had him all trussed up by the time he fluttered back to life a few minutes later.

"What happened here?" he said.

"Not what you planned," Jesse said.

"You have me wrong."

Jesse smacked him in the face with the .45 and ordered me to gag him with a biker's bandana. Then Jesse and I walked up the road to get the truck. I parked in the driveway, and we carried Beaumont out to the camper and locked him in the crate.

Back in the house, Jesse got a blanket out of one of the bedrooms and took it to the patio. He wrapped up the body of a girl whose throat had been cut and told me and Edgar to take her out. He was holding Czarnecki's .45 on me, but his gun hand shook as we laid her in the camper next to the box.

"Where to?" I said when we were all in the cab of the truck.

"Just drive," he said.

I'm going to quit for now, baby, hopefully get to the rest later. It's 2 p.m. Beaumont's in the camper, and the brothers and I are in my room. Jesse's guarding me from the table with the .45, Edgar's asleep on one of the beds, and I'm on the other, feeling like Daniel in the lions' den.

If I die helping this kid go after the bikers, you'll never see what I'm about to write next, but I want to set it down anyway, say it in my mind, and send it out into the universe: I love you, baby. You've always been better than me, smarter than me, stronger than me. Remember the good times, that's all I ask. Because that's what I'll be doing, seeing your sweet smile as I take my last breath.

24

WHEN ANTONIA RETURNS BEAUMONT'S PHONE CALL, SHE'S thinking he has another job for them. People come to him for help, and if it's a problem the Fiends can solve, he acts as go-between for ten percent of whatever they get for handling it. This call isn't about a hit or a robbery, though. It's about something better.

Unaware of Beaumont's connection to the Fiends, the rover who dusted Bob asked him to contact them to see if there was some way to make amends. What the fool didn't know is that Beaumont has been harboring his own grudge against him for years, something about a woman they both knew in the past. He's coming to Vegas to meet with Beaumont, and Beaumont suggests the Fiends travel to Vegas, too, where he and they will settle both their scores at once.

Antonia agrees to make the trip, and the gang erupts at the news, cheering and punching and hugging one another. They ride for Vegas the next night with a plan to crash at Bull's motel on the outskirts of town, a ten-cabin motor court so dilapidated it doesn't even have a sign anymore, just a red neon arrow. Bull isn't a rover, but he's fine with accommodating them as long as there's no killing or feeding on the premises. He'll even run daytime errands for a price.

He steps out of his cabin barefoot, shirtless, and wearing Bermuda shorts when they ride up, a big, bald fat man who claims he used to be a mobster in New York.

"Do you have room for us?" Antonia says.

"Enough for them," Bull says. "But you'll have to bunk with me."

"Shit," Antonia says. "You can't even see your pecker over that gut."

Bull grins around the joint in his mouth. "That's okay," he says. "You can tell me if it's still there."

"We need three cabins. We'll be staying two, maybe three days."

There's no registration book, Bull just tosses them their keys. Only one other cabin is occupied, by a professor from Germany who's come to the desert to study scorpions.

"I don't know how serious he is," Bull says. "He's usually fucked up on schnapps by noon."

Antonia uses Bull's phone to call Beaumont. He says the rovers they're after, a man named Jesse and his retarded brother, have arrived in town, along with the girl who stole the baby. He's invited them to his house for dinner tomorrow night, and how he's got it figured is that the Fiends will show up before they get there and lie in wait for them. His only request in exchange for letting the gang exact their revenge at his place is that he be allowed to keep the girl.

Antonia runs this by the other Fiends. They're fine with giving him the girl, but Bob pitches a fit at having to delay his vengeance for even a short while, wants Antonia to call Beaumont back and find out where the rovers are staying. A quaalude and a few beers mellow him out, and soon they're celebrating their good fortune, all of them gathered around a picnic table under a tamarisk tree at the edge of the motel parking lot. Bull's drinking with them, and so's the German. Johnny keeps throwing him the Nazi salute and barking, "Heil Hitler," and the German keeps saying, "Fuck Hitler."

"Is that jump joint still open, out toward the lake?" Bob asks Bull.

"Last I heard," Bull replies.

"What's the name of the girl you liked there?" Bob says to Pedro. "Blond hair, big ass."

"Jenny?" Pedro says.

"Let's pay her a visit."

"I'm in too," Johnny says.

"How about you, Colonel Klink," Bob says to the German. "You like zee puzzy?"

"You will go on the Harley Davidsons?" the German says.

"How else?"

"Wonderful!"

They ride off a few minutes later, Pedro and Bob on one bike, Johnny and the German on another. Bull goes to bed, and Antonia, Elijah, Real Deal, and Yuma play five-card stud. They talk about going to New Orleans when this is over, and Elijah tells stories about when he lived there back when Spain still claimed it.

"Just like now, whatever you wanted, someone there had," he says. "Every way to kill yourself you could think of."

Bob and the others get to the cathouse, which is really a trailer park strung with Christmas lights, a double-wide serving as parlor and bar. Jenny's long gone, but Pedro finds another girl to his liking, and the others choose from the rest.

The men gather in the parlor afterward to drink, play pool, and flirt with the whores. The German teaches them a drinking song, "*Ein Prosit, ein Prosit, der Gemütlichkeit, Ticky Tocky Ticky Tocky, Oi oi oi,*" and they sing it so loudly so many times, the bouncer tells them to hit the road.

Back at Bull's, the card game winds down. Antonia and Elijah go to their cabin, and Antonia settles into bed to read.

"What's *The Other Side of Midnight?*" Elijah asks about the paperback in her hands.

"It's trash," she says. "Rich people doing each other dirt. She loves him, he doesn't love her, he loves her, she doesn't love him, they marry the wrong people. It goes on and on. The writer must've been being paid by the word."

"We sure got lucky, didn't we?" Elijah says. "The way this worked out with Beaumont?"

"At least we won't waste any more time searching," Antonia says.

"Or dealing with Bob's tantrums."

Bob and the others return, and Antonia turns out the light and pulls the shade.

"I don't feel like dealing with a bunch of drunks," she says.

"Me neither," Elijah says.

He lies down beside her and drifts off to the whisper of turning pages.

After a long, fidgety day, the Fiends bust out of their cabins as soon as the sun sets. Bull grills hamburgers and sells them for a quarter—fifty cents with chili and cheese—and Bob passes a bottle of tequila.

"Where's the Kraut?" Johnny says.

"He took off this morning," Bull says. "Looked like hell."

Fed and buzzed, the Fiends mount up and ride to Beaumont's

place, stashing their bikes in the garage. Beaumont invites them inside. They shoot the shit on the patio in the middle of the house while waiting for Jesse.

Antonia can tell Beaumont is uncomfortable. Dealing with the gang over the phone is one thing, having to talk to them face-to-face is another. He minces around with a phony smile and flapping hands like he's worried they're going to track mud on his carpet while a costumed servant named Tommy passes out drinks.

"You shine the man's shoes too?" Bob says to Tommy.

"I'm Monsieur's driver and houseman," Tommy replies, picking up an empty glass.

"Ooh la la," Bob says and turns to Pedro. "You want Tommy here to bring you anything?"

"Got any more beer?" Pedro says.

"Hop to it," Bob says. "Fetch the man a beer."

At 11 p.m., an hour before Jesse and the others are supposed to arrive, the Fiends go out to the garage, where they'll wait to make their entrance. Yuma sits on the floor next to Real Deal. She draws her revolver, swings out the cylinder, and spins it.

"There was a little man who had a little gun, and his bullets were made of lead, lead, lead," she chants. "He went to the brook and saw a little duck and shot it right through the head, head, head."

"What's that?" Real Deal says.

"Something my mama used to recite."

Johnny farts.

"That's something Johnny's mama used to recite," Bob says.

"Quiet," Antonia says.

She's sitting on her Harley, the gasoline fumes in the garage making her nauseous. Elijah is straddling his bike, too, arms crossed over his chest. His wristwatch has glow-in-the-dark numbers, and after a while everyone's staring at them, mesmerized.

The sound of an approaching car gooses them out of their reverie. They drop to the floor as headlights flash through the little window in the garage door and sweep across the ceiling. Doors slam, someone tells someone to comb his hair, and a girl laughs. The new arrivals go to the porch and ring the bell. Beaumont lets them in.

Another half hour passes, during which the Fiends hear singing, muffled conversation, and Beaumont calling for champagne. Their pistols are out, their knives ready. One of them knocks over a broom, and the crack of the handle hitting concrete is as loud as a gunshot, but the party inside continues.

The overhead bulb finally flashes three times, the signal for them to come inside. Antonia opens the door to the living room, and one by one they slip through.

Beaumont, Jesse, his brother, and the girl are sitting at the table on the patio. The Fiends glide like black smoke to their positions behind the glass sliders, passing Tommy as he hurries for the front door. At a sign from Beaumont, they all step out onto the patio at once.

An hour later those of them still alive are back at Bull's, sitting at the picnic table again and passing the tequila as they piece together what just went down.

"Why did you kill the girl?" Antonia says to Bob.

"I could tell Jesse cared for her."

"But we promised her to Beaumont."

"I wanted him to hurt like I do."

"Okay, but what's that say about our word?"

"I don't give a fuck. It was worth it to see the look in his eyes. It's not my fault the rest of you couldn't hold him and the retard."

"What happened after they got loose?" Elijah says. "After the big one got you by the throat, and Jesse laid into us?"

What happened was, Bob fell to the ground, coughing blood, his windpipe crushed, and Edgar ran for the living room. Jesse head-butted Elijah, then went after Antonia, smashing her face into the table, snatching her pistol, and shooting Elijah between the eyes. That's when Johnny jumped in to battle Jesse for the gun.

Real Deal picks up the story. "Me and Pedro and Yuma chased the retard into the living room, and Yuma put a bullet in him. I went to dust him, and someone started pounding on the door. Beaumont ran out of the house, and a rover wrapped in chains and a black dude ran in, the motherfucker that shot me and Yuma."

Meanwhile, on the patio, Johnny was getting the best of Jesse, had him bent over the table backward, when Jesse dug a thumb into his eye and pushed until something popped. The two of them slipped on the bloody concrete and went down together. Jesse grabbed a knife and dusted Johnny, then picked up Antonia's gun and ran for the living room.

"And Pedro?" Elijah says.

Real Deal reaches up to scratch his head. His fingers come away bloody. "I was still half out of it, but I saw him tackle the brother that shot me," he says. "He was about to finish him when Jesse ran in and blew out his candle. Right then Yuma came to, and Jesse heard. I tried my damnedest to get up, but…" He slams his fist on the picnic table, making the tequila bottle jump, then growls his next few words. "Jesse took her out, and brotherman dusted Pedro."

"Jesse came for us after that," Antonia says. "Me and Elijah and Bob were still on the patio. We'd all healed and were ready to run when he appeared. Bob backed him off with a couple of shots, and we headed out."

Real Deal managed to join them as they passed through the living room, and they fled to the garage. Antonia got Elijah settled behind her on her Harley, Real Deal straddled his ride, and Bob started Elijah's. The four of them made their escape, roaring out of the garage and down the driveway. They cranked their throttles when they hit the street and raced away without looking back.

When they were miles away and certain nobody was following, they pulled over behind a boarded-up gas station to take stock. They looked like they'd been swimming in a lake of blood. Real Deal sat shaking on his bike, his head in his hands.

"Can you keep going?" Antonia asked him. "We shouldn't be out, looking like this."

"We should be riding back to burn that fucking house down," Bob said.

"We're too beat up right now to think straight. Let's go to Bull's and get our shit together."

"I'm fine," Bob said. "I'm a hundred percent ready to throw down."

"Throw down by yourself then," Antonia said. "I'm not gonna be pushed into something stupid."

"You'll come, Elijah, won't you? For Johnny and Pedro and Yuma."

"Antonia's right," Elijah said.

"Of course she is," Bob snarled.

"She is," Real Deal said. "How long till daybreak? We go off half-cocked, we'll all get caught out and never have a chance to get even."

He started his bike and rode off. Antonia and Elijah followed. Soon enough so did Bob, cussing under his breath.

Sitting at the picnic table, the story finally straight, Antonia sips from the bottle of tequila.

"And now here we are," she says.

"I'll stand guard till dawn," Bob says.

"Who are you expecting?"

"The kid and the spook who helped him."

"You think they'll show?"

"That French fucker knows we're staying here. He'll give us up real quick."

"Maybe they've had enough."

"After what I did to the girl? Jesse's coming for me."

"If that's the case, we should take off, find new rooms, and hunt them down tomorrow night."

"Like we hunted them down in Phoenix?" Bob says. "No. I'm not leaving, not playing any games. I'm betting the kid'll try for me here, and I'll be waiting."

"I'm not leaving either," Real Deal says. "If you think they're coming, I'm staying too."

Antonia has a belt of tequila. Nothing she says will change their minds, so it's only her and Elijah she has to worry about. They've got an hour before the sun comes up—enough time to make a quick getaway. Her pride hangs her up, though.

She and Elijah have been leading the Fiends for seven years. And while it's true she's sick of wrangling psychos and true she's dreamed of splitting from the gang, to run off now, after the deaths of Yuma and the others, and leave

Bob and Real Deal to face what's coming next on their own doesn't sit right with her. She'll be nothing but trash if she abandons them.

"Go in and get cleaned up," she says to Bob. "I'll hang out here." She turns to Real Deal. "You too. Sleep if you can."

Real Deal locks himself in his cabin. The ten years he was with Yuma were the best of his life. He told her that he turned because he knew it'd take a long time to find the perfect woman, and when he did, he wanted to be with her forever. "And it was you I was waiting for," he said. He hasn't cried in a hundred years, not since his brother was killed, but now thinks he might never stop.

Seated at the picnic table, Antonia checks herself for damage. The gash on her head where it hit the table is gone, and there's no pain when she wiggles her nose.

"You didn't try very hard to sway them," Elijah says.

"They're spoiling for a fight," Antonia replies.

"And we're fighting with them?"

"We've been riding together a long time. We've got to see this through."

Elijah picks at a splinter on the table. "We'll send Bull for more ammo," he says. "And a shotgun. You can use that other pistol of mine."

"Are you mad?"

"If it was up to just me, I'd leave. We're sitting ducks, and I don't like putting you in danger."

"Isn't that sweet," Antonia scoffs.

"It's selfish," Elijah says. "I'd be worse than dusted if something happened to you."

Antonia presses her forehead to his and looks into his eyes.

"Everything comes to an end, old man."

"Not me, not you," Elijah says. "Not before we go to

Italy. Not before you see the—what the hell was it?—Birth of Venus?"

They watch the road until the last star winks out. Two cars and a power-company truck pass by. Safe in their cabin as the sun rises, they drop off immediately but are wakened later by sobs—Real Deal's, rising and falling like some strange bird's sorrowful song, a terrible thing to hear.

25

Jesse stops digging and sits. Johona's grave is only two feet deep, but all the strength drains out of his arms, and he can't keep hold of the shovel. Edgar takes his place in the hole, though, and he and the black man who showed up at Beaumont's, Charles Sanders, keep working, so the dirt keeps piling up. Sanders didn't kick when Jesse made him pull over to bury Johona. "I'm a Christian," he said, "I understand," and even picked up a shovel and pitched in.

Johona's body lies next to Jesse, blood seeping through the blanket he wrapped her in. He touches the bundle, finds her corpse has gone cold, and feels sick to his stomach thinking how twelve hours ago she was resting in his arms. She was like some small, soft thing that got torn apart between two dogs. He should've taken better care of her.

"My brother's the best gravedigger there is," Edgar tells Sanders. "And I'm second."

"Is that right?" Sanders says.

Jesse makes himself stand. "You two take a break," he says. "I'll finish up."

When the hole is deep enough, they lower Johona into

it. Sanders asks Jesse if he wants to say anything. He doesn't, doesn't have the words.

"I'll do it," Edgar says.

"Leave it be," Jesse snaps. He's had enough of his brother's jabber for tonight, enough for a lifetime.

He and Sanders fill the grave while Edgar sulks.

Sanders drives the truck back into town. Jesse keeps the .45 he took off the man pointed at his belly. No more mistakes.

"Where are you staying?" he asks Sanders.

"A motel near the Strip," Sanders replies.

"Me and Edgar will be holing up with you for today."

Sanders frowns but doesn't protest. A while later he says, "How will you find the bikers?"

"The Fiends," Jesse says. "They call themselves the Fiends."

"Do you have a line on them?"

"I've got Beaumont. He knows where they are."

"Then what? You and me and your brother go after them?"

"He'd be no help."

"I can fight good as you," Edgar says.

"Shut up."

"So it'll be two against four," Sanders says.

"We did all right against seven."

"That was luck," Sanders says. His face is swollen from the beating he took at Beaumont's, and there's a cut on his forehead. He dabs at it with a rag. "If I get shot, I die."

"I'll turn you, if you want," Jesse says. "Then they can shoot you ten times, and you'll keep coming back."

"I guess you think that's funny," Sanders says.

Jesse doesn't reply. He has the man stop a few blocks from the motel where he, Edgar, and Johona have been staying.

"Give me the keys and your wallet," he says.

Sanders hands the items over. Jesse opens the wallet and sees a photograph of a woman holding a child. "Is this your family?" he says.

"My wife, my son," Sanders says.

Jesse points at the address on the driver's license. "And this is where they live?"

Sanders turns to stone, doesn't answer.

"If you're not here when I get back, I'll go to this address and kill everyone there," Jesse says. "You understand?"

"I'll be here."

"Where you going?" Edgar says.

"Stay with Mr. Sanders. You'll be fine."

It's past 4 a.m. The street is deserted. Jesse hurries along, but not so quickly he'll attract attention. When he reaches the motel, he scans for Fiends. There doesn't appear to be a lookout, so he jogs to the room, unlocks the door, and pushes it open. Drawing the .45, he steps inside and checks the bathroom. All clear.

He gathers his and Edgar's belongings and shoves them into their suitcases. He has one grip, Edgar two, the second for his toys and other junk. Jesse can only carry two bags, so he leaves most of the toys behind, fitting what he can—Matchbox cars, a few picture books, a deck of cards—into the case with Edgar's clothes. Then there's Abby to deal with.

The cat hisses and recoils when he reaches for her. He considers leaving her, but Edgar will already be upset about the other missing items. He strips the case off one of the pillows and, after a battle that leaves him bitten and scratched, manages to shove the animal inside it.

The sunglasses Johona bought him are on the table. All the strength goes out of him again when he sees them, and he sits on the bed while he pulls himself together. He's got to be tougher. If he's going to get revenge for the girl, he's got to ball up his grief and bury it, can't have it blindsiding him. So he should leave the glasses. But he can't. He slips them into his pocket and peeks out the door.

Nobody's waiting, nobody raises an alarm. Carrying the suitcases and cat, he makes his way back to the truck by a different route. Sanders is there like he said he'd be. Jesse stows the grips in the camper and hands the pillowcase to Edgar when he returns to the cab.

"Keep her in there," he says.

Edgar reaches inside to stroke Abby.

Sanders drives to his motel, parks, and gives Jesse the keys.

"Take Edgar inside," Jesse says and goes to the camper for the grips. He leans in and bangs on the crate that Beaumont's locked up in. "It's gonna be a hundred and ten today," he says. "I hope you fucking roast in there."

He locks the camper and carries the grips to the room.

"Where's the other?" Edgar says when Jesse hands him the single suitcase.

"You've only got one now," Jesse says.

Edgar sits on a bed and opens the case. He unpacks it and separates his clothes from his other things, then turns on Jesse in a fury.

"Where's my seashells? Where's my sword?"

"I couldn't bring that and Abby too."

"I need my stuff!"

"And I need you to be a help and not a burden."

"It's your fault I got shot. It's your fault that man near cut my ear off."

"And it's your fault Johona's dead," Jesse says.

It's been eating at him since Beaumont's, the notion that if he hadn't been hurt trying to help Edgar, he might have been able to get to the Fiend before he cut the girl's throat. His anger boils over, and he storms into the bathroom and turns on the shower. "Get your ass in here!" he barks. "Wash that blood off."

"I need my stuff."

"Now!"

Edgar pops up and lurches toward him, maybe to take a swing, Jesse thinks, but he pushes past into the bathroom and slams the door.

Embarrassed about squabbling in front of Sanders, Jesse says, "Excuse me for that."

"It's been a long night," Sanders says. He pulls the rag away and touches the cut on his head.

"Looks like the bleeding's stopped," Jesse says.

"Will you let me put a bandage on it?"

"Go on ahead."

Sanders roots in a duffel bag and comes up with a small first aid kit. He wets a washcloth in the room's sink and cleans the gash.

"You haven't been at this long, have you?" Jesse says.

"What? Bleeding?" Sanders says.

"Killing rovers."

"I didn't even know there was such a thing until a few days ago, and I wish I'd stayed ignorant," Sanders says. He dabs antibiotic ointment on the cut and fashions a dressing out of cotton balls and tape.

"What brought you to it?" Jesse says.

"One of you devils killed my son."

"And killing us makes you feel better?"

"Not yet."

Sanders presses the bandage into place and checks it in

the mirror. "How many people have you murdered?" he asks Jesse.

"One or a thousand, it's all the same, isn't it?" Jesse replies.

"I suppose so," Sanders says. "You were damned after the first." He lies on one of the beds with a Bible. Jesse sits at the table, the .45 close at hand.

Morning has come up, the room's drapes barely holding it back, by the time Edgar emerges from the bathroom and stretches out on the second bed with Abby.

"I'm hungry," he says.

"You can hold off until dark," Jesse says.

Edgar points at Sanders and says, "Send this boy out for something."

"That's Mr. Sanders," Jesse says. "He's not your boy."

"I have bread and lunch meat," Sanders says. "You're welcome to it."

"Thank you," Jesse says.

Sanders lays out a loaf of Wonder Bread, a jar of mustard, and a package of salami. Jesse tells Edgar to get up and make his own sandwich. Sanders makes one for himself when Edgar finishes.

"You want me to leave this out for you?" he asks Jesse.

Food is the furthest thing from Jesse's mind. Now that they're settled, he's focused on going after the Fiends.

"What kind of weapons have you got?" he asks Sanders when the man comes out of the bathroom after taking a shower.

Sanders runs down the items in his arsenal: the .45 Jesse took from him, a new shotgun, and ammo for both; a knife; a few ice picks; a hacksaw. Jesse's got two pistols he picked up at Beaumont's, a .38 revolver and a 9mm automatic, and his hunting knife. That should be enough. In the end it won't come down to which side is better armed anyway, it'll be who fights hardest.

Edgar wants to watch television. All that's on are Sunday-morning church services and Bicentennial specials. Today's the Fourth of July, the 200th anniversary of the USA, but Jesse couldn't give two shits. His country has no flag, no anthem, no chorus girls dressed in red, white, and blue. It's a wasteland where lost souls prey on other lost souls. It's the hunger, the hunt, and the blood that comes after.

Edgar and Sanders are asleep before long. Jesse is exhausted too, but doesn't trust Sanders not to make a move if he naps. He sits at the table, and the hours crawl past. To keep away thoughts of Claudine and Johona, he concentrates on the faint *pop pop pop* of distant firecrackers and the rumble of the maid's laundry cart on the walkway outside, on the twitching of Abby's tail and the fluttering of the pages of Sanders's Bible in the breeze from the air conditioner.

Despite his best efforts, he dozes off. When he jerks back to wakefulness, Bob Hope is on television, dressed like George Washington. Jesse turns off the set and paces the room to get his blood flowing.

Sanders wakes and spends some time writing in a notebook.

"What's that?" Jesse asks him.

"A letter to my wife," Sanders replies.

"How long's it been since you've seen her?"

"Too long," Sanders says. He closes the book and puts it in his bag. "This room's given me a chill," he says. "Can I go sit by the pool?"

"I can't let you do that," Jesse says.

"You've got the keys to the truck, my wallet, and Beaumont. I'm not going to run off. I give you my word."

"What's that worth to me?"

"It's everything to me."

Jesse stares at Sanders long and hard, trying to read his mind. Sanders stares right back.

"Don't be gone long," Jesse says.

"I thank you," Sanders says.

"Just so you know," Jesse says before he steps outside. "I called a friend. If he doesn't hear from me in twenty-four hours, he'll go to your house in my stead." This is a lie, but even if Sanders doubts it, Jesse figures it'll make him think twice about trying anything.

Edgar sits up.

"Jesse."

"What?"

"I pissed myself."

"Goddamn it," Jesse says. His patience has been worn down to nothing. "Take the fucking sheets off."

"You," Edgar says.

"I'm through doing for you. From here on in, if you piss, you clean it up yourself. Get moving."

"No," Edgar says.

Jesse yanks his arm, pulling him to his feet. "Strip the bed and put the sheets in the tub."

"I'm wet," Edgar wails. "I don't want Mr. Sanders to see me."

"Then you best finish before he gets back. You can wash up afterward."

Edgar tugs half-heartedly at the top sheet. It brushes against him, and he recoils and drops it to the floor.

"What are you, scared of your own water?" Jesse says.

"I hate you," Edgar says.

"I don't care."

"I hate you for throwing my things away, I hate you for

getting me hurt last night, and I hate you for putting the Little Devil in me."

"You must hate Mama too, then, because she's the one who made me turn you."

"She didn't know how it'd be."

"She knew," Jesse says. "And she hears everything you're saying, up in heaven."

Edgar shouts at the ceiling. "He don't care nothing about me, Mama, only his little whore Miss Johona."

Jesse pushes him, sprawling him across the bed. "Shut your mouth, or I'll rub your nose in your mess."

"You should never have brought that bitch along," Edgar says. "It was bad luck. Now I ain't got my sword, I ain't got my soldiers, and my best shirt's ruint."

Jesse's anger gets the better of him again. He leaps at Edgar and slaps him across the face.

"You fucking idiot," he says. "You'd forget to wipe your own ass if I didn't remind you. I've kept you alive for fifty years, but if not for promising Mama, I'd have ended this a long time ago. I'd be at peace, and Johona would be alive."

"That girl's cunny made you cuckoo," Edgar says. "I'm glad she got killed."

Jesse grabs his brother by the throat and squeezes. Edgar puts up a fight, but Jesse's hands are wolves' jaws, his arms iron bars. Edgar's eyes bulge, and his face flushes crimson as Jesse forces him onto his back. His grip on Jesse's wrists weakens, and Jesse watches life leaving him like he's watched it leave hundreds of others. He's so goddamned tired of death. Right before his brother's spark goes out, he releases him, and Edgar draws a rattling breath.

Jesse spies Abby sitting in a corner. He scrambles off the bed, gets the cat by the scruff, and carries it to the door.

"No!" Edgar shouts.

Jesse grimaces against the blast of sunlight when he opens the door. He tosses the cat out onto the hot asphalt of the parking lot, where it spins like a dog chasing its tail, yowls and spits, then collapses into a heap of gray dust.

Jesse steps back into the room, face and hands scorched. Edgar tries to push past, but he wrestles him to the floor and kicks the door closed. Edgar's panting, sweating, blubbering. Good. Jesse wants him to suffer. He wants him to wake up, reach for Abby, and have her not be there. He wants him to know loss, the only wound that scars a rover.

He holds his brother down until he stops thrashing, then says, "If you ever speak of Johona again, I'll dust you. Do you hear me?"

"Yes," Edgar says.

"Now, finish cleaning up."

Edgar carries the soiled sheets to the bathroom. Jesse stands over him, giving instructions. Fill the tub. Pour in shampoo. Squeeze the sheets and swish them. When the bedding has been hung on the towel rod to dry, Jesse lets Edgar shower. He brings in britches and undershorts and leaves them next to the tub and flips the mattress himself.

Edgar comes out and lies on the bed without a word. Jesse sits at the table and plays Klondike.

There's a knock at the door. Sanders. If he saw what happened to Abby, he doesn't say anything. He goes into the bathroom, comes out a few minutes later, and says, "Doing laundry?"

"My brother wet the bed," Jesse says.

Sanders takes a bag of potato chips out of his food box. "You want some of these?"

"No, thank you."

"I believe I'll lie down."

"Suit yourself."

Jesse plays cards through the rest of the afternoon. When he feels the sun set, it's like coming up for air after being underwater. Edgar is asleep, and Sanders is back at his Bible.

"Get me one of your ice picks," Jesse says to him.

Sanders pulls a pick from his duffel and hands it over.

"I'm going out to talk to Beaumont," Jesse says. "You're coming with me."

Sanders puts his Bible away. He and Jesse walk out to the truck. It's barely dusk, but already rockets are booming and crackling.

"I never could wait either," Sanders says. "The Fourth, man, that was a big one."

Jesse gives him the keys and has him unlock the camper. The air inside is hot and rank. Beaumont glares up at them when Sanders opens the crate. His face glistens with sweat. Jesse sticks the point of the ice pick into his ear.

"I'm only asking once," he says. "Where are the Fiends?"

He slips the bandana Sanders gagged the man with off Beaumont's mouth. "A motel on the road to Lake Mead," Beaumont says. He licks his lips and swallows hard. "I need water. Please."

Sanders points to a jug on the counter.

"Not yet," Jesse says. He pushes the pick in deeper, tickling Beaumont's eardrum. "Where on the road? How far out?"

"I'm not certain, but I know it by sight," Beaumont says. "I'll take you there."

Jesse jiggles the pick to scare him before withdrawing it. He nods to Sanders, who puts the jug to Beaumont's mouth and holds it while he drinks.

"Thank you, brother," Beaumont says when he's had his fill.

"I'm not your brother," Sanders says.

A fly lands on Beaumont's cheek and laps at the blood smeared there. Beaumont shakes his head, but the fly just hops to a new spot.

"May I use a toilet?" Beaumont says.

"Not until you take me to the motel," Jesse says.

"Some food?"

"No. Nothing."

Jesse slides the gag back and closes the crate. He checks the padlocks after Sanders snaps them shut.

The men leave the camper. Children are playing with sparklers in the motel's parking lot, twirling them, tossing them, fighting fiery duels.

"*God bless America*," a girl sings, marching like she's in a parade. "*Land that I love.*"

"We're going after them tonight," Jesse says to Sanders.

"Do you have a plan?" Sanders asks.

"Dust them all," Jesse replies.

A bottle rocket explodes, loosing a swarm of sparks. The last of the sunlight is draining from an orange cloud becalmed above Charleston Peak, and the sky is getting darker by the second.

26

Jesse don't know but I don't believe in heaven no more. When I died last night I didn't see no mansions nor streets of gold nor angels. And no good God would've let Jesse kill Abby so he's bunk too. The sun burned like lye when I run out the door after her. I wasn't thinking. I heard her crying and wasn't thinking. There wasn't no sense in me going out there. You can't bring nothing back from ashes.

We was in Houston Texas when I found her. Jesse was out hunting. I'm to keep to the room when he's gone but I sneak out sometimes. I know what fifteen minutes looks like and I never go more than that. I walk to the swimming pool if we got one to a washing place to McDonald's. Once I stood outside a drive-in movie and watched a show about some boys in jail and once I peeked into a tavern where a lady dancing with her titties hanging out called me sugar. Come in and enjoy the show, she said and I said, No ma'am I got to get to work.

In Houston I was on my way to a market with a quarter to buy me a Hershey Bar. Abby was sitting under a car in the parking lot. I called her to me but she wouldn't come till I spent that quarter on jerky and gave her some. Then she followed me all the way back to the room purring and rubbing on my legs.

The row me and Jesse had over keeping her went for days. I had to make a thousand promises. And I thought he was gonna stomp me a new asshole when he found out I turned her. I couldn't bear to think of her dying.

I was the only one could pet her feed her or pick her up. She slept next to me and kept watch like a guard dog. She liked it when you scratched her chin but couldn't abide you touching her paws and if her tail was swishing watch out. Her favorite food was tuna fish out of a tin but she'd eat grapes peanut butter soda crackers—most anything. And after I fed we didn't have to do hardly any cleaning she was such a pig about lapping up spilled blood. She'd even gobble at the dead girls' throats and chew on their fingers.

Jesse didn't kill her 'cause of what I said about Johona. He killed her 'cause he lost his sweetheart and couldn't abide me having Abby still. Pure meanness is what it was. When he pulled me back after I went after her my heart hurt more than it did when Mama died but I knew he'd dust me if I fought him. The Little Devil told me so. *That cocksucker's looking for a reason to throw you out there too,* he said, *don't give him one.* So I did what Jesse wanted. I washed the sheets like he told me to yes sir yes sir. I took myself to bed keeping my sadness hid and whetting my anger like a blade.

What I got left: my cards my train book most my cars some of my dinosaurs a puzzle I can't work a sack of fake gold nuggets my Mickey Mouse flashlight.

Mr. Sanders comes back from the swimming pool and quick as a dog can lick a plate clean Jesse tells him I pissed the bed. I fall asleep for a while and wake to find them going out to talk to Monsieur Beaumont. I pull the curtain aside and watch them climb into the camper.

Folks are setting off fireworks for the Fourth of July. Jesse always says he won't get me none but always does for a surprise. He won't let me light firecrackers but I can do sparklers and fountains if I'm careful to run away before they go to spitting. Some kids out there got sparklers and I'm thinking I might go over and say howdy and see can I have one but Jesse and Mr. Sanders come out of the truck and I get scared and close the curtains. They come inside and Jesse opens a can of pork and beans for me. Mr. Sanders asks do I want bread and gives me a slice. I don't ask for butter. I want it but don't ask.

Jesse and Mr. Sanders lay out their guns. Mr. Sanders has got a brand-new shotgun in its box. Daddy let me shoot his shotgun once. It was like a mule kicking me in the chest. Him and Uncle Offutt laughed when I cried. More meanness.

Jesse loads the shotgun. I pick up a shell and sniff. Smells like fireworks. Put it down, Jesse says. I don't want to speak to him but I want to know. I ask what's happening and he says him and Mr. Sanders are fixing to do away with the Fiends. I go to shaking. I don't want no more trouble nobody shooting me nobody stabbing me. I say, You're gonna get me killed. No, I won't, Jesse says, I'll see you're safe.

I don't trust him. I quit the beans and get back into bed. Jesse asks do I want to watch television. I don't answer but he puts it on anyway. A soldier band is playing and there's fireworks in Washington DC. Washington DC's where the president lives in his white house.

Daddy took us to see President Teddy Roosevelt in Wheeling. He come in on the train rode in a parade and give a speech. There was so many people I couldn't see nothing but a man yelling on a balcony. Daddy bought me a candy apple. On the way home we laid over for the night outside Littleton in the barn of Daddy's friend Breezy. Breezy had a dog named Red that'd sing when he played the fiddle. The president now is a man named Ford same as the car.

I don't care about the fireworks on television. I'm feeling sick to my stomach and the Little Devil won't quit griping. Get up, Jesse says, we're leaving. I don't want to. Get up, Jesse says again and his voice means business. I go to pull on my shoes and there's blood all over them. My fingers get sticky tying the laces. Stop putting on a show, Jesse says when he sees me crying.

Me and him and Mr. Sanders walk out and climb in the camper. Mr. Sanders opens the box back there and I go to shaking again when I see Monsieur Beaumont lying in it wrapped round with chains.

Jesse puts his pistol to Monsieur Beaumont's head. We're going after the Fiends, he says, I don't want to hear nothing from you but directions. Monsieur Beaumont with a rag in his mouth can't do nothing but nod. Jesse and Mr. Sanders lift him out of the box. He stinks like he shit hisself and his fancy suit is black with blood.

You're riding back here, Jesse says to me, there's no room up front. I don't want to. It's dark and it's hot. Jesse says, Buddy do what I say or I'm gonna lock *you* in that box. I can't let him put me in there. He's like never to let me out.

Him and Mr. Sanders take Monsieur Beaumont with them. The door shuts and I'm all alone. Sweat's running down my face and crawling down my back. The truck starts and we're agoing. Through a little window I see cars lights people. Fireworks are popping and fading and leaving spidery ghosts.

We stop at Kmart and Jesse runs inside and then we're driving again.

The road's long and straight and empty after that. I open drawers and come upon some silverware a hammer and nails a box of pencils and two Christmas candy canes. I put one candy in my pocket and tear the plastic off the other. I'm sucking on it when the truck all of a sudden slows. I go sit at the table and hide the candy under a cushion.

Out the window's a red arrow and a motel. The truck goes past them but stops down the road. Mr. Sanders opens the door and Jesse brings Monsieur Beaumont in and lays him back in the box. Mr. Sanders sticks the rag in his mouth and closes the lid and locks it.

Him and Jesse strap on their guns and knives. Sit tight, Jesse says to me, don't open the door no matter what you hear. I ask what about Monsieur Beaumont. He can't get at you, Jesse says, he's all locked up and no more dangerous than a sack of spuds.

Him and Mr. Sanders step out and I watch through the window at them walking off toward the red arrow. I hear Monsieur Beaumont breathing in the box his chains jingling. Keep still you sonofabitch, I say. You was our friend but you ain't no more.

I take the candy from under the cushion and go to sucking it again. It's real quiet just flies buzzing until Monsieur Beaumont commences to moaning like a haint and kicking inside the box like he means to break out. *Boom boom boom.* I go to the drawer and get a knife and yell that I got it but that don't settle him. *Boom boom boom.* I kick the box myself. I pound it with my fist. You best lay off, I say, I'll dust you I will. *Boom boom boom.* I go to singing loud as I can to drown him out. *We got a great big convoy trucking through the night. We got a great big convoy ain't she a beautiful sight.*

I'm singing and he's kicking for I don't know how long but when we're both finally quiet another sound gives me goose bumps gunfire rattling like marbles in a can. There's a bed up a ladder. I climb into it pull a blanket over me and stick fingers in my ears deep as they'll go.

27

July 5, 1976, Las Vegas

To get to where I find myself now, it's easiest to pick up where I last left off.

After the fight with the bikers—the Fiends, they're called—at Beaumont's place, we buried the girl Jesse had wrapped in the blanket. I helped with the digging, the work a relief from worrying about what might be coming next. It struck me that it was the second grave I'd dug in less than a week.

Jesse said he and Edgar would be sharing my room with me. As he was pointing Czarnecki's .45 at my head at the time, I didn't argue. First, though, he had me park near a motel where he and his brother had been staying so he could pick up their belongings.

As soon as he was out of sight, Edgar started to talk. He's slow somehow, retarded, and seemed to be saying any old thing that popped into his brain. He told me he hit a jackpot on a slot machine, was lucky that way. He said he wanted to go to Dallas because someone called Icky Twerp showed Popeye cartoons there. He asked if I had a CB radio and said I should get one and he'd show me how to use it.

When I could finally sneak a word in, I asked who the dead girl was. He said she was Jesse's sweetheart and one of the Fiends had killed her. He said she was nice but dumb, and something about her stealing a baby. He was back on cartoons by the time Jesse returned and handed him a pillowcase with a cat in it. At that point nothing was strange to me.

The brothers started bickering before we'd even settled in my room. I bandaged the cut on my head, ate a sandwich, and took a shower to wash the blood off myself. The sun was up when I finally lay down with my Bible, but morning didn't bring me back to life. I nodded off within minutes and slept for a long while.

I was sore when I woke—my head, my back—and still at a loss as to how to handle the situation I was in. I had a powerful urge to escape the room even if only for a few minutes. Jesse let me walk out to the pool.

The sun was a blazing arc in a bleached sky, and the only other people braving the hottest stretch of an ungodly hot day were a white couple on chaises in the shade of an overhang. They were drinking beer and watching their kids play in the water. I pulled a chair into another sliver of shade and sat facing the room, so if Jesse checked, there I'd be.

The children, a boy and a girl, took turns dunking each other, the drone of traffic drifted over from the Strip, and a maid's radio hiccupped a Mexican song. I'd never felt so alone surrounded by so many people. A hot wind ruffled the water and rolled one of the couple's empty beer cans across the deck. It ended up under my chair.

"Sorry about that," the man, a freckle-faced redhead with permanent sunburn, called out. He brought over a full can of Coors and said, "Take this. You're gonna cook in all those clothes."

I thanked him.

He asked if I was winning big.

"I'm here on business," I replied.

"We're just passing through ourselves," he said. "On our way to California. I start a job in Bakersfield next week."

I tore the tab off the beer and raised the can. "Good luck to you," I said.

"I expect it'll be a big change from Oklahoma," he said.

"For the better, I'm sure," I said.

"You from there? California?" he asked.

"San Diego," I said.

"I hear it's nice there," he said.

His wife, as redheaded and sunburned as him, shouted, "Rodney, haul the kids out. We've got to go."

"Yes, hon," he drawled and winked at me. "I hear divorces come easy in California too," he said.

He rounded up the kids, his wife draped towels around them, and the family dashed across the parking lot to their room, the little boy crying, "Ouch, ouch, ouch," with each step on the hot asphalt until his dad scooped him up.

Keep those babies close, I thought. *Keep them safe.*

I don't believe any beer I've ever had tasted as good as that one. Probably because I thought it might be my last. I was fairly certain Jesse was rushing me to my doom, and I couldn't see any way out of it that wouldn't lead to something worse.

This feeling grew stronger when the door to the room flew open and Jesse appeared. Smoke rose off him as he stepped into the sun. He flung Edgar's cat into the parking lot, where it screeched and turned to ash, then he and Edgar grappled on the threshold before he pulled his brother inside and slammed the door.

The wind whirled the cat's ashes into a dust devil—all the maid saw when she poked her head out of the laundry room.

I sipped my beer slowly, not wanting to return during a battle between the brothers.

Edgar was asleep when I got back, and Jesse was playing solitaire. I crawled into bed thinking I'd get more sleep, but it never came. Every tick of my watch was like a hammer on a railroad spike.

As soon as the sun went down, Jesse and I went out to the camper to talk to Beaumont. Jesse quickly got out of him where the Fiends were and told me we were going after them that night. I asked if he had a plan. He didn't. More than ever it looked like a suicide mission.

Back in the room, Jesse laid out the guns. He loaded the shotgun and slid a fresh magazine into the .45.

"I hope you're planning to let me carry something," I said.

"You won't be any use to me unarmed," Jesse said.

He stowed the guns in Czarnecki's duffel, all except the old man's .45, which he stuck in his waistband like a liquor-store robber. He put on his jacket, I put on mine, and it was time to go.

We pulled Beaumont out of the box so he could steer us to the motel. The King of the Rovers, shaking in his soiled disco suit, was a pathetic sight. Jesse hustled him up to the cab and locked him to the bolt on the floor. I drove.

The Fourth was in full swing, fireworks going off everywhere. The loudest had me jumping like I was being stung by bees. We needed ammunition. Jesse directed me to a Kmart. He took the keys before going into the store and reminded me he had our address.

Beaumont began rocking and moaning behind his gag. He seemed to be in some distress. Worried that if anything happened to him Jesse would blame me, I slipped the bandana out of his mouth.

"Why are you helping this man?" he said.

"Why did you try to kill him?" I replied.

"He was responsible for the death of a woman I loved."

"And now you're responsible for the death of a woman he loved."

"He lies," Beaumont said. "Don't listen to him."

"Should I listen to you?" I said.

He lifted his shackled hands, showing them to me. "In your heart, you know that you and I, even with our differences, are more alike than you and he. We have the same blood. We've known the same hatred, the same fear, the same humiliation."

"You might have once been like me, but you're not anymore," I said. "You're a viper now, from the same nest as the rest of these monsters. I've got nothing in common with any of you."

"Help me escape and I'll make you rich," Beaumont went on. He negotiated like a man still in power, still in control. He has no idea how much his situation has changed. There'll be no more fancy houses, fancy clothes, fancy cars. No more respect or obedience. As Sally's replacement, he'll be imprisoned in that box day and night except for the few hours when I pull him out to finger his own kind for extermination.

Some might get a kick out of seeing the tables turned on a beast like him, might revel in holding the future of such a devil in their hands. I don't. It's just another burden added to my load.

"You're wasting your breath," I said. "Money can't buy anything I need now."

"Jesse is using you. He has no loyalty to you."

"And you do? You won't betray me like you betrayed him?"

"Don't be a fool."

"Too late for that," I said and put the gag back in his mouth.

When Jesse returned he loaded the revolver and the automatic with the bullets he'd bought. The click of the cartridges sliding into place sent a chill through me. He put the automatic to Beaumont's head and pulled the bandana down.

"Which way?" he said.

"East toward the lake," Beaumont said. "On the old highway."

We were soon rolling through open desert. One star lit another, and the sky filled quickly. We saw only one other vehicle, a car going the opposite direction. Now and then we passed the ruins of a gas station or motel.

"This man tried to enlist me to help him kill you," Beaumont said out of nowhere, addressing Jesse.

I clutched the wheel tighter but didn't speak.

"He's going to dust you and your brother at his first opportunity."

"What do you have to say to that?" Jesse asked me.

Inwardly, I was panicking, but my voice was calm. "I told you I'd never do anything to put my wife in danger," I said.

"Such a touching lie," Beaumont said.

"Which of us is more desperate?" I said.

Beaumont hissed when Jesse smacked him with the gun. He replaced the gag and told him to grunt when we got to where we were supposed to be. We drove in silence until a red arrow appeared ahead of us, part of an old motel sign. Beaumont made a noise and pointed with his chin.

"Keep going," Jesse said to me. "Don't slow down and don't look over."

As I sped past the motel, I glimpsed a cluster of cabins and a gravel parking lot. Half a mile down the road Jesse told me to kill the lights and take my foot off the gas. The truck slowed without me using the brakes, and I steered onto the shoulder.

Jesse released Beaumont from the bolt in the floor while I unlocked the camper. The wind had died, and the night was hot and still.

"You sure you want to take this sonofabitch with you afterward?" Jesse asked me when he brought Beaumont back. "We're done with him, can dust him right now."

"I don't want any of this," I said. "But I need him."

Edgar was sitting at the table in the camper. We locked Beaumont in the crate, and Jesse pulled the guns out of the duffel bag. He handed me Czarnecki's .45 and the holster.

"You seem to know how to use this," he said.

He gave me the revolver from Beaumont's, too, and took the shotgun and automatic for himself. I strapped on the holster and buckled the knife to my shin. The revolver and extra rounds went into the pocket of my jacket. I grabbed an ice pick and tossed another to Jesse.

"Do you need to pray?" he asked.

I told him I guessed it was too late for that.

We climbed out of the camper. Jesse locked the door and kept the keys.

"I'll come from the front," he said. "You go around back and set yourself up to catch anyone who tries to run when the shooting starts."

He took off down the road, sticking to the brush on the shoulder. I walked a hundred yards into the desert before turning toward the motel. The moon and stars gave enough light to navigate by, and the neon arrow served as a beacon. I drew the .45 and felt less scared with it in my hand.

The motel was dark when I got close. I paused every few steps to listen for anybody moving around. A burned-out trailer sat at the rear of the property and seemed a perfect spot to take cover. Whatever it was that scurried across the floor when I stepped inside stopped me for a second, but I made my way to an empty window frame with a view of the back doors of the cabins and the three motorcycles parked behind them.

My heart banged against my ribs, and fear gummed my mouth so that it was hard to swallow. I rested the elbow of my gun arm on the sill to brace it. Squinting down the barrel of the .45, I swung it from cabin to cabin, alert for any movement. It was like waiting for a bomb to go off.

The first shot made me jump. The fusillade that followed, coming from the front of the motel, had me holding my breath. The back door of one of the cabins opened, and a fat man I hadn't seen at Beaumont's ran out. My orders were to gun down anyone trying to escape, so I pointed the .45 and pulled the trigger. The bullet hit the fat man in the leg, and he screamed and went down. I shot two more times. He stopped screaming.

More gunfire clattered, and the door to another cabin opened. Jesse backed out, shooting his pistol, the muzzle flashes a bright tongue flicking. The gun ran out of ammo, and Jesse tossed it aside and pulled a knife. A biker pointing a shotgun limped out of the cabin. I fired, hit him, and he dropped the shotgun as he fell.

Suddenly, I was under attack. Bullets punched through the aluminum skin of the trailer and whizzed past me. A round tore the .45 from my hand. A second bullet slammed into my thigh. The gust of pain knocked me off a cliff and set me adrift on a sea of fire.

28

I'VE GOT ALL MY CHIPS ON YOU.

Real Deal is lying on his bed, as barren inside as the desert outside, his and Yuma's motto echoing in his head.

I've got all my chips on you.

He's still covered in blood from last night's shootout but doesn't give a damn, may never wash it off. Some might be hers. As the sun sets he walks out the cabin's back door to where his Harley is parked so it can't be seen from the road. He digs in his saddlebags for the .22 semiauto stashed there, something to replace the gun he left behind when they fled Beaumont's.

Bob comes out the back door of his cabin with his pistol and a cigarette.

"I heard a noise, almost blasted you," he says.

Real Deal shows him the .22 and says, "I hope you're right about that motherfucker looking to get even."

"I'm right," Bob says. "Elijah's keeping watch up front. We'll switch off every two hours."

"I'll sit out there all night," Real Deal says. "I need something to do besides drive myself crazy."

"It's best we stick to the plan," Antonia says. She steps

out of her and Elijah's cabin, where she's been eavesdropping. "Stay inside, keep it dark, keep the bikes hidden. Anybody snooping around will have to come right to our doors."

"That's all hunky-dory," Bob says. "But if any shit goes down, I'll be doing my own thing. Don't get in my way."

"We'll all be doing our own thing at that point," Antonia says, "but until then, shut your cabin light off."

Bob hits his cigarette, waiting for her to go back inside before he says, "I've about had my fill of that bitch."

Real Deal doesn't have time for Bob's bullshit. He makes sure the .22's magazine is full.

"That blood's gonna start to stink if you don't clean up," Bob says.

"It's my war paint," Real Deal replies.

Bob goes into his cabin and switches off the lamp next to his bed. He opens the front door and whistles. Elijah whistles back, the all clear, and Bob jogs across the parking lot to the clump of tamarisk where Elijah's hunkered down with a chair, a jug of water, and the shotgun Bull brought back from town earlier today.

"Did you eat something?" Bob says.

"I'm not hungry," Elijah says.

"I'm starving."

There's still some pink in the sky, but it'll soon be full dark. A nightbird chirps, another answers. A vehicle approaches from the west, and Bob ducks beside Elijah.

"Don't stare at the lights," he says.

A Dodge rattles past, whipping up dust. The men swivel to watch until it disappears in the distance. Elijah slaps his forearm and squints at his palm.

"Are there mosquitoes out here?" he says.

"Probably an ant," Bob says. "There's plenty of those. The biting kind."

Elijah lifts his boot in search of an anthill. Bob walks over and knocks on the door of Bull's cabin. Bull, shirtless, opens up and asks what he wants.

"You have anything to eat?" Bob says.

"First you make me run all over town getting you guns, and now you want to raid my refrigerator?" Bull says.

"I'll pay."

"There's leftover fried rice and a couple hot dogs."

"Boil the franks and throw them on the rice. I'll give you two bucks."

"The stove'll make a light."

"I'll handle Antonia."

"Yes, sir. Right away, sir. Kiss my ass, sir," Bull grumbles on his way to his fridge.

Bob steps into the cabin. It's a pigsty, trash everywhere. Stacks of porno magazines, rusty tools, old glass telephone insulators. Smells like a pigsty too. Bull dumps the rice in a skillet and drops the dogs into a pot of water.

"Put a shirt on," Bob says. "I don't want hair in my food."

"I'm tired of you fuckers telling me what to do," Bull says. "And now this Fort Apache bullshit."

"Take off till it's over. Nobody's stopping you."

"This is my fucking place." Bull turns and waves a spatula. "You take off. Settle your beef elsewhere."

"Stir some ketchup in there if you got it," Bob says and goes outside to sit on the old couch on the porch.

Antonia's at the table in her cabin, trying to read by the glow of the neon arrow. It's more effort than it's worth, and she's too tense to concentrate anyway, keeps looking out the window to where Elijah's hiding, keeps jumping at noises that make her think someone's creeping up on them.

She hopes to hell this thing gets resolved tonight. She hates these ratty shacks and Bull and the idea that Bob and Real Deal's thirst for revenge has put her and Elijah in danger. On top of that, twinges of bloodlust are rippling through her like someone's strumming her veins and arteries. She's still a couple weeks out from having to feed, but the stress of the past few days has screwed up her clock. She checks the magazine of her pistol for the tenth time and gives the book another chance, hoping the story will take hold.

Elijah, standing guard, knows everything she's feeling. He heard it in her voice this evening and saw it in the set of her jaw. Nothing he can say will calm her, though, and he doesn't want her calm anyway. He wants her on edge, he wants her ready to fight. He looks toward the cabins. The only movement is at Bull's place. Bob's out front. Bull hands him a plate of food. The two men talk quietly.

Elijah turns back to the road. From where he's hidden he can see all the way up and down the strip of asphalt to where it disappears in both directions. Across the road buzzing power lines are strung between steel towers. These, too, extend as far as he can see. He aims the shotgun as if preparing to fire. "Boom," he whispers. He lowers the gun and brings it up again.

"Boom."

Because Antonia made them turn off their noisy swamp coolers, Real Deal's cabin is sweltering even with all the windows open. There's a .22 cartridge on the table. He flicks it to set it spinning, but the sound is too loud in the enforced silence.

He feels he's close to snapping, and God help the world if he does, now that Yuma's not here to rein him in.

Bob finishes his grub and walks out to the lookout post. "Private Pyle reporting for duty," he says to Elijah.

"Come back in twenty minutes," Elijah says.

"Go on. Throw Antonia a bone. Seems like she needs it."

Elijah hands Bob the shotgun and goes back to his cabin. Bob settles into the chair. Not five minutes later headlights rise like twin moons in the west. Bob sinks to one knee. As the vehicle draws near, he lifts the shotgun, ready to send a load of buckshot through the windshield. An old pickup—Ford, with an over-the-cab camper—drives past and off into the night. Bob sits again. These false alarms are gonna kill him.

Bull sprawls on his bed, a plastic bag filled with ice pressed to his forehead. Fuck the fucking rovers for dragging him into their shit. The fight they're waiting for could wreck this joint, and the few bucks he's made off them won't be compensation for that. He's been thinking about moving to the Keys, and tonight's convinced him he should. He's got enough money stashed to buy property there, another motel, a legit one this time. Of course in Florida there's always the danger of running into someone holding a grudge, but plastic surgeons can work miracles, and if he lost some weight, his own mother wouldn't recognize him.

Outside, Bob stands and stretches. He's never been able to sit for long, couldn't even make it through a movie when he was a kid without getting up two or three times. He leaves the cover of the tamarisk carrying only his pistol and walks out to the road. There's not a car in sight.

He thinks about what he'll do if Jesse doesn't show up tonight. If the Fiends couldn't find the guy in Phoenix, they won't find him here. It might be time for him to go out on his own. He won't have anyone watching his back, but he also won't have to follow Antonia's orders or worry about anybody but himself. He'll be able to put all his time and energy into tracking down and dusting Jesse before Jesse finds and dusts him.

He stands on the dotted line in the center of the road and lights a cigarette, takes in the glow of Vegas on the horizon. Gravel crunching in the parking lot snaps his head around. It's Jesse, toting a shotgun, creeping up on the cabins.

"He's here!" Bob shouts and fires his pistol. Jesse turns the shotgun on him. He drops to the ground, but enough pellets get him that his knees won't work. He drags himself out of the road using only his arms.

Real Deal, Antonia, and Elijah fling open their doors. They spot Jesse and cut loose with their guns. Jesse sends a blast Antonia and Elijah's way then charges Real Deal, firing at him on the run.

Bull, cowering on the floor of his cabin, decides *Fuck this* and flees out the back door. Someone shooting from the old trailer hits him in the leg. He howls in pain and falls hard. He's still howling when another bullet destroys his heart.

Real Deal dives sideways in time to avoid too much damage from Jesse's hail of buckshot. With a joyous roar, he leaps on him when he barrels into the cabin, and they go down in a snarl of arms and legs, falling into the narrow space between the bed and the wall, Jesse's shotgun sandwiched between them.

Real Deal wrenches one hand free and throttles Jesse. "Yuma," he shouts. "You watching this, baby?" Jesse comes up with a pistol from somewhere. Real Deal grabs for it, and the round ends up in the ceiling. He forces Jesse's arm down, Jesse fighting the whole way. His other hand is still on Jesse's throat, but he's having trouble choking him and controlling the gun at the same time.

Jesse pulls the pistol's trigger again. This time the bullet burrows into Real Deal's leg until it hits bone. He gulps the scream that wells up but can't stop his hand from going to the wound. Jesse pushes him aside and scrabbles to his feet, headed for the back door. Real Deal grabs the shotgun he left behind and uses it as a crutch to lift himself. The pain in his leg is intense, but he manages to raise the shotgun. Jesse turns in the doorway before he can pull the trigger and fires the pistol at him. One of the rounds nicks his collarbone, and the arm holding the barrel of the shotgun goes numb, fouling his aim.

Jesse's out back by then, and out of bullets. Real Deal reaches the doorway and sees him toss the pistol and pull a knife. Real Deal roars again and brings the shotgun up one-handed, propping it on his hip. Before he can shoot, a bullet fired from the trailer gets him in the chest. As his mouth fills with blood, he recalls a cloud shaped like a duck that he saw when he was a kid. He drops the shotgun and falls to his knees.

Antonia and Elijah open up through their back door on whoever's shooting from inside the trailer, then turn their guns on Jesse when he takes hold of Real Deal and drags him into the walkway between two of the cabins.

"Cover me," Elijah says to Antonia.

"Stay here."

"I'm going after him."

No gunfire comes from the trailer as he runs to the walkway, but he's too late. Real Deal's been dusted, and there's no sign of Jesse. Elijah moves up the walkway, keeping his shoulder against the cabin to his right and his pistol up. *Where the hell's Bob?* he wonders.

"Are you okay?" Antonia shouts.

He's about to respond when something tears into his right leg above his boot. Looking down, he sees a knife buried in his calf. In the same instant Jesse reaches out from the crawl-space under the cabin, takes hold of the ankle of his other leg, and pulls hard, toppling him. Elijah rolls onto his back and points his pistol, but Jesse wrenches it out of his hand and turns it on him.

One round hits him in the stomach, two others miss. He cringes, anticipating another shot, but Jesse has a new target. It's Bob, shotgun in one hand, pistol in the other, who's appeared at the front end of the walkway. Bob cuts loose with the pistol, and Jesse returns fire with Elijah's gun, then turns and flees to the back of the cabins.

He runs smack into Antonia, who's come looking for Elijah. They fire at the same time. Antonia's shot misses, but Jesse's gets her in the face, the bullet entering under her right cheekbone, exiting over her left ear, and knocking her off her feet. Elijah screams her name as she hits the ground.

Jesse snatches up the shotgun Real Deal dropped and makes for the ruined trailer at the back of the property. Bob dashes out of the walkway, chasing him and already in his mind catching him and twisting off his head with his bare hands. Jesse whips around and fires the shotgun. The blast tears away Bob's shirt and most of the skin from his chest to his thigh on his left side, exposing red muscle, yellow fat, and white bone. Tough as he is, he almost faints. A man's not meant to see that much of his insides. He falls behind Real Deal's Harley as Jesse disappears into the trailer.

Elijah staggers from between the cabins, grabs Antonia, and pulls her back into the walkway. He wipes some of the blood off her face. Her bulging right eye settles into its socket, and the hole in her cheek is closing, but she's still unconscious.

The sound of the shots fades and the smoke drifts away. A fraught calm falls over the battlefield. Bob's wound is healing but still hurts like a motherfucker. He reloads his pistol to take his mind off the pain and retrieves the shotgun he dropped when he was hit. When he's back behind the bike, he hisses loudly, a signal. Elijah pokes his head around the cabin.

"Real Deal?" Bob mouths.

Elijah picks up a fistful of sand and lets it sift through his fingers.

"Antonia?"

Elijah wobbles the same hand. So-so.

Shotgun and pistol fire pour from the trailer, lighting up the night. Bullets and buckshot ping off Real Deal's Harley and chew up the cabin behind it. Bob curls into a ball. When the salvo dies down, he realizes he's been hit in the foot. Blood pours out of a rip in his boot. The guns roar again, the target this time Elijah's ride. Sparks fly, bullets ricochet, and the bike topples over.

Bob sits up when the shooting stops. He'll be damned if he's going to cower like a frightened rabbit until he's picked off. Hissing again to get Elijah's attention, he throws him the pistol and aims the shotgun over the seat of Real Deal's Harley.

"Hit 'em!" he shouts, and he and Elijah blast the trailer until their guns are empty.

A moan from the trailer breaks the silence that follows. Bob drops behind the bike, pulls some shells from his pocket, and reloads. It's time to end this bullshit standoff, and he's the one who'll have to do it. He calls out to Jesse.

"I hear you," Jesse replies.

"Do you surrender?"

"That's not how this is going to go."

"You're outnumbered, and we've got better position. We'll either make you use up all your ammo and rush you or keep you pinned until morning and let the sun take care of you."

"Or you might talk me to death," Jesse says.

"What if I give you a chance to better your odds?"

"Why would you do that?"

"This is really just between you and me. You dusted my partner, and I killed your girl."

"Go on."

Bob checks the shotgun wound. It's almost healed. "Give my people time to ride out of here, and I'll let whoever you've got with you leave too," he says. "Then you and me'll go toe to toe with knives, finish what we started on the mountain. You'll have a fifty-fifty shot."

In the walkway between the cabins, Antonia has healed enough that she can sit. She and Elijah listen to the negotiation and wonder what Bob's up to. It seems like a needless gamble.

"He take a bullet to the head too?" Antonia says.

"Hurry and make up your mind," Bob shouts at Jesse. "This is a limited-time offer."

"Your people go first," Jesse says.

"Fine," Bob says. "I'm gonna get up and go talk to them."

"Talk to them from where you are."

Bob rolls over so he's facing the cabins. "You hear all that?" he says.

"That's not how I'd play it," Antonia says.

"Well, that's how I'm playing it."

"You expect us to just ride off and leave you?" Elijah says.

"Go on and don't look back," Bob says. "The Fiends are through. It's every man for himself now."

Elijah looks at Antonia, eyes asking if he should try harder.

"Sounds like he's got his mind made up," she says. She's seen the end coming for a long time but hadn't pictured this. Elijah helps her stand.

"We need to get our things," she calls out.

"Leave it," Jesse says. "And your guns too."

"We're supposed to trust you?"

"If you're going, go now."

Elijah tosses the pistol, and he and Antonia step out into the open, hands in the air. They walk past Bob crouched behind Real Deal's ruined bike.

"Good luck to you," Elijah says.

"See you down the road," Bob replies.

They sit on Antonia's Harley. She starts it, and they ride slowly around to the front of the motel. Bob hears the engine clatter as they set off and thinks, *Good riddance.*

"Your turn," he shouts to Jesse.

The black man from Beaumont's limps out of the trailer with a blood-soaked rag tied around one of his legs. He walks between two cabins toward the road. When he's gone, Bob says, "I'm getting up now."

The shotgun wound hardly hurts at all when he stands, and his foot's okay too. He keeps his gun pointed at the ground.

Jesse appears in the doorway of the trailer, carrying a pistol and a knife. "Drop the iron," he says to Bob.

"You too."

Jesse flings his pistol into the scrub. Bob does the same with the shotgun. As the men advance toward each other, Bob frees his knife from its sheath on his belt. They stop ten paces apart.

"One," Bob says, going into a crouch. He's grinning, can't wait to cut this motherfucker to pieces.

"Two."

Jesse twists his feet to plant them in the dirt.

"Three!"

Bob rushes Jesse, going hard, but Jesse sidesteps and jabs with his knife. He misses and has to spin around. Facing each other, the men shuffle sideways, circling. Bob waves his empty hand, and when Jesse glances at it, lunges, slashes him across the chest, and skips out of reach. This is his plan: Get in, strike, get out. If he keeps it up, Jesse'll soon be so weak, he won't be able to dodge.

They go back to circling. Bob feints a few times, but Jesse doesn't take the bait again. Instead he speeds up, shuffling faster and faster, forcing Bob to speed up too. "Haw!" Jesse shouts, like he's steering a mule. "Haw!" When he stops suddenly and reverses direction, Bob trips trying to mirror him. Jesse's on him in an instant, stabbing and pulling away before he can strike back. The pain's not bad enough to bring him down, but he tastes blood, and every breath is a struggle. He's got to keep circling, though, keep his eyes on Jesse. The fucker knows he's hurt and isn't going to give him time to heal.

Sure enough, he moves in again, knife raised for an overhand strike. Instead of trying to get out of the way, Bob shifts just enough so that the blade sinks into the fleshy part of his shoulder instead of his chest. He then grabs Jesse's wrist with his free hand to stop him from pulling the knife out and at the same time stabs him in the back. Jesse lets go of his knife, jerks his arm free, and stumbles backward.

Now both of them are hurt too badly to keep circling. They glare at each other as Bob pulls Jesse's knife from his shoulder and tosses it aside. Bob means to say something smart but can't speak, so spits instead. In ten seconds he'll go in for the kill. Ten seconds of healing. *Nine, eight, seven.* He almost groans out loud when Jesse reaches into his jacket and pulls out an ice pick. The fucker is putting up more of a fight than he expected. *Four, three.*

Jesse walks toward him but stops out of striking range. Bob waves his blade, and Jesse watches it like it's a swaying snake and he's calculating when to reach out and grab it. Bob lunges and jabs to foil any attack the man might be cooking up, and Jesse backs up a step. Bob lunges again, and again Jesse retreats.

The third time Bob tries the move, Jesse deflects his strike with a sweep of his arm and counters with a jab of his own. The tip of the ice pick barely pricks Bob's chest, but the sting is enough to flood him with fresh anger. Strategizing on the fly, he pretends to fumble his knife, drops it, and bends to pick it up. Jesse falls for the ruse, rushing in with the pick aimed low, meaning to get him in the throat.

Bob stops him in mid-thrust by grabbing his forearm, snatches up his knife with his other hand, and stabs upward toward Jesse's chest. The bastard clamps onto his wrist, though, before the blade finds its mark.

They wind up face-to-face, chest to chest, Bob clutching Jesse's right arm, Jesse hanging on for dear life to his. A slap-stick tango ensues as they try to knee each other in the balls, spinning round and round until their legs tangle and they topple over.

Bob lands on the shoulder Jesse stabbed, and a bolt of pain nearly blacks him out. By the time the static clears Jesse's got the ice pick between his ribs and is probing for his heart. Bob realizes his knife is still in his hand and thrusts it into Jesse's belly. The last thing he hears before his body finally gives out is Jesse scream.

When he comes to who knows how long later, Jesse is facedown and out cold beside him. His head whirls when he sits up, but there's no time to waste. He grabs his knife and rolls Jesse onto his back, straddles the sonofabitch, and lays the blade against his neck. He's two strokes into dusting him when Jesse's eyes pop open. *The ice pick,* Bob thinks. Too late. Jesse shoves the pick up through the bottom of his chin, through his mouth, and into

29

Jesse uses the ice pick embedded in the Fiend's head to guide the body to the ground. The wound in his stomach makes him feel like he's drunk acid, and he lies back and waits to heal more. When the worst has passed, he dusts the biker with the biker's own knife.

He still doesn't feel safe, though, not with the last two Fiends in the wind. He gathers all the guns he can find and carries them to the truck in a bindle made from a bedsheet, taking it slow, watching the road and listening for a motorcycle. When he gets close to the pickup he pauses to look for signs of trouble. Everything seems to be fine. Sanders is even behind the wheel. Jesse wasn't sure he'd make it back.

He was lying in a puddle of blood when Jesse ran into the trailer, not moving. Assuming he was dead, Jesse went to the window and watched the big, dark Fiend he'd stabbed drag the blond woman he shot to safety. Sanders groaned, startling Jesse.

"Where are you hit?" Jesse asked.

"My leg," Sanders said.

A bullet had passed through his thigh. Jesse cut a sleeve off Sanders's shirt and tied it around the leg. It was no kind of fix, but it would get him through the next few minutes, when Jesse would need him. He groaned again as Jesse hauled him to his feet, but the leg supported his weight. Jesse had him take up a position at the window, and he crouched in the doorway.

After striking the deal with the Fiend who killed Johona allowing Sanders to go, he told Sanders, "Wait in the truck. If I'm not back by dawn, take off."

"And your brother?" Sanders asked.

There was only one alternative. "Put him down," Jesse replied. Edgar not being able to fend for himself, it'd be a mercy killing.

Jesse waves at Sanders now as he approaches the truck, says, "You alive?"

"Barely," Sanders says.

Jesse walks back to the camper. Edgar peers down from a bed in a nook above the cab.

"Monsieur Beaumont went crazy," he says. "He like to have kicked that box to kindling."

"Come up front," Jesse says. "Everything's settled."

Sanders keeps drifting in and out of consciousness, so Jesse drives. Edgar rides between them. Nobody says anything on the way back to Vegas, not even Edgar. Instead of gassing about cartoons or begging to turn on the radio, he stares out the windshield, his big, knuckly hands clutching the dash. Jesse and Sanders reek of blood, gunpowder, and exhaustion. Jesse opens all the vents, flooding the cab with fresh air.

Sanders needs help walking to the room. Jesse lays him on the bed and strips off his trousers to examine his leg more closely. Through and through, as he thought: one hole in the front of the thigh, one in the back, both barely bleeding now. He's in a lot of pain, and Jesse feels that patching him up is part of their bargain. He goes through the man's first aid kit, but he'll need more than what's there to do the job right.

Edgar's on his bed, watching television. He doesn't look over when Jesse starts making himself presentable enough to go out.

"You want a hamburger?" Jesse asks him.

"Two Big Macs," Edgar says. "And French fries."

"What about you?" Jesse says to Sanders.

"I'm fine."

Jesse walks to an all-night drugstore for peroxide and gauze and buys a few extra burgers from the McDonald's next door in case Sanders changes his mind.

Sanders, lying in the bathtub, hisses when Jesse pours peroxide into the bullet holes and bloody froth boils out. By the time Jesse bandages the leg and gets the man back to his bed, Edgar is asleep. Sanders nibbles at a hamburger and is soon sleeping too.

Jesse stretches out on the floor with a pillow. It's the first chance he's had to relax in two days, but rest doesn't come easy. Whenever he closes his eyes, a vicious montage unspools. Him stabbed and shot and stabbing and shooting, guns and knives and blood, rovers collapsing into dust. He and the Fiends fight on the mountain, he and the biker fight at the motel, and Johona dies over and over. It's light outside before exhaustion finally shuts him down.

The first thing he hears when he wakes is laughter. The television. Edgar's watching from bed, and Sanders is writing to his wife. The sun is down, he can feel it. He stands and stretches. Besides being parched, he's doing okay. He drinks three glasses of water and takes a long shower, keeping his mind on the night ahead and not letting it stray into sorrow.

He tells Edgar to pack his things and is surprised when he fills his grip without kicking.

He walks to the nearest casino and cases the parking lot. Spotting an old Galaxie 500, he sidles up and jams a screwdriver into the door lock. A few taps with a hammer, a hard twist, and he's in the driver's seat. After a bit of work on the ignition cylinder, he touches the starter wire to the battery wires, and the car comes to life.

All Edgar's got to say when he walks back into the room is that he's hungry again. "We'll get something on the way," Jesse tells him and sets about packing his own suitcase. It doesn't take long. The shirt and jeans he's wearing are the only clothes he's got not covered in blood. He takes Sanders's .45 from the bundle of guns and lays it on the table.

"You might need this," he says to Sanders.

Sanders doesn't respond. He looks even more miserable than usual, like he could either cry on someone's shoulder or kill them, depending on the direction of the next breeze. Jesse's felt the same way a thousand times but doesn't have any sympathy to spare. He's running along his own tightrope, keeping moving to keep from falling. He stashes his knife in his jacket, picks up the guns and his grip, and takes one last look around to make sure Edgar hasn't forgotten anything he'll be whining about an hour down the road. Then it's a quick goodbye to Sanders, and he and Edgar are out the door.

Edgar's got the mulligrubs, too, hasn't said three words all night. Jesse points him to the Galaxie and puts their grips and the guns in the back seat. They're going to Seattle. He's tired of the heat, wants to see mountains, smell trees.

"What about Disneyland?" Edgar says.

"We'll go soon," Jesse says.

Edgar snickers. "You're a liar, and the truth ain't in you," he says.

They stop at A&W for supper. Edgar tells the carhop she's pretty and asks for his own tray. The girl brings one out and hangs it from his window. The food livens him up. He guzzles his root beer, burps, and licks at the foam on his upper lip. He's messing with his fries in a way Jesse's scolded him for in the past, rolling each in ketchup, dirtying his fingers, before popping it into his mouth. Jesse ignores it this time. He'll never forgive him for what he said about Johona, but he also can't see riding him too hard after what he's been through.

A Little League game is in its fifth inning on a baseball diamond next to the drive-in. A kid hits a fly into left field, the *thwack* of the bat on the ball not reaching Jesse's ears until the boy's already running for first. The fielder gapes at the sky and punches his glove. The ball goes to him like it was meant to, seeming to slow almost to stopping as it drops into his mitt.

"I'm gonna get me a motorcycle," Edgar says.

"No, you're not," Jesse says.

"I'm gonna ride with the Fiends. They're tougher than you."

"You sure about that?"

"I seen them fight."

"So how come they're all dead, and I'm still here?"

Edgar drops a fry into his puddle of ketchup and flips it with the tip of his finger. "I'll start my own gang then," he says.

"What'll you call it?"

"The Pirates."

Jesse goes to piss before they hit the road. The car is running when he gets back, Edgar behind the wheel.

"What the fuck are you doing?" Jesse says.

"Touch the one wire to the two," Edgar says. "I remember."

"You don't mess with the car without my permission. You know that."

"Can I have permission to drive?"

"Get back on your side."

Edgar acts like it takes everything in him to slide across the seat.

They head north. Jesse figures they can make it to Wells, or even Jackpot, before having to stop for daylight. An hour into the drive, Edgar, who's been sulking, turns on the radio. Jesse shuts it off.

"Please, sir, may I play the radio, sir?" Edgar says. His resentment at having to ask is obvious, even behind the funny voice he uses.

"You may," Jesse says, rewarding him for following the rules.

Traffic is sparse on the highway. When they meet another vehicle, it's usually a big rig, some as festooned with colored lights as Christmas trees. Hank Williams's "I'm So Lonesome" comes on the radio. After the first verse about the whip-poorwill being too blue to fly and the moon hiding behind a cloud to cry, Jesse changes the station. The only way he'll get through the next few nights is to keep one step ahead of grief.

The Galaxie blows a tire an hour past Ely. Jesse manhandles the car to the shoulder, kills the engine, and lucks out when he finds a flashlight in the glove box. His luck continues when he pops the trunk with his screwdriver and there's a jack and a spare.

"Give me a hand," he calls to Edgar, still in the car.

It's the left rear tire that failed. Edgar holds the light while Jesse loosens the nuts with a lug wrench and jacks up the car.

Jesse's sweating as he pulls off the ruined tire and slips on the spare, has to dry his hands on his pant legs before replacing and finger-snugging the nuts. Edgar can't stand still. The flashlight beam keeps jumping around.

"Quit fidgeting," Jesse snaps.

He lowers the car, tightens the nuts, and carries the jack to the trunk. The engine starts, and he slams the trunk shut and, through the rear window, sees Edgar in the driver's seat again.

"Goddammit!" he yells.

Edgar puts the car in reverse and hits the gas. The back bumper shatters Jesse's left knee. He falls to the ground, and the Galaxie crushes his right ankle as it rolls on top of him. The car stops then, but Jesse's stomach is against the muffler. The hot steel sears his flesh. That's what finally starts him screaming.

He's still screaming when Edgar shifts into drive and takes off. His shirt catches on the bumper, and he's dragged out into the road before the fabric tears and he skids to a stop. The Galaxie speeds away, its taillights visible long after the sound of the engine has faded.

30

THE LITTLE DEVIL STARTS IN AS SOON AS JESSE SPRINGS ME FROM
the camper after he and Mr. Sanders come back from the red
arrow motel. *He don't care nothing about you,* he says. *He killed
Abby. He tried to kill you. You can't trust him.* He keeps spitting
poison until I fall asleep in Mr. Sanders's room. Ruins my
hamburgers ruins my French fries.

I wake up thinking about Abby. When I recall what
happened to her I feel like crying. I feel like taking a knife to
Jesse and dusting him. *Do it!* the Little Devil whispers. I turn
on *The Brady Bunch* to drown him out. Mr. Sanders is writing
in his book. He says, Do you have to play it so loud? He'd
best watch himself or I'll off him too.

Soon as Jesse gets up he tells me to pack my bag we're
moving on. Stacking the little I have left in my grip steams me
even more. There's my cards but I want my checkers. There's
my dinosaurs but I want my sword.

We're going to Seattle. They got Brakeman Bill there and
JP Patches and Gertrude. The new car Jesse stole is a Galaxie.
A galaxy is stars you need a telescope to see. I looked at the
moon with a telescope. There's a face on it. Sometimes the
moon's out during the day. What you call a Judas moon. Judas

betrayed Jesus for thirty pieces of silver. Jesse betrayed me for a piece of ass.

A&W ain't gonna make up for that. Every time I look at Jesse I get mad all over again. He goes to pee and I slide over and start the car. *Drive off,* the Little Devil says, *get away.* Jesse comes back before I make up my mind. He yells at me in front of the waitress girl.

When we get going he makes me ask permission to turn on the radio. I do but ain't ever gonna again. The Little Devil keeps talking over the music about revenge. The car swerves and Jesse says it's a blowout. He tells me to come help him change the tire. I want to tell him to fuck himself but I'm scared. I remember him choking me. I remember fighting to breathe and not getting air and fighting to breathe and almost swallowing my tongue and fighting to breathe and forgetting how.

I'm shaking such I can't hold the flashlight still. Jesse yells at me and the Little Devil's yelling too. *If a dog bites once he'll bite twice,* he says. *Careful he don't brain you with that wrench.* I can't think straight with all the noise in my head. When Jesse goes to put the jack in the trunk I walk up and get in the driver seat. That's when the Little Devil takes over. It's him who touches the one wire to the two to spark the engine. It's him who puts the Galaxie in *R* and gives it gas. It's him who runs Jesse over and drives off. *Don't look back,* he says, *keep your eyes on the road.*

I don't think about nothing but driving. I ain't never done it alone before. You got to do all the concentrating yourself. You got to steer and work the gas and watch what's coming all at the same time. The Little Devil goes back in his hole. Got nothing more to say.

I stop at the first motel I come to. Jesse's wallet's in the glove box and there's money in it. The lights are out in the motel office. I knock on the door and ring the bell. A Chinaman answers grumbling about it's late. I tell him I had a flat tire. He comes back with a key and says there's no hot water in the room but it's the only one he's got on account of there's a highway crew staying there. I say cold water'll be fine.

The room's on the second floor. I get my grip and Jesse's out of the car and carry them up. I take the guns too. The room smells sour and there's a bug in the sink. The television goes on but no channels come in. I get my cards out and deal two hands for Crazy Eights. It's no fun playing myself.

I open Jesse's grip and look through it. His shaving kit the photo book and them sunglasses Johona give him. I hear him telling me to leave his gear be. I hear me saying, *Why? You ain't got nothing anybody'd want to steal.*

I stick his wallet in one pocket and one of the pistols in the other and go out on the walkway. The parking lot is full of pickup trucks. Past them is the highway and a truck stop all lit up on the other side. Alamo it's called. Davy Crockett king of the wild frontier got killed at the Alamo. I draw the pistol and point it at the gas pumps. You close one eye to aim. Pow. I pretend this time but if Jesse finds me I'll shoot him for real. I'll practice till I can knock a bean can off a fence post till I can hit a silver dollar throwed in the air. 'Cause I'm sure he'll dust me if he gets the chance. He ain't never believed me about the Little Devil.

I cross to the truck stop. They got every kind of potato chips in the store there every kind of candy every kind of soda pop. There's hula girls for your dashboard fishing poles and tackle and Wile E. Coyote belt buckles. They even got CB radios.

I pick one up and ask how much. The cash register man says, Seventy-five dollars plus tax. Does it work? I say. We wouldn't be selling it if it didn't, he says. Jesse's wallet is fat with twenty-dollar bills. I hand the man four to make eighty. He gives me back one and some change.

There's slot machines by the bathroom. Star Spangled Sevens. I hand the cash register man another twenty-dollar bill and ask for quarters. He gives me a paper-wrapped roll and ten dollars back.

I sit at the game and tap it three times. Three times for three sevens. It don't work. I drop coins and pull drop coins and pull but the damn thing doesn't hit. The cash register man comes over smoking a cigarette. Mind if I watch? he says. I tell him there ain't much to see but he's welcome.

I only got two quarters left when three BARS come up and some coins jingle into the tray. The cash register man says, I'd quit while you're ahead, and I say, I guess you're right, and stuff the quarters in my pocket.

I take my CB into the diner and sit at the counter. The waitress lady is as old and fat as Mama but's got yellow hair. She calls me handsome when she brings the menu. How are ya handsome? I tell her to give me hotcakes sausage and scrambled eggs. And orange juice. A big glass not a little one. I ask if they got blueberry syrup. Better places got blueberry syrup. Nope sorry, she says, only maple but it's just as sweet. She asks me, You with the road crew? No ma'am, I say, passing through.

I set my quarters on the counter and stack them four high. Four makes a dollar and I got four dollars and fifty cents worth. I ask the waitress what time the sun comes up. About five thirty, she says. What time is it now? I ask. She looks at her watch. Five oh five, she says. I shovel my food in and get back to the room when it's coming light. I got to be more careful. I hang the DO NOT DISTURB sign on the doorknob. I make sure the curtains is shut.

There's cartoons on now. Gigantor on one channel Bugs Bunny on the other. I put on Bugs but don't pay attention 'cause I'm worried. It's day so if Jesse ain't here he ain't coming. Could be he ain't even looking for me. Could be he's dusted. I wanted that when I was mad but I ain't so mad anymore. He ain't been all bad. I know how to do some things but not all of it. I ain't never hunted. I ain't never killed. Jesse always took care of that.

The dark where I see things comes. This time all it is is blackness. Blackness and me crying. Crying and saying no. When it lifts I'm shaking like a goose walked across my grave. Where am I gonna go? What am I gonna do? The only one I got to talk to is the Little Devil and all he does when I ask is belch.

I feel like if I don't do something good I'll do something bad. I take my CB radio out of the box and set it on the bed. I turn the knobs and nothing happens. It's got a book of how to work it but the letters are too small and the pictures don't make sense.

I pick up the microphone and press the button. Breaker breaker this here's the Wolfman, I say, come back good buddy. I press the button again. This here goes out to Jesse, I say, I know it was your mama's favorite. And then I sing.

Oh let me die in winter
When the night hangs dark above
And cold the snow is lying
On bosoms that we love
Ah! May the wind at midnight
That bloweth from the sea
Chant mildly, softly, sweetly
A requiem for me

31

July 5, 1976, Las Vegas (cont.)

I CAME TO HEARING JESSE ASKING WHERE I'D BEEN SHOT. HE used my shirt to bandage a wound in my thigh. We'd been pinned down by the bikers, but Jesse wasn't about to give up. He propped me at the window with the .45 and wedged himself in the doorway with the shotgun, and we proceeded to turn two of the Fiends' Harleys into scrap metal.

We were about to blast the last one when the bikers opened up on us. Knowing the walls of the trailer wouldn't stop anything, I dropped to the ground. The pain in my leg was so bad, I thought I'd been hit again.

When the shooting petered out, I struggled to find some way to sit that didn't hurt. The Fiends must have been in bad shape, too, because the next thing I knew, Jesse and one of them were going back and forth, negotiating safe passage for the other bikers and myself. I was too dazed to feel much relief about leaving and worried I wouldn't have the strength to get back to the truck.

A motorcycle carrying a pair of Fiends drove off, and then it was my turn to go. Jesse said if he wasn't at the truck by dawn, I should leave without him. In that case, I asked, what about Edgar? He quickly and coldly told me I should kill him.

My God, I thought, *this truly must be hell.* I was dealt another blow seconds later, as I prepared to leave the trailer. I warned Jesse not to forget about the fat man I'd shot, said he must be close to healed by now.

"He won't be healing," Jesse said.

I asked what he meant.

"He's not a rover."

Hoping he was mistaken, I made a beeline for the body as soon as I limped out of the trailer. There the man lay, wide-eyed, open-mouthed, and dead, dead, dead, and I was confronted with the awful fact that I'd killed a human being.

I'm not sure how I kept going after that. Some instinct for self-preservation kicked in and powered me out to the highway. Every step was agony, and my existence narrowed to the task of keeping moving. Prayer helped, but my plea got simpler and simpler, until in the end it was just, "Jesus, Jesus, Jesus," repeated over and over.

I hardly recall reaching the truck, Jesse's return, or the ride to the motel. The trek had done me in. I truly believe I was straddling life and death, and death seemed like the better option. Jesse dressed my wound properly, and a long, dreamless sleep followed. My leg still hurt when I came to, but I could sit up without feeling like puking, and I managed to hobble to the bathroom on my own.

The sun set while I've been writing this. Edgar's watching television, and Jesse is stirring on the floor. I killed a man helping him get his revenge and was almost killed myself, so I hope he keeps his promise to let me go. I'll say a prayer now for the soul of the dead man and another begging forgiveness for his murder. I doubt they'll earn me any grace, but maybe they'll get me through the night.

July 7, 1976, Outside Truckee, California

Czarnecki's cabin is the last place I thought I'd find myself, but here I am. In a way, I guess, it's appropriate: This nightmare will end where it began.

To backtrack a bit, Jesse was a man of his word. The night after the shootout at the trailer, he returned my wallet and Czarnecki's .45, and he and Edgar drove off in a stolen car. My first thought was that I should leave the motel too, put some distance between me and the scene of my crime, but my leg still ached, and I needed more rest. My appetite was back, so I had a pizza delivered. After eating my fill, I thought of Beaumont chained in the camper. He'd been without food or water for nearly twenty-four hours.

He didn't say anything when I lifted the lid of the crate, didn't reach for the jug of water I offered him.

"I won't beg you," I said.

"I need to use the toilet," he said.

I told him to go on. He stood slowly, awkwardly, chains jingling. I turned away while he squatted over the bucket.

"May I stand for a bit?" he said when he finished.

I let him lean against the counter while he ate a couple of slices of pizza and drank some water.

"Where is Jesse?" he asked.

"Gone," I replied.

"But I'm still a prisoner."

"For as long as you earn your keep," I said. "You're going to help me hunt rovers."

"While living in a box and shitting in a bucket?"

"Better than you'll do in hell."

"I'd rule hell in a week."

I took his arrogance as a warning. After being surprised by Sally, I'd never again let my guard down around a rover, but I'd have to be extra cautious with Beaumont. I could tell from his sneer, from the tilt of his head, that even in chains he thought he was superior to me and would always be scheming to escape. The first chance he got—when I was feeding him my own blood to keep him alive?—he'd be on me like a tiger. I hurried him into the crate and didn't feel safe until he was locked inside.

Back in the room I changed the dressing on my leg. It didn't look any better, but it also didn't look any worse. I tried to get lost in a ballgame on TV, but you know how that goes. Whatever's bedeviling you always wins out.

That I'd killed a man, even mistakenly, weighed heavily on me. Rovers were soulless demons, and with not much twisting I could convince myself that putting them down was doing the Lord's work. Killing a human being, though. Even if the man I shot was a killer himself, murder is a mortal sin.

And then there was the matter of the future. If I continued down the road I was on, I'd be hunting rovers in earnest, carrying on Czarnecki's crusade, a crusade that had always felt more like a curse. Driving around night after night with a monster beside me searching for other monsters, then becoming a monster myself in order to put a bullet into the brain of what was once a man, to stick a knife into the heart of what was once a woman, to saw the head off of what was once a child. Doomed to darkness, doomed to danger, doomed to death.

I couldn't think of anything else but to put it in God's hands. They say Jesus prayed so hard the night before he was crucified, he sweated blood. I don't know if that's true, but at

4 a.m., after hours of beseeching the Lord for forgiveness, for direction, for a sign he was even listening, my leg started to bleed again, a red rose blooming on the bandage, and at the same moment I heard a voice in my head, a voice saying, "All debts are paid."

I've been a prayerful man all my life, a questioner, a petitioner, but I've never experienced anything like that. I don't know if it was God speaking *to* me or *through* me. I don't know if the debt was to Benny or to God or to the dead man, but I do know this: I received permission from someone I needed permission from to change course, to abandon the brutal path I'd found myself on.

I slept a few hours. My mind was clear and quiet when I woke, and the rock that had filled my gut ever since I learned of Benny's death was gone. I decided to leave immediately.

There was one final horror to be lived through, though.

Beaumont, knowing it was day, was uneasy when I opened the crate. He tried to sit up, but I pushed him back.

"Don't do it, Brother," he said. "I've lived too long and suffered too much to have it end like this."

"I'll pray for you," I said.

"Unchain me, and we'll pray together," he said. "That's what God wants, Brother. Listen to God."

I stuck an ice pick in his chest. His eyes widened, his heels drummed on the wood of the crate, but then he stilled. I used a hacksaw to take off his head, and he collapsed into dust, a king no more.

I loaded my things into the truck and drove north, arriving here at Czarnecki's cabin around 4. I mean to be gone before dark, which isn't far off now. I only came back to get the Econoline and cover my tracks some.

I sank the .45, the murder weapon, in the first lake I came to and scrubbed everything here that might have my fingerprints on it with a bleach-soaked towel. Doorknobs, the dishes I ate off, the lock on the shed, even the shovel I used to bury the old man. I wiped down the camper and truck, too, cleaned the shoe polish off the van, and burned the posters of Benny and my scrapbook.

When the work was done, I ate a can of tuna and took a nap, and I've spent the last hour writing this, the final entry in this journal, which started as a chronicle of my search for Benny's murderer and ended up a killer's confession. Afterward I'll burn it too, because there's no reason for you to read it, no reason you should be burdened with such awful knowledge.

When the pages have turned to ash, I'll drive to Reno, check into a nice hotel, and eat the biggest steak I can find. And then I'm going to call you. I'm going to call and tell you I've finally accepted that I'm never going to find the person who killed our son, and I'm going to ask if I can come home.

If you say yes, I'll be in San Diego before you know it. I'll wrap my arms around you and hang on for dear life as I thank you for taking me back. I'll start teaching again, I'll go to dinner at Chuey's with you on Saturdays, and to church with you every Sunday. And the only thing I ask is that if I ever wake up screaming, you forgive me when I don't tell you what the dream was, and if some night we're out and you catch me staring at someone and I suddenly grab your hand and say, "Let's go," you don't ask why, you just come along, quickly and quietly. Hopefully that won't happen too often. Hopefully, with the Lord's help, I'll become very good at forgetting.

TODAY'S PASSAGE: Remember ye not the former things, neither consider the things of old. Behold, I will do a new thing. Now shall it spring forth. Shall ye not know it? I will even make a way in the wilderness, and rivers in the desert.

—Isaiah 43:18–19

32

ELIJAH SQUINTS AT ANTONIA'S ITALIAN PHRASEBOOK, RUNS HIS finger down the page. He can barely see the words in the dim light of the church but finally finds what he wants to say.

"*Ho fame,*" he whispers into Antonia's ear.

She's staring at a statue of Mary cradling Jesus. A mother and her dead son. One of the most famous sculptures in the world by one of the most famous artists, she said. Elijah whispers again.

"*Ho fame.*"

"What's that mean?" Antonia says.

"I'm hungry."

"*Un momento.*"

It's been five months since the shootout at the motel and the end of the Fiends. In the aftermath, Antonia and Elijah threw away their leathers and dumped the Harley. Elijah shaved his beard and cut his hair; Antonia grew hers long and has taken to wearing embroidered Mexican dresses and turquoise jewelry. New identities, new beginnings. They've had a few.

They took a night flight from New York to London and another to Rome, where they've been for a week. Every afternoon at 4:30, when the winter sun sets, they leave their hotel to visit sites on Antonia's list, and every one of them has been more beautiful than she imagined. Her knees shook in the Sistine Chapel, the Trevi Fountain made her dizzy, and now this, Michelangelo's Pietà. The marble figures are so lifelike, she wouldn't be surprised to feel a pulse if she put her fingers to Mary's throat, wouldn't be shocked if Jesus's flesh was warm to the touch.

The sculpture is surrounded by bulletproof glass. A few years ago a madman attacked it with a hammer, breaking off one of Mary's arms and her nose. Luke used a hammer when he went crazy too. Went crazy and beat little Abigail to death. Went crazy and murdered wee James. She came home right after, had been to the grocer, was carrying a sack of onions and potatoes. Luke greeted her naked, bloody, raving. "Hello, wife. I've done for your piglets, and now I'll have you." Because she'd threatened to leave him, to take the children and go.

She went crazy herself then, got hold of a kitchen knife and stabbed him twenty times. If she hadn't discovered that she had killing in her that day, that she could kill and not care, would things have been different? If she hadn't been shown that all men were beasts, would she have so readily become a rover, a beast of all beasts?

She blinks away the questions. She blinks away the past. Those babies died of the pox. Her eyes climb a column to the church's vaulted roof, to the dome hazy with scented smoke from an earlier Mass. All the pain of her life has been worth it if that's what it took to get here, to see the candles flickering like fireflies in front of the chapels.

She and Elijah walk to the statue of St. Peter. Visitors, kissing rosaries and crossing themselves, are lined up to touch its foot. They join the queue.

"You're not getting religion, are you?" Elijah says.

"It's tradition," Antonia says.

When it's her turn in front of the statue, she gazes at its toes, worn shiny and shapeless by the caresses of countless pilgrims seeking mercy. *Fools,* she thinks, before reaching out to stroke the foot herself.

She and Elijah eat at a restaurant on a little square with a fountain. Their table is against a window fogged by the warmth of the room. Elijah uses the edge of his hand to clear a patch so they can watch people rushing past, bundled against the cold, their breath puffing and trailing like steam from locomotives. Christmas lights are everywhere even though it's only a week into December.

The waiter, with his droopy gray mustache, speaks enough English to guide them through the menu. Elijah orders spaghetti carbonara for the third time. Antonia frowns at his lack of imagination and asks about the specialty of the house.

"Saltimbocca," the waiter says. "This means it will jump into your mouth."

"I'll have that," Antonia says.

She opens her guidebook.

"The Coliseum is open late tomorrow," she says. "That's something we've got to see."

"All right," Elijah says.

"It's where gladiators fought. Sometimes it was man against man, and sometimes they fought lions and tigers and elephants."

Elijah's staring out the window, watching a bum in a ragged coat stagger to the fountain and splash water on his face. Antonia sees the bum too.

"You're not that kind of hungry, are you?" she says.

"Not yet," Elijah says.

"Did you notice the camp by the river, those drunks?"

"Are you telling me not to worry, there's plenty of good hunting?"

"I'd like to stay here a while. And then we'll go to Madrid. You can show me where you were born."

"You're the one with the memory," Elijah says. "I've forgotten everything about the place."

"You don't know what'll happen when you see it again," Antonia says. "It might all come back to you."

She signals the waiter.

"I believe I'll have wine after all. Do you want some?"

"Sure," Elijah says.

She smiles and opens her phrasebook to see how to say "red."

33

J ESSE HAULS HIMSELF OUT OF THE ROAD AND INTO THE SCRUB, his fear of being spotted worse than his pain. The effort exhausts him. He can't do anything afterward but stare up at the glittery web of stars spun across the sky.

He should've anticipated trouble. Edgar's been getting more and more sneaky and defiant and at the same time more strange, all his talk of visions and the Little Devil. If he hadn't been distracted by Johona and the Fiends, he'd have seen this coming. He let his guard down, and now he's paying the price.

It's 3:30 by the time he can stand. Two hours until sunrise. Wells, the nearest town, is an hour's drive. His best guess is Edgar will stop there. He'll need to get a ride soon if he's going to make it by dawn.

He retrieves his denim jacket from where he tossed it while changing the tire and buttons it over his torn and bloody shirt. The guns are in the Galaxie, but he's got his knife. He sets off along the shoulder.

He's been walking fifteen minutes when headlights finally appear. He steps into the road and waves his arms. A semi charges out of the darkness like a rhino. The driver sounds his horn but doesn't slow down. Jesse is nearly bowled over by the blast of hot wind as the truck passes. He fingers grit from the corner of his eye and keeps walking.

Ten minutes later another truck comes along, from the opposite direction this time. Jesse crosses the highway. Again, the rig blows by like the driver didn't see him, as do two more that pass during the next half hour.

Time is growing short to reach shelter before daybreak, and panic nibbles at Jesse's edges. More headlights. He stands in the road, waving madly. It's a car this time, a dusty Gremlin. It slows and comes to a stop twenty feet away.

"What's wrong?" a man calls out.

"I had an accident," Jesse yells back.

He reaches into his pocket for his knife as he hurries to the car.

"Hold up," the driver says. "Keep your distance."

Jesse ignores him and goes to his window, which he's desperately trying to roll up. He's an old man with thick glasses and buck teeth. An old woman cowers in the passenger seat, clutching a little old dog. Jesse grabs the edge of the window and stops it from going any higher.

"I need a ride into Wells," he says.

"Let go of the glass," the old man says, still trying to turn the handle.

"I'm hurt," Jesse says.

"Let go of the glass."

Jesse yanks the door handle, but the door is locked. He reaches through the window for the knob. The woman screams, the dog barks, and the man stomps on the gas. Jesse is spun around when the Gremlin takes off, twirls and falls to the ground.

The realization that it's too late to make it to Wells settles over him like a leaden shroud. He starts walking again. False dawn comes and goes. He keeps walking. Another truck barrels past. He doesn't try to flag it down, just keeps walking.

The sky is paling when he spies an abandoned homesteader cabin. He makes his way to the windowless, doorless shanty and sticks his head inside. It's not the sanctuary he was hoping for. The roof has collapsed, leaving only one corner of the interior covered, and there's no chance of cobbling a shelter out of the debris. Someone's burned it all in the center of the dirt floor.

He scans the surrounding desert. Would a thick enough blanket of brush protect him from the sun? Might he dig a hole and cover himself with earth? He steps outside, drops to his knees, and begins scooping a temporary grave, but it's only a foot deep by the time the sun crests the hills to the east and sends a wave of orange fire rolling across the desert.

He returns to the cabin and crouches under what's left of the roof, can't do anything but watch helplessly as sunlight slides toward him, a deadly incoming tide. Closer and closer it creeps, until he's forced to stand with his back to the wall. The shadow of the remaining bit of roof holds back the brightness, but in an hour, when the sun rises above the cabin, there'll be no escaping it.

He charts the sun's ascent by the light descending the walls, his desperation increasing as one by one his benchmarks—the bent nail, the stain that looks like a ten-gallon hat, the top of the *f* in the spray-painted *fuck* next to the window—are illuminated. His anxiety peaks when the scrap of shadow beneath his feet starts to fade. His legs quake, his teeth chatter, and he wonders if he'll shake himself to pieces before the sun incinerates him.

Then, suddenly, mercifully, a great calm blooms in his chest.

The wisest man he ever met was an old sailor who held down the end of the bar at the Whale, a lowdown San Francisco saloon later destroyed in the quake. Snipe, as this sailor was known, would, for the price of a rum, answer questions about matters both practical and philosophic, everything from what to do to unstick the lid of a pickle jar to how to woo a woman above your station.

One night, as a lark, Claudine bought him a drink and told Jesse to ask him something. On the spot, Jesse struggled to come up with a question. Snipe noticed his difficulty and said, "I know what you want to know. You want to know what happens to you when you die." This was actually the furthest thing from Jesse's mind. He was a rover and didn't anticipate ever dying. But he humored the old man, telling him to go on.

"When you die, what you *believe* will happen to you is exactly what *will* happen to you," Snipe said. "If you want angels, you'll get angels. If you think you're headed for hell, you'll end up there. And if you think this sad slog is all there is, it'll be all there is."

Jesse scoffed at the words then, but remembering them now, he's filled with new courage. He moves from the shade into the sunlight and walks out the door of the cabin. His flesh smokes, and the pain is everything he feared, but he doesn't fear it anymore. After twenty feet his body is dust, but the rest of him keeps going. The rest of him steps onto the road and heads down it. The rest of him watches a cloud drift, a jackrabbit run. The rest of him sniffs sage and kicks an empty can. The rest of him sees Claudine materialize out of a watery mirage and runs laughing to her.

ACKNOWLEDGMENTS

Thank you to my team: Henry Dunow, Sylvie Rabineau, Jill Gillett, and Peter Dealbert. And thank you to Asya Muchnick and everyone at Mulholland Books.

ABOUT THE AUTHOR

Richard Lange is the author of the story collections *Dead Boys* and *Sweet Nothing* and the novels *This Wicked World, Angel Baby,* and *The Smack*. He is the recipient of a Guggenheim Fellowship, the International Association of Crime Writers' Hammett Prize, a Crime Writers' Association Dagger Award, and the Rosenthal Family Foundation Award from the American Academy of Arts and Letters. He lives in Los Angeles.